Praise for *A Country You Can Leave*

"[An] impressive debut . . . Lara is an enchanting protagonist, equal parts skeptic and romantic . . . Angel-Ajani's book is breathless and beautiful, and Lara is a gloriously brave American hero."
— Courtney Eathorne, *Booklist*

"Extraordinary." — Karla J. Strand, *Ms.*

"Angel-Ajani's unflinching portrait of this hypernuclear family is captivating and complex, with a richly drawn supporting cast and occasional arch humor that leavens the intensely emotional backdrop." — Thane Tierney, *BookPage* (starred review)

"[A] sharp, observant debut novel, which deftly blends humor and hard truths while examining economic inequities and the emotional toll they take." — *Kirkus Reviews*

"Angel-Ajani captures a delicate mother-daughter relationship that is fissured from both internal and external forces . . . *A Country You Can Leave* is about love in the face of American precarity, oppression, and violence." — Sarah Neilson, *Shondaland*

"This remarkable debut focuses on the turbulent and complicated relationship between a Black, biracial teen and her erratic, fierce Russian mother . . . [It's a] gripping coming-of-age novel."
— Margaret Kingsbury, *BuzzFeed News*

"*A Country You Can Leave* is an enthralling and heartfelt novel. In this striking debut, Asale Angel-Ajani's phenomenal skills shine on every page. This book will leave you profoundly moved and feeling like you better understand the word *loneliness*."
— Sarah Jackson, author of *A Bit Much*

"*A Country You Can Leave* shattered me with its pain and sweetness. At its heart are a mother and daughter like none I've read before, each striving for selfhood in a world that seems bent on crushing them. It's rare to encounter a debut so fearless and insightful and truly new, but here is Asale Angel-Ajani to show us what's possible in the landscape of American fiction."

—Tania James, author of *Loot*

"A journey through the California everyone should know, a place America needs to see, a world of desperation and beauty, collaboration and redemption. In the best tradition of fiercely perceptive daughters fighting to survive dangerous lives, from Betty Smith to Janet Fitch to Helena Maria Viramontes, the debut of Asale Angel-Ajani was ever surprising, a novel I read in one day."

—Susan Straight, author of *Mecca*

"Refined and raw, cosmopolitan and claustrophobic, *A Country You Can Leave* is a novel of contrasts, built around a mother and daughter who see themselves as nothing alike. Asale Angel-Ajani portrays the complexity of the whole world through this one core relationship. Her debut is as loving as it is demanding, as vulnerable as it is merciless, and its complications will break your heart."

—Julia Phillips, author of *Disappearing Earth*

Sylvie Rosokoff

ASALE ANGEL-AJANI

A COUNTRY YOU CAN LEAVE

Asale Angel-Ajani is a writer and a professor at the City College of New York. She is the author of two nonfiction books, *Strange Trade: The Story of Two Women Who Risked Everything in the International Drug Trade* and the forthcoming *Intimate: Essays on Racial Terror.* She has held residencies at Millay Arts, the Djerassi Resident Artists Program, and Playa and is an alum of VONA and Tin House. *A Country You Can Leave* is her first novel.

A COUNTRY
YOU CAN
LEAVE

A COUNTRY YOU CAN LEAVE

ASALE ANGEL-AJANI

MCD ⊗ PICADOR

FARRAR, STRAUS AND GIROUX   NEW YORK

MCD
Picador
120 Broadway, New York 10271

Originally published in 2023 by MCD / Farrar, Straus and Giroux
First paperback edition, 2024

The Library of Congress has cataloged the MCD hardcover
edition as follows:
Names: Angel-Ajani, Asale, author.
Title: A country you can leave : a novel / Asale Angel-Ajani.
Description: First edition. | New York : MCD / Farrar, Straus and
  Giroux, 2023.
Identifiers: LCCN 2022044456 | ISBN 9780374604059 (hardcover)
Subjects: LCGFT: Novels.
Classification: LCC PS3601.N554463 C68 2023 | DDC 813/.6—
  dc23/eng/20220916
LC record available at https://lccn.loc.gov/2022044456

Paperback ISBN: 978-1-250-32166-4

Our books may be purchased in bulk for promotional, educational, or
business use. Please contact your local bookseller or the Macmillan
Corporate and Premium Sales Department at 1-800-221-7945, extension
5442, or by email at MacmillanSpecialMarkets@macmillan.com.

Picador® is a U.S. registered trademark and is used by Macmillan Publishing
Group, LLC, under license from Pan Books Limited.

For book club information, please email marketing@picadorusa.com.

mcdbooks.com • Follow us on social media at @mcdbooks
picadorusa.com • Follow us on social media at @picador or @picadorusa

P1

For

JAH, EAH, and LAH,

my lovely disruptors,

and for

Lira, who once knew a girl named Lara

I would prefer the country you can leave
to the country you cannot.

—JOSEPH BRODSKY, *Conversations*

A COUNTRY
YOU CAN
LEAVE

This is as much as I ever told you and yet you are not here.

PART I

LESSONS IN RUSSIAN LITERATURE

**Mother was The Woman
the whole world had imagined to death.**

—DEBORAH LEVY, *Things I Don't Want to Know*

1

*There is no release from life's turmoil, so put your
back into it.*

In a gulch somewhere between the San Jacinto and Santa
Anas, my mother, Yevgenia, slows the car at the sign wel-
coming us to the dubiously named Oasis Mobile Estates. She
cuts the engine behind the property manager's battered truck
and goes about the task of cleaning herself up. She pulls a
rubber band out of her stiff, dyed-black hair. She scrunches it
back to life. Tweezers in hand, she yanks the rearview mirror
down to brutalize her already emaciated eyebrows. When she
smell-checks her armpits, I know there is a man inside.

"Don't I get a vote?" I ask, watching Yevgenia resuscitate
her breasts by scooping them up in her bra. Our drive from
Nevada to California has been nonstop. For miles, nothing
but hot dust, windswept trash, and nameless mountains closing in on our resentments.

My mother ignores me. Instead, she looks through the
bug-splattered windshield, her eyes turned to the heaven she
doesn't believe in. She blows hard through her mouth. Traces
of old beer and tobacco stir in the narrow space between us.

"People who cast votes decide nothing. People who *count*
votes decide everything." Pushing the car door open with her
shoulder, she says, "Stalin. Look it up."

"Hey," I call out as she heads to the manager's trailer,

her red tank top plastered to her back with sweat. "Use a condom."

There's a brief pause in her step. Her body tenses. Then I hear it. The source of what I yearned for most in childhood, her husky laugh, etched by decades of chain-smoking.

Waiting for her to score whatever it is she thinks she'll get from a place like this, I crane my neck to survey the Oasis Mobile Estates. Nestled in shriveled patches of yellow desert grass wedged between boulders heavily scarred by acid rain, this "oasis" is a decrepit collection of rusted metal boxes lined up along small tributaries of roughly hewed roads. The only sign that I'm in the year 2000 is a flat-roofed Circle K squatting a half mile outside the trailer park. Fiery air blasts through the open car window from the direction of the Mojave. I shove my hand down the back of my jeans to pull my sweat-drenched underwear out of my crack.

Eventually, the door of the property manager's tin hut opens. My mother emerges with a man in tow. Her skirt is straight, her tank top tucked in. They hadn't done it. This is a bad sign. It means she's serious about the place. They approach the car and I overhear Yevgenia casually lying about where we have just been, saying Denver and not Las Vegas. That she's leaving a job rather than leaving yet another guy who turned out to be broke. The property manager, with his tangled waist-length black hair and weathered brown skin, is smitten. He follows my mother, eyeing her swaying hips.

"Don't just sit there like a dum-dum," my mother says to me through a fake smile. Her voice comes from the earthy place deep between her legs. It drips with allure, turned up by the presence of a man who has something she wants. "Get out of the car. Say hello to Carlos."

Out of habit, I do as she says. But inside I smolder. I raise my hand in a half-hearted greeting. Yevgenia glares.

"This is my daughter, Lara," she says. And I wait for it. Maybe secretly, Yevgenia does too. The scrutiny of a white woman with a Black child.

There. Carlos's eyes flick between me and my mother. The appraisal of biological proximity. Her straight hair to my curly, lopsided Afro. Her rounded, fleshy curves to my limp, flat lines. Her light, white skin, the known story, to my dark, open question.

"Call me Papa Bear," he says, straightening his face, giving us a pass. "Everyone does."

He's got a bum knee, so we follow Papa Bear's slow, limping figure down the cracked asphalt road. He heads with purpose toward the main artery of the Oasis. *Dead Man Walking* isn't a film I've seen but the title comes to mind. I try not to notice Papa Bear's disability, but his lurching movement ignites an involuntary jumpiness within my own body. I hate myself for it and glance at my mother. Her attention is on two women standing next to the trailer we're approaching.

"Don't Minnie look silly?" says an older white woman. She's standing in the carport on a step stool, attaching a rainbow umbrella hat over a yellow baseball cap worn by a second, taller old woman. They wave at Papa Bear.

Papa Bear smiles at them, polite and exaggerated. To me he says, "She's Mickey and the other is Minnie. Get it?"

"Yeah." I don't get it, but I know it's easier to just go along.

"Their names. Their *actual* names." He's shaking his head, as if he's looking at the eighth wonder.

I grunt a false half laugh, not confused by their names

but by the winter clothes they're wearing. Shapeless jeans and baggy sweatshirts, and neither of them is sweating.

Several trailers down we stop next to a cramped front porch with steep carpeted steps. It looks the same as all the others except in the covered carport there are black plastic garbage bags flung one on top of the other like bodies in an open grave.

"Don't mind that crap," Papa Bear says, his eyes on the swell of my mother's breasts. "They'll come 'round to collect in a day or two."

My mother considers the place, shaking her head. Fishing her cigarettes out of her fake Chanel, she lights up carefully. Yevgenia always takes her time before haggling over the rent. It's her game. Acting as though she's deliberating from a long list of nonexistent options. She sighs, annoyed, glancing at the mess in the carport, pretending those bags interrupt some big plan of hers. Amid the dilapidations and failures, my mother, Yevgenia, a woman who accidentally defected from the Soviet Union in the 1980s, is at her most Russian. She will make anything work. A broken washing machine, a flat tire, a foreign country. This.

I don't want to be here but it's not like I'm at risk of running away. Though my mother wouldn't care. The truth is, she's tethered to me by weak strings of obligation. Nathaniel "Nate" Basmadjian taught me this, and how to scrunch my body into a tiny ball on the floor of the car, while he and my mother drove around town. One night, Nate hinted that if my mother "lost the Black kid," he'd marry her and within a few days, they were off. I was five at the time so the recollection is vague. What I do remember of my life without Yevgenia is time spent with the strange people my mother pawned me off on. The Polish Seventh-day Adventist couple who liked to show me pictures from their missionary trip to Botswana, saying, "This is your culture, dear," until I nodded my head like I understood. The pretty Canadian coke addict who made me lie on the floor at the foot of her bed while she talked to me about her married boyfriend until I fell asleep. Then there was the large family from Guam who worked me like a slave and called me *nekglo ñamu*, black mosquito, in their Chamorro language, which was "amazing that they even knew those words," the eleven-year-old cousin told me, since the U.S. burned all the dictionaries in his country.

So not exactly foster care, but something like it.

Acquaintances from Yevgenia's various jobs. People who owed her a favor. She exhausted everyone with promises she would send more money, be back soon. She was gone for nearly two years. Supposedly embarking on a new life in Scottsdale as a blonde named "Evie" who played mixed doubles every Saturday. When my mother returned to me in California with brown roots and an allergy to shrimp cocktail, she didn't speak too much about tennis or Nate or Arizona, so I didn't ask.

Those years without her created a savage hunger in me that's hard to shake. When I was eight, nine, and ten, Yevgenia had to cleave me from her body whenever she left for work or to go to the store. At twelve, thirteen, and fourteen, I yoked my mother, leaving little space between us as she sat to read, on the sofa or in a chair. If she closed a door, my back would be pressed against it. I was the inextricable daughter, physically and mentally. But now, as we arrive at the Oasis during this Indian summer, as I enter what will be the merciless year of sixteen, I am ready for the grip of longing to finally loosen. And there's relief, like letting go of a sweaty hand.

THE DESERT HEAT is powerful, an unrelenting foe of the living. Papa Bear and my mother seem unfazed by it. I wipe my brow with the back of my hand, my eyes on the cigarette strangled between Yevgenia's two fingers. She sucks smoke deep into her lungs, frowning. Papa Bear is not looking at her face so he can't see her dissatisfaction. Yevgenia clears her throat, loudly. She motions her cigarette in the direction of the piles of trash in the carport; he jerks his eyes away from her chest, nervous.

That's the thing about her. Her powers of seduction specialize in lonely, sexually frustrated men, and Papa Bear fits the bill. In my mother, he sees a drinking partner, hot sex, the chance to introduce her as his "old lady."

Papa Bear has no idea.

He blathers panicky explanations about the trailer, like he needs to change her mind. "You know, the former tenants had to beat a hasty retreat."

A hasty retreat. Our calling card, my mother and I. In those Hefty bags filled with whatever junk didn't make the cut in the rush to get out before the cops or Immigration or a murderous ex broke the door down, I imagine lie rotting artifacts from a taxonomy of restless belonging. A yearbook from the school three moves ago. A green dress bought and never worn for a party whose invitation never arrived. A salvaged mirror, cracked but still pretty. A letter with a father's last known address.

And if those bags aren't an ominous sign, the boy directly

across the street, nine or ten years old, is. He's sitting on the curb with his bike thrown on the ground behind him. His white hair is a perfect polished tooth next to his shabby, yellowed mobile home. He's disconcerting, this boy. It's like his face is out of place here in the desert. The freckles, the bright white hair, the upturned nose of privilege, and the astute blue eyes all belong to a clean-cut Caucasian kid in a cereal commercial. But from the neck down there are signs of neglect. Dirty ripped clothing, bloodied knuckles, filthy bare feet. He's throwing rocks in the middle of the road, tracking us: me, Papa Bear, my mother. When he catches me looking, he freezes. Then he thrusts his middle finger in the air.

Caught off guard, I stammer, "That . . . that kid."

"Oh yeah," Papa Bear says, turning to give the kid a quick wave. "That's Brody. He's alright."

"Yeah, well, he just flipped us off."

"Don't make an elephant out of a fly." A standard Yevgenia idiom. She stamps out her second cigarette.

"But he's an *asshole*," I say, hating the whining tone in my voice but unable to rein it in.

My mother sighs. She turns to Brody. "Hey, asshole."

His blue eyes turn toward her and she flips him off. His mouth twists into a sneer and he laughs, high-pitched and phony.

She brushes her hands on her jean skirt, turning to me. "Better now?"

"Much." There is more to say. There always is between my mother and me.

Her jaw clenches, communicating. *Don't screw this up.*

I shrug her off with an eye roll.

Her eyes lock onto Papa Bear, who seems uncomfortable.

Stepping a little closer to him, she starts her negotiation boldly. "One hundred fifty a week."

Papa Bear shakes his head. "No can do. Two hundred forty cash and it's already a huge discount."

"Two hundred, cash. Best and last." Yevgenia's brows are thin, uneven arches, making her look fierce and slightly psychotic. She jams her hand in her purse and pulls out her ring of keys. She's ready to leave if she has to.

Papa Bear's hand trembles slightly as he rubs his chin. He is trying to figure out if she means it. Yevgenia shifts her weight to one leg, arms crossing under her breasts. The round flesh of her boobs pours out from her shirt. It's a beckoning. I've seen her practice this move in countless bathroom mirrors, been a witness to its effects on gas station attendants and motel clerks. The pit of my stomach burns. I look over at the kid across the street. I am neither religious nor superstitious, but I throw myself at the feet of whatever higher power is out there. *Please. Not the fucking Oasis.* I can't live in this penal colony. This refuge for losers. Across the street, the blond kid picks his nose, balling up his boogers between his fingers. *Fucking gross.* This is all my mother's fault. Before California was Nevada and Utah and Colorado and Texas. But before all of that was Mexico, a place I was learning to call home, and she took that away from me. And I'm pissed. Now here we are, at what feels like our last chance. Because it's not hard to miss that the Oasis is just a pit stop on the way to the bottom.

"Oh, damn it to hell." Papa Bear kicks at the ground and puffs of dust plume. "Don't mention what you're paying to anyone," he says, reaching into his pocket. The keys clink together as he softly tosses them to my mother.

Yevgenia turns to me, her face flush with victory. "Get the suitcase."

My shoulders drop.

If an inanimate object can bully, it's the blue suitcase. Since Yevgenia never takes a standard approach to anything, I have learned to watch the case. Before she buys groceries, or stops reusing the same plastic utensils, or thinks about getting any furniture, Yevgenia will put the blue suitcase in the corner of a room with a door, marking her territory. If she leaves it in the car, I know we will be moving on. But it's not just the suitcase itself and what it represents that bullies. It's what is contained inside. The multicolored spiral-bound notebooks, their torn pages like slim fingers slipped through prison bars, taunt me. In these notebooks live my mother's authoritarian edicts, philosophies, and communiqués, mostly regarding sex and men and politics and reading habits. The notebooks will be the sum total of her legacy and my meager inheritance. When she's bored or drunk or both, she gets the suitcase, rummages past Technicolor photos of herself smoking with friends outside a drab apartment block in Cheryomushki or posing arm in arm with lecherous-looking Italian men in front of the Colosseum, and reads out loud from her lists.

Yevgenia claps her hands at me. "Chip-chop."

I hate when she says that. It's so colonial. "It's chop-chop," I mutter, walking to the car.

◆

Shun men who are actors. Or models. They are looking for validation. Their lives are all about hoping and waiting,

which means they will make you hope and wait for a good
orgasm too.

Armageddon arrives at the Oasis on the first of the month.
It starts early in the afternoon with the TVs turned up at top
volumes, mariachi music piping from radios, and hard rock
or hip-hop blaring too much treble from busted car speakers.
It is only a matter of hours before all the day drinking tran-
sitions to sloppy drunken parties spilling out of trailers to
carports and into the narrow streets. A fight starts, a tremor
that turns into an all-out brawl until the cops come and shut
it down. After a night of reckoning, the part of the Oasis that
slept through the chaos wakes, too early, to grab hold of the
cool Saturday morning before the sun starts scorching. This
time belongs to the Oasis's elderly residents. Ms. Eunice, a
trim African American woman who keeps busy riding up
and down the streets on her bright red electric mobility
scooter, the basket on the handlebar stuffed with papers and
plastic bags. Her cane is jammed in the basket too, aluminum
knocking against aluminum as she rides over the potholes
and cracks in the road. Then there's Lourdes's husband, Gus,
tinkering under the hood of his truck, his small transistor
playing Spanish talk radio. The white-haired sisters, Mickey
and Minnie, speed-walk the neighborhood in their pink and
pale blue sweatpants. Papa Bear, though not elderly, sits out
under his carport, a lawn chair backed up against the bumper
of his truck as if he's tailgating, drinking a cup of coffee.

"You're up early," he calls to me. I am trudging down the
road from the Circle K. Yevgenia is still out from the night
before and there was no bread for toast.

"Yeah, too early," I say, because he is the landlord. But I'm lying—9:00 a.m. is late for me. The truth is, I have been up for hours, keeping vigil for my mother, as I often do. I can't sleep when she's not home.

"Ask your mom for the killer hangover cure she has. It works." He chuckles, raising his coffee mug, in salute.

"Sure." I guess he doesn't know I am five years away from the legal drinking age. Or maybe he thinks, given how Yevgenia is with liquor, that I'm the same way. I always find it curious, the idea of what traits or behaviors a parent passes to their child. I don't do the things my mother does. I don't drink or smoke or have sex. The no drinking and no smoking parts of my monastic life are easy. I hate the taste. But sex? This is not a question I will solve on my walk home from the Circle K.

The Toyota is in the carport. Yevgenia returned while I was out. Not that I was too worried. My mother can't stomach more than seventy-two hours with a man. Any more than that is too much domesticity. Of course, the men never see it coming. Yevgenia is a deceptive lover. Attentive to needs of a sexual nature, but don't ask her to pass a pack of smokes, get a beer from the fridge, or scratch that hard-to-reach spot in the middle of your back. By the time someone might look at her and wonder if she will be the intense, clingy type, she vanishes, leaving bruised egos and blue balls in her wake. It's brilliant, really, the way my mother gets what she wants from people, men in particular.

I was eleven when I finally paid attention to Yevgenia's lessons about men. It was after I told her about seeing one of her "friends" sitting on my bed, sniffing a pair of my underwear. Yevgenia's reaction was surprisingly satisfying. We drove out from Burbank to a barren tire shop in Castaic in search of this guy.

Not finding him, she went after his car. "Fucking pervert!" Yevgenia shouted as she brought the crowbar down over her head into the windshield. At first, the smash of glass was anticlimactic. Small fractures extended moderately from the epicenter. My mother hit the window again and again until she was sweating and bits of window sprayed over the dashboard. Even after all the windows of the car were broken she kept hitting, and I knew she was beating back a history that had nothing to do with me.

Later, by the side of the road, Yevgenia took a swig from her makeshift flask. I stared at the small cut across her cheek where a bubble of blood swelled and ran toward her jaw. She seemed oblivious to it. Instead, she gripped the old perfume bottle filled with dark bourbon tightly, until her knuckles were white. "Sex before puberty is a bodily violation," she said. "It will age you. If a man touches you when you're not ready, you tell me and I'll kill him."

That was the extent of my sex-ed talk. I understood then, between me and my mother, this kind of violence was an act of love.

AN UNFAMILIAR MOTORCYCLE is parked in front of Brody and his mother Terri's trailer. Since our first run-in, I stay away from the kid and take to watching him from the kitchen window whenever he is outside. Or, like now, I create a wide berth whenever I am walking near his house. I don't trust him. He seems like the type of kid who could set whole neighborhoods on fire and watch gleefully from the sidelines.

"Hotel California" wafts up from their backyard. My mother hates this song. A guy she dated once called it "America's Dirtbag Anthem," and now that's what she calls it too. I stop for a minute to listen. Hoarse male laughter fills a gap in the music. I turn toward my house, not all that interested in the lives of my neighbors.

"What are you looking at, you stupid pussy?" It's Brody's voice behind me. He's standing at the edge of the street with his arms across his bare, concave chest.

"Fuck off, kid. Go brush your teeth or take a bath or something." I scramble quickly into my yard.

There's the metallic clang of Brody's screen door snapping shut, the shuffle of feet on the landing.

"Hey, is this little dude causing you grief?" The voice is genial.

I turn despite my embarrassment at being heard cursing at a little kid. The man standing on the top step of Brody's trailer is smiling. He is clearly not from the trailer park. First of all, he looks clean. Clean jeans, clean white T-shirt, clean motorcycle boots. His blond hair is long enough for him to tuck it behind his ears. He's a little older but beautiful enough to be a model.

I feel my palms start to sweat.

"I'm Steve, Brody's dad." He comes walking over with the confidence of a salesman. "I met your mom yesterday. Evie, right?"

I roll my eyes. His voice doesn't give anything away. But knowing my mother, she tried to give him a lap dance in the middle of the road.

"Yeah, my mom's real name is Yevgenia. She tells people to call her Evie, so it's easier for them. Evie is such a dumb name."

Steve's eyes drift over to his trailer, like something more important is calling him back.

"I mean she's Russian," I say.

"Yeah, Russian, that's cool. Listen, I was wondering if

you'd watch Brody sometime. I'll pay you. Not much, you know, a little walking-around money . . ."

I don't hear the rest of what he's saying because I am already nodding my head, "Yeah, sure, I'll do it."

"Okay, great." He gives me another smile.

I hurry up my trailer steps. I shut the door and the plywood-paneled walls of my living room threaten to cave in around me. I come to my senses. The last thing I want to do is babysit some devil kid. "Fuck," I say out loud.

"Ah, you met our neighbor." There's a hint of laughter in my mother's voice. She's sitting on the sofa in a purple bra and black underwear, disdainfully plucking through the English edition of Tolstoy's *Resurrection*. The book isn't the source of her scorn. For Yevgenia, there is nothing better than the Russians in all things, especially literature. Pushkin and Tolstoy, which seems a bit obvious, and Gogol were the greats according to her. I think her appreciation of Gogol is a nod to a shared biographical footnote. He spent a few years in Rome and so did she. But Russian stories in English? "Can't be translated," my mother always says.

I bend to collect her discarded clothes and drape them on the back of the hideous and uncomfortable Russian imperial-style chair she found at a swap meet. Dark wood with an ornately carved high back. The seat, a small square of padded red brocade held by several broken brass nails, offers a parody of comfort. I want to move toward my room, but Yevgenia stops me by saying, wistfully, "You know, our neighbor Steve is movie-star sexy but he's still just a normal guy. Makes you think we can all fuck Brad Pitt." She arches her back and, still holding *Resurrection*, stretches her arms over her head. "Do you want to fuck Brad Pitt?"

"Gross," I say, watching her carefully, knowing she's about to pounce. This fight between us over men or sex or sex *and* men is constant, always ending with her breaking out one of her stupid notebooks, flipping to the page she wants, and reading one or two of her "rules" out loud.

Yevgenia carefully folds Tolstoy down beside her with a tenderness she reserves only for books. "You can have him when I am done."

I have come to think of the rivalries she spits at me as the residual effects of her childhood spent as a third-rate ballerina trained under the Soviet system. That, and our natural inclination to regard everything between us as a competition.

"That's fucked-up, *Evie*, talking to your daughter that way," I say, lilting my voice in what I hope is a suggestive and mildly threatening tone. "This time, you may have to eat my leftovers."

Surprised laughter oozes out of her and she swings her bare legs, sitting to attention. I think I've got her, and for a moment it's a tiny win.

"Well, my little virgin, you may see a penis in this lifetime after all." She stretches her hand out toward the kitchen, pointing to the counter where a glass of vodka stands sweating. "Reach me my drink, before you disappear."

Don't chase after a man who has an elaborate hairstyle. No good.

"If I teach you anything, it's that the way to a man's heart is not through free labor. You make him work for this," Yevgenia says, patting her crotch, after I tell her I am going to babysit Brody. "That's the power of feminism."

I know sex isn't connected to feminism but she is right about the free labor. And yet, I do it to be near Steve. Since meeting him, hours of fantasy have been logged. Us, going to the beach, or riding the Catalina ferry together, and other, less mundane things. So I'll watch Brody, as a "favor," which means I won't get paid. Again. But Steve asked me to come over and I'm not saying no.

When I arrive, I hear Steve and Brody in the kitchen making something to eat.

"Okay, B.," Steve says. "I'm working tonight. Mom will be home later. Lara is here, so you ask her for whatever you need."

"Do you have to go?" Brody sounds sad, even a little scared. I don't know what Steve does for work. He's around for a few days and then he's gone. I imagine he's a model on a photo shoot or a stunt double or a pilot on a private jet for a rich guy.

"Yeah, sorry, bud." Steve pats Brody on the shoulder. "I'll be back later. And I bet your mom is home in an hour. Just watch. I'll leave and she will come strolling through that door." They both look expectantly at the door where I am standing.

Brody's face hardens when he sees me. "Yeah, whatever."

"Alright, kiddo. I'll be back in a bit." Steve tussles Brody's hair. "Your mom should be home soon." The more Steve says it, the more I know it's a lie. Brody's mother isn't anyone I keep tabs on, but her car hasn't been in the driveway for at least two days. Steve grabs a stuffed black backpack and his helmet. I am on his heels.

"Bye, Steve. See you when you get back." I sound too eager.

"Hey, thanks, Lara. You're saving me." The way he stands, slightly awkward, distracted by thoughts of work or leaving, makes me forget myself. I jump at him, throwing my arms around him and giving him a tight squeeze.

"Oh, um, okay." Steve uses his free hand to extract one of my arms and lightly pats me on the back. He steps away from me, his eyes evasive and guarded, like they are fencing him in. My cheeks burn.

After his dad leaves, Brody stands in the threshold between the kitchen and the living room trying to decide what's next. "I'm hungry," he says finally.

I roll my eyes. "Didn't you just eat?"

"I don't like it."

"God, you are so spoiled." I go into the kitchen and look at Brody's food.

"Try some. It's fucking gross."

"What is it?" I ask, swirling lumpy gray bits around in the bowl. It smells yeasty, like wet white bread.

"I don't know. My dad stuck it in the microwave for me."

"Okay, go sit down. Let me see what you got." Brody goes into the living room, turns on the television, and flops down on the floor in front of it.

Their refrigerator is nearly as empty as ours, the cabinets equally bare. I manage to find a dried heel of bread, a handful of macaroni, and old bacon grease saved in a mug. I mix it together, microwaving it in a bowl. I'm not sure he'll eat it, but he does.

Brody's Nintendo game is a narcotic. While he's under its spell, I make my way freely around the house. The interior of Steve and Terri's trailer seems disconnected from their reality. The layout is the same as all the others at the Oasis. A combined living and dining room, the kitchen, and then a bathroom followed by two bedrooms. The "master bedroom" takes up the entire back of the trailer and the other tiny bedroom is squeezed in next to a closet. They all have the same flat industrial carpet and plywood-paneled walls. The first time I went to their house, I expected to find Terri's empty liquor bottles strewn on the floor or piles of rocks and sticks and dirt brought in by Brody. Instead, their home contains phantom dregs of their previous, more successful life. A worn cream-colored leather sofa, a chipped glass coffee table, bookshelves with dusty glass geometric objects, and four framed black-and-white photos—two of Brody as a chunky, towheaded baby smiling with two teeth; one of the family with the ocean glistening behind them; and a photo from their wedding, Steve in a tux facing the camera, Terri, healthy looking and full faced, leaning in, gazing intently at him, ecstatic.

I roam their house unimpeded, passing Brody's bedroom and heading straight back to where Steve and Terri sleep. With all the decorative pillows and the spiced potpourri, their room smacks of suburban refugees. The bed is unwrinkled and the clothes, mostly Terri's, hang in the closet like they haven't been touched in forever. A sweater and two shirts still have tags on them. On top of the dresser sit an empty jewelry box and a large bottle of pink perfume. I try to pull the cap off to take a whiff, but it is sealed shut by hard yellowed lumps. I open Steve's disorganized drawers. They're disappointing. All he seems to have are a few pairs of old tube socks and tighty-whities. It's in Terri's drawers that I find an untouched trove.

Matching lace bra and underwear sets, garter belts, skimpy, sheer nightgowns.

I pull out a bra from the back of her neatly constructed stack. It is a black bra with lace along the satin cups. Yevgenia never brings home anything that's been bought at a department store. Of course, bras have always been optional for my mother, even at her age. If there is lace in my mother's clothing, it's the shiny, cheap, highly flammable kind. I rub the lace of Terri's bra between my fingers.

As the TV blares from the living room, I take my chances. I pull my sweatshirt over my head and tug off the light blue sports bra that's tight enough to make my breasts even smaller. I stand, naked down to my waist, and look in the mirror above the dresser. I examine Terri's bra. She is at least one or even two cup sizes larger than me. My heart is thumping. I clasp the bra into place on the tightest row, spin it around to the back, and slip my arms through the straps. The bra bags and gapes. I will have to take in the straps, and the cups, to make it fit me. It doesn't matter. I turn, examining it from all sides. It's my imagination but my breasts seem bigger, my skin seems softer, even my hair seems to be longer and to cascade down my back. I could be pretty in this bra. I think, briefly, of returning it to the pile of Terri's unworn clothes. But I want it. It's beautiful and out of place in this ugly trailer park, just like Steve is, just like I want to be.

"CAN I HAVE something more to eat?" Brody calls from the living room. Scrambling, I throw my sports bra on over the lace one.

"Yeah, okay. Hold on." I tug my sweatshirt back on, starting

for the door. I do it without thinking and once I realize I'm going to steal the bra, I start justifying my actions. I am taking
payment for watching their kid. Then I go over to the dresser
and take out a pair of black lace underwear. I jam the panties
and a glimmering pearl slip into the waistband of my jeans.

IN MEXICO, there was an encyclopedia where I read all about
how the ancient Greeks had at least four different words for
love: *eros, philia, agape,* and *storge.* I know all about eros from
watching my mother and Saturday-morning reruns of an
old 1970s show called *Charlie's Angels.* I gather from these
sources that guys—if they're not trying to make you fall in
love with them so they can steal all your money—will force
their temperamental affections on you. They press up on you,
panting fetid cigarette breath and soured alcohol fumes in
your ear. I also know eros humiliates, especially if you are a
brainy, mannish brunette.

But after I read Aristotle's *Nicomachean Ethics,* I am drawn
to the idea of "philia." It's more than the physically rooted
eros. Anyone can have eros. But not philia. For Aristotle, it's
a profound love. The love shared between two like minds. For
me, philia is a sanctified, mutual love. It's the kind of love I
think about whenever Yevgenia says love causes nothing but
pain and suffering. She thinks love is absurdly optimistic.
"Optimism is a lack of information," she always says, quoting
the famous Russian actress Faina Ranevskaya, as she takes a
long, dramatic drag on her cigarette and makes a ponderous,
searching expression I always find so fake.

———

THE NEXT MORNING, my mother is sitting at the dining table, with a pack of smokes and a cup of tea in front of her.

"'Morning, sunshine." Her voice is a harsh, crackling whisper.

"Hey." I have learned to approach my mother cautiously in the mornings. She may still be drunk, for all I know.

The sound of Steve's motorcycle starting up across the street causes us both to look toward the window. He will be gone, probably to the main road, by the time I walk out my front door. I freeze as I catch a glimpse of a shiny black helmet blur past.

"With fake Brad Pitt, you and me, we are like the Soviet and U.S. space programs' race to the moon." Yevgenia laughs, a forced, open-mouthed laugh. "And you know, we Russians got there first."

"Technically," I say. "But it was an *unmanned* mission, wasn't it?"

I'm not sure if Steve knows or cares one way or the other about the cold war between me and my mother. What's certain, though, is in almost every situation—parenting, career, money management, any nonsexual relationship— Yevgenia is a catastrophe. However, the woman is a master at getting a man into her bed. And from the way Steve watches my mother slink into her car in the evening on her way to work, it's only a matter of time before he ends up in hers. Of course he would, because eros is the simplest form of all the kinds of loves and it's also the most fucked-up because eros will make me do things I generally do not condone, like allow myself to take the bait and compete with my mother for Steve's attention. At the time, I'll want to think that Steve is the real contest. Later, I'll tell myself it has to do with Mexico, how I wanted to stay when she was ready to leave. It's neither. Both Steve and Mexico are only bit parts in a much longer campaign between me and my mother. We've been trying to save ourselves, and maybe each other, from a slow disintegration that actually began with the first sighs of my birth.

2

Don't trust men who recite the poetry of others or repeat jokes or read aloud long passages of books, especially if they wrote them. All they want is your attention and the bone you throw them will never be big enough for their egos.

The desert mist rolls down from the San Jacinto Mountains, scattering tiny silver beads over the quiet, sleepy homes of the Oasis. I am listening to an errant coyote sniff around our trailer on its way home to the foothills.

I start school in a few hours, another first day, for the fifth or maybe sixth time in two years. I brace myself for what lies ahead. For the remedial and ESL classes I will sit in for weeks before a teacher realizes I do not belong there. For the notes from the principal's office reminding my mother to send my academic records. For the other students, who have no reason to notice me. To them, I will reek of car exhaust and roadside rest stops, the smell of an itinerant kid. They know I will be nothing but the mute witness of their unraveling lives. Then I am on to a new town, a new state.

THE TRAILER PARK is split down the middle by the school district and I am glad for it. Just a couple of mobile homes over and I would end up at Kennedy, also known as "Killer" Kennedy. Since Yevgenia takes her sweet time enrolling me, I sit at the kitchen window for a couple of weeks watching the kids from Kennedy fight, fuck, and get high with all the drama of an after-school special.

I already feel better than them for no reason other than the zoning mistake that allows me to attend Canyon Lake High, a school built for the gated community of the same name, but someone forgot to put the school inside the actual gates. I am bused in over the ridge just like the other poor kids. In a matter of days I too will perform the ritual of everyone on the bus—as we crest the peak, we look back. Down to the valley, over the places we are forced to call home. The buildings scattered like chalky bones smashed against the bulge of dirt hills. On the bus with me are Black kids, a few Native kids who everyone thinks are Samoans, and actual Samoan kids who all live in squat, single-story government housing. There are also Mexican and Central American kids living in tiny, neat houses with yards like parking lots and a few white kids with houses adorned with broken stoves or mattresses so filthy they are iridescent with implausible greens and browns. If any of us is lucky, we share classes with other kinds of white people who seem to have lives like the Rockefellers.

Approaching the bus stop I see a girl. From the way she stands, slightly hunched, shoulders sloped, her black, uneven, bowl-cut bangs covering her eyes, I figure she is like me—a loner who might cling to other people if given the chance.

"Hey," I say, wanting to believe that I am, somehow, good enough to befriend.

She nods, still staring at the road. She is brown-skinned but her cheeks are red and inflamed with acne. I figure she's either Native or maybe Central American. It will turn out that I'm wrong. She's Filipina.

"I'm Crystal," she whispers. I notice her hand goes to the wooden cross she wears around her neck, a talisman.

"Lara," I say. My smile is meant to be reassuring, but she's not looking. Instead, she's watching a bright white Lexus roll up to the stop sign. From the open window, Mariah Carey croons sap. At the wheel is a white girl with bleached blond hair twisted into a messy beehive. Her passenger is a Black guy who reminds me of that actor, Marlon Wayans, with his deep brown skin and aquiline nose, only skinnier and with a low fade. I have never seen them before. The girl is chattering loudly, bits of her voice blasting through the music. My ears catch clips of words. *Fucking. Homework. P.E. Commoners.*

Commoner. That's me. When the car turns right onto the road leading out of the valley and continues beyond the hills that imprison me, it seems like those kids are actually going someplace.

I turn to Crystal and see her with new, discerning eyes. Her shapeless jean skirt, the no-name white shoes of an orderly. I decide her parents are recent arrivals, indoctrinated with the idea that an American education and hard work will save a person from whatever patchwork version of life is on offer in the old country. Thankfully, Yevgenia feeds me none of this crap. She is an atheist when it comes to the scriptures of the immigrant future. "Don't hope for shit, because you get what you get," she always says. So I learn there is nothing to work for, no specific thing I need to be. I go to school because it's free and keeps the social workers away, but mostly because my mother wants me out of the house.

Crystal scrambles onto the bus when it arrives like she is scared she will get left behind. I give her enough room so no one will mistake us for being together. She slips into the first seat, right behind the driver. I pause on the second step, shaken for a moment by the raucous shit talking coming from the back of the bus.

I take a deep breath before being thrown into the pit of my peers.

The driver, a dark-skinned man wearing a silver durag, looks down at me. The hole from his missing canine tooth is almost endearing. "You better get your ass in a seat," he says, closing the door behind me.

JULIE AND CHARLES, the kids in the Lexus, are terrible together. They have a friendship of convenience. Charles needs rides, as well as an excellent source of free, off-the-rack clothing— which Julie steals for him—and Julie needs a friend who her parents will frown upon. She also likes to have another excuse to shoplift. The two of them bring me into their lives with the fierce intensity of an unhappy couple who gets a new puppy.

"You look a lot like that girl Raquel Kamaka. The two of you could be sisters or something," Julie says to me the first time we meet, when a rare rainy afternoon sweeps her and Charles into the library at lunchtime.

I admit, at first, I think Julie is an idiot. Because I know who she's talking about, and no, Raquel and I are far from looking like sisters. At fifteen or sixteen, whatever age she is, Raquel is petite and womanly where I am tall and angular. Raquel's straight black hair is in either two aggressively tight cornrows or long box braids. Raquel's skin is the flesh of a walnut where mine is the color of wet sand. My hair is lighter, a deep brown, curly, and I can't be bothered to wear it any way but pulled out of my face. Raquel is the kind of girl guys talk about. She has boyfriends and Monday-morning hickies. I have a single raunchy Marquis de Sade book my mother picked up years ago at a yard sale.

Charles comes up behind her, talking loud: "For real, Julie? Raquel is Hawaiian Syndicate. Have you seen her ink?" He waves his hand apologetically at me. "The two of you are nothing alike."

I shrug. I am going for nonchalance but wonder if it comes off as misanthropy. At lunch, I hide in the sorry English lit section, deep in the farthest corner of the library. The kids at school don't talk to me and I don't talk to them. I've never questioned the arrangement so I regard Charles and Julie warily.

"We have Kim's class together." The chair scrapes across the industrial linoleum floor as Charles sits down.

After weeks of what amounted to an academic gladiatorial circuit where I battled it out and proved my mettle among the lower ranks, I finally landed in Ms. Kim's AP English class. Ms. Kim is not like any of the other teachers. First, she isn't white. She isn't old and she isn't boring. Her parents immigrated to the U.S. from Korea and she has traveled all over the world. The class is less a class than a cult following with Charles at the helm. While I sit in Ms. Kim's presence, dumb and speechless, Charles dominates and steers every and all discussions with his critiques. *I found his characters fulfilled a metonymic function*, or, *Her play of images really challenges the hegemony of the signifier.* He seems to have access to some specialized knowledge, turning the rest of the class into neophytes. Perhaps this comes with the territory of a person who refuses to be shaped by the opinion of others.

Because this is for certain: in the part of California where we live, on the edge of the desert surrounded by urine-colored weeds and speckled brown boulders, Charles is unlike anyone, male or female. Everyone knows it. Charles wears tweed sports jackets, penny loafers, tapered slacks, fake black-rimmed glasses, plaid scarves, a trench coat in the rain. He carries books with complicated titles by authors with hard-to-pronounce names. All of this gives the impression of him as a foreign exchange student, visiting from a place far more interesting than our puny, go-nowhere desert town. And since Charles is poor and Black and smart and gay, he creates a future for himself that includes none of the shit around us. Understandably, this makes him completely full of himself.

Julie glowers at the back of Charles's head. She sinks down in the chair next to him. Her T-shirt is strategically torn at the collar, the hole large enough to expose the curve of her shoulder.

Charles juts his chin to the book in my hand. "What are you reading?"

I flash the cover of the book. "*Things Fall Apart*," I say.

"Right. It's pretty good. Is that what you're doing for the paper?"

"Well, I'm trying to decide." My face is burning. Charles acts like he doesn't notice. It's hard to tell if Julie does. Her eyes are empty.

"I'm writing about existentialist immanentism," he says. "You know, reading Jean-Paul Sartre and Elizabeth Bishop side by side. Ultimately, the paper will be about Bishop's work. How she rejects participation in experiences and how her poetry is all about the articulation of being in the world, right? You know, intentionality."

I nod my head, though I don't know what he's talking about.

Julie groans. "Oh, come on, can we get out of here?"

"In a minute." Charles puffs out his chest a little. "I write poetry, so I find it interesting." He glances at Julie like he's making a point. "What about you?" He turns back to me.

"Me?"

"Yeah, do you write?"

It feels strange to be asked this, as if I am the kind of person who might have a desire for self-expression. As if I am the kind of person who observes or wants my words to be observed. "A little." I hear myself tell the lie.

Charles snaps his fingers. "I knew it." There is real excitement in his voice. "What? Do you write poetry too or short stories or something like that?"

I think about the only writing I've ever done, a year or two ago, in a diary my mother once took from me, marking it up with a red pen, handing it back, amused at what she called "asinine drivel"—words I had to look up. I nod. "Something like that."

"LET'S GET OUT of here." Julie is stretched out on her stomach. Her feet bounce against the sofa's armrest like Ping-Pong balls, first the right, then the left.

Charles, Julie, and I start hanging out together after school. Then Julie and I start leaving school at lunchtime, or like today, ditching altogether.

"Let's go to the beach," I offer.

She wrinkles her nose. "Too far. My dad clocks my miles so he'd know I wasn't in school. We need someplace close."

I have been to Julie's house once. Charles and I waited in her car while she ran in. Even from the outside, I could see she comes from a world differently ordered than ours. She lives in Bella Vista, Canyon Lake's gated community. It's the gated community's gated community. Bella Vista's Tuscan-style homes are coral-colored dominoes circling a fake waterfall. There is a guardhouse and speed bumps and real grass that can't be grown over two inches and can be watered only between 6:00 and 6:30 a.m. It is so unlike the Oasis, it might as well be in Italy. Charles asks Julie if we can ever hang out at her place, use her pool, eat her food for a change, but she says her parents are assholes and she goes on and on about their strict rules. I don't doubt it, but all I can see is the car they give her, the spending money, and the phone they pay for.

"We'll go shopping." Julie sits up on my sofa. "Let's get ready."

I groan. I know what shopping means to Julie. It's two hours crammed into my bathroom, me sitting on the toilet while Julie puts makeup on me. I let her do the makeup because I don't own any. But I've moved so much I've never really had friends, so I'm eager to please. Once I even let Julie "fix" my hair despite myself. When she touched it, she was surprised, saying, "Oh, it's so fluffy, like a poodle's." She then ratted it with a comb, knotting it, breaking it, and making me look like the bride of Frankenstein.

For Julie, shopping also means casing a store, watching out for plainclothes security, finding the cameras' dead spots, and detagging clothes in the changing room. The first couple of times, I pretend not to notice. Then one afternoon at my house, after we have been at an Eckerd's, I see she has taken four or five bottles of cheap nail polish.

"Why do you steal? I mean, aren't you worried you'll get caught?" I don't look at her when I ask. We are still new friends, after all.

When Julie laughs, it's a short, uncomfortable sound that comes out like a yelp. "I don't know," she says after a long pause. "I'm good at it and also it's kind of fun."

"Yeah, but what if you get caught?" I look at the nail polish she lines up on my kitchen table. I can't understand it. What's four or five dollars to someone like her? She probably has more than enough cash in her wallet and a few of her parents' credit cards.

"Oh, I've been caught before," she brags. "A couple of times. I just cried, said it was my first time, or I'd tell them my parents are splitting up or my mom was in the hospital or something. Then I say I am sorry and it won't happen again."

"Really?"

"Yeah. I mean, I get the lecture about not throwing my life away and how it's all a slippery slope to prison, yada, yada. But they haven't called my parents or anything. I just pay for whatever it was and that's it."

"That's it," I repeat. I think about me stealing, getting caught. The stuff I stole from Terri still crumpled in the corner of my drawer. I can barely look at it.

"YOU ALMOST DONE in there?" Yevgenia leans against the bathroom door in her robe, running her fingers through her hair. "Some of us have jobs, you know."

Julie goes rigid. She steps to the side of the toilet, like she is trying to put me in between her and my mother.

It's hard for Yevgenia to conceal her pleasure at Julie's

discomfort. When they first meet, my mother asks Julie her usual newcomer question: *What books do you like to read?* Julie says, "Do magazines count? Just kidding. I'm more of a movie and TV person."

My mother nods silently at Julie and then turns to me, an eyebrow raised. "So your friend is a real American intellectual. How charming." From then on, Yevgenia goes out of her way to make passive-aggressive comments whenever Julie's around, like *It's a shame money can't buy people brains*, or, *The rest of the world knows how dumb Americans are, that's why they let you call yourselves a "superpower."*

"We're done. It's all yours," I say to Yevgenia.

She eyes me suspiciously as I step past her. I smile grimly, wishing for once my mother might ask where I'm going or why I'm not in school.

Instead she says, "That color lipstick is no good on you. Makes you look like a bozo," and shuts the bathroom door behind her.

IT'S ON ONE of these afternoons, while Julie, Charles, and I are ditching class, that we spy Steve leaving his mobile home. We are sitting on the front steps of my trailer. Charles is reciting a poem he has written that sounds very much like a droll to-do list. Julie and I are bent over our feet, painting our toenails. The heat and chemical smell of lacquer makes me light-headed. When Steve steps out onto his landing our attentions turn in unison.

"Hiya," Steve calls out to us, raising his helmet in a quick greeting before fitting it on his head. He swings his leg over his bike. He revs the engine twice as he passes, slowly, the roar of the machine loud enough to thrum within us. Do I imagine a smile behind his dark visor?

"Whoa, who's *that*?" Julie asks.

Charles sucks his teeth hard. "An overrated teen idol."

Julie slaps Charles on the leg. "Come on, you'd do him."

A smile leaks from him. "If I had to."

"That's Steve," I say to Julie, unsure if our stage of friendship requires me to say more. Charles and Julie glance at each other.

"And?" Charles leans in closer.

"He's . . ." I haven't articulated out loud what I like about him, so I stumble. "Yeah, I guess, I kind of like him, you know." I sound stupid. It's the consequence of not telling the truth. Because really, I hardly know Steve.

"Oh God, are you going to have sex with him? I mean you totally should." Julie is flapping her hands up and down in front of her.

"Nope, he's married and has a kid." This is a version of a conversation I keep having with Yevgenia. It leaves me feeling exhausted.

Julie claps her hands on her thighs. "You're joking, right? Okay, he's old. But he's hot."

"Yeah, if you are going to have sex," Charles offers, "might as well have it with someone who knows what they're doing."

"I guess." I wonder if they can figure out that I'm a virgin.

"So your big plan is to stalk him from up on this ratty-ass porch?" Charles laughs into his fist. "Is that what y'all count as 'trailer-park seduction'?"

Charles makes a habit of pretending he doesn't live at the Oasis too. "Isn't your porch as ratty as mine?" I throw back at him. I've never been to his place but I know they are pretty much all the same. "Besides," I add quickly, "I'm not trying to seduce him. I just want to go to the movies or something."

"Oh, you scoundrel." Charles clutches his imaginary pearls, his voice a quick falsetto, before turning peevish. "And bitch, I live in a double-wide."

Thankfully Julie has an appetite for attention. "Hey, did I ever tell you about Tony Martinez?" She launches into a story about her first time having sex with the pimple-faced JV basketball player. The crux of it is that while they were doing it, she never told Tony he didn't get his penis into her vagina.

"Where'd he put it then?" I'm confused.

"Do you have to ask?" Charles says, shaking his head like I am a lost cause.

◆

It's always the one who laughs too much who is the first to stick a knife in your back.

It's past midnight when Yevgenia moans "*bozhe moi*" into her pillow before falling into bed after closing at Rusty's. The noise wakes me. Her bedroom light is on and from where I lie on the sofa I get a straight shot of her bare, pale ass. It's a deflated beach ball washed up on her bedspread. I want to close her door, but I won't. Yevgenia's bedroom is off limits. When I was younger I would sneak into her room just to sit among her things. From her bedroom in the apartment in the rundown Victorian in San Francisco, to the room in the coral 1950s complex in Los Angeles, or her space in the three-room ranch house in Portland, Oregon, they all undoubtedly look like her bedroom at the Oasis.

Two cardboard boxes stacked and covered with an old lace tablecloth. The gaudy imitation Tiffany lamp she bought at a yard sale when she first arrived in California. Its cartoonish stained-glass effect more made-by-local-kindergartner than handcrafted-by-skilled-jeweler. Still, Yevgenia carries that lamp from place to place, all carefully wrapped as if it is the real thing. And then there are her books, stacked or lined against the wall, never in a bookcase. Some books, hard-covers with call numbers printed on white tags and taped to the spine, are hostages taken from the quiet libraries my mother ransacks. Other books, paperbacks with soft covers torn completely off and their value, diminished to twenty-five cents, boldly marked in black Sharpie on the front page, are orphans she rescued from garage sales and garbage bins. In the years when I was more curious about her, I sat among these books, some with titles in languages I will never speak, others with titles I wouldn't understand for years, and imagined what each volume contained within its pages. I dare not remove a book without carefully marking its place in the ordered chaos of my mother's filing system. Books are her private conversations, she says, so Keep Out. And I do.

Screw church and all religion. The library is the most important institution.

In the afternoon, Yevgenia is at the dining table, her tabernacle, an open book and overflowing ashtray in front of her. Cigarette smoke curdles the air. It circles like a vulture around her head.

It's her fault I am home this morning and not at school, so I glare at her.

She doesn't notice.

When my mother reads, it is an all-consuming endeavor. She goes for a day or two, stopping only for the toilet, a drink, a bit of food, a cigarette, sleep, and, if she absolutely must, her shift at work. A while ago, I studied her in one of these loops. She makes a book look so tantalizing, so interesting, I ended up thinking, I'm going to borrow it when she's done. Then I saw that it was Gogol's *Dead Souls*, a book she had read before, only this time she was reading the Italian translation. Months later she read it again in Spanish. My mother reads for nostalgia. The same twenty or maybe twenty-five books year in and year out, in the original and in translation. Once I know this, I understand that what my mother seeks from books isn't what I seek. I want to be lifted up, carried away. She wants to be anchored. The exact opposite of what each of us wants from our real life.

I hover closer and closer to my mother until she gives a loud sigh. She closes the book carefully. "Are you queen of England now, waking up at noon?" she asks, glancing at the stove clock even though it's broken.

"If the queen's mother ever fucked up by forgetting to send the queen's immunization record to her school, then yeah, I guess so."

After weeks of warning letters and phone calls from school, I am suspended until I bring in proof of vaccination, signed by a doctor or some sort of official exemption. Yevgenia keeps saying she's handling it, but of course she lets it slide.

———

MY MOTHER, who thinks intelligence is more important than wealth and even sex, claims not to grasp the utility of what she calls "the state's education system." In my early years, she chose to school me in the libraries of whatever town we happened to live in. For as long as I can remember, my mother would roll up to the library, rattle off a list of books she wanted me to read, and remind me to talk to no one. Then she would drive off, promising to come back to get me later. This worked until I was nine. Then the librarian in some small town in Arizona noticed I was in the stacks for three straight days, unsupervised, during the dead hours of midday. I tried to warn Yevgenia. Even I knew it wouldn't be long before someone looked up to see a brown-skinned child sitting alone in the corner reading books, no matter how much I tried to hide myself. As I feared, on the third day, the librarian approached me as I sat reading on the floor, wedged between the stacks.

"You speak English?" the woman asked, scrutinizing my face.

This was not a question I was prepared to answer. While Yevgenia told me to not talk to anyone, she also said, *Never tell anyone anything about yourself, your name, where you live, or where you come from. And say absolutely nothing when it comes to me.*

I hesitated. Was language personal information? If I said yes, would I give away too much? I nodded as a compromise.

This seemed to satisfy the librarian, who gestured with her chin. "Yeah, I figured you weren't an illegal with that hair of yours." I didn't know what to do so I just stared.

"Well, this isn't a romper room and I'm no babysitter, got that?" She brushed her hands on her thighs like she was wiping them free of dirt. Then she walked back to her desk, leaving me alone until my mother appeared at the entrance, hours later. Yevgenia looked like a flaming matchstick with her dyed-red hair. When my mother motioned me to come with her, the librarian was out of her seat, heading off my path, getting to my mother first.

"Listen, ma'am." I remember how the librarian stood with parted feet, hands on her hips. Yevgenia was wearing a pair of sunglasses. She moved them from the bridge of her nose to a resting place on top of her head. My mother cast her hazel eyes over the librarian, a dumpy woman in a rumpled white shirt, baggy khaki shorts, comfortable thick-soled sandals— all wardrobe choices of certain American women my mother derides.

Yevgenia expertly raised a judgmental arched brow. "Yes?" It was in the way she spoke, the way she could cut you with a look, that made me fear my mother. It was as if just beneath Yevgenia's short, tight dress there lived a demonically cruel beast that thought nothing of bludgeoning you to death. The librarian saw it too, because she took a step back and softened her voice.

"Um, well, it's about the child. She needs to be accompanied by an adult." The librarian looked at my mother, who stared at her coldly. "It's just that I, or we, will have to call the authorities. You know, liability issues."

My mother said nothing, purposely dragging her gaze to look beyond the woman's shoulder, locking on to me. Yevgenia's eyes smoldered. I was in deep trouble.

"Well, did you call them?" my mother asked. Perhaps it was just the situation, but Yevgenia's English was more deliberately "Russian," as if she was trying to sound more villainous to an American ear.

"Call who?" And maybe it occurred to the librarian at that moment that she should mind her own business.

"The authorities."

"Oh no, I didn't call this time." The librarian gave my mother a chummy smile, lowering her voice slightly like they were exchanging secret recipes. "Think of it as a favor."

"Oh, good," Yevgenia said, her face expressionless. "Then I won't have to put your head in a box." She pulled her sunglasses down onto her nose. "Think of it as a favor." It was an over-the-top gesture, and I was just young enough to be impressed. So on our way back to the car, I must have said something like, "You're so glamorous," or, "You're like a movie star," or some such compliment because I remember she laughed, briefly squeezing me close, before saying, "Never let anyone say where you do or don't belong. Especially at the library and especially not by people like her."

From then on, whenever we moved, my mother always, eventually, enrolled me in school.

I THINK ABOUT that Arizona librarian as I stand staring at my mother, waving my letter of suspension. Maybe because Yevgenia is not yet dressed for the day, still in her threadbare tank top, her breasts distending the word *pink* across her chest, she needs a moment to consider the timeliness of an argument. She rests her jaw in the palm of her hand. Her face turns toward the feeble gray light from a small window in what might be called the dining room. The view from there is of the roof of the car, and beyond that, the rusted chain-link fence of the empty dirt lot next door. Then a peek of the road and the base of the mountains. I get it. My mother will make me wait.

I shrug my shoulders. "Okay then. I guess I won't get a high school diploma. I'll sit around all day." I purse my lips together. It's not like Yevgenia cares if I am in school, as long as I stay out of her way.

The vinyl under my feet feels leathery as I walk past her. "You forgot the bread," I say, staring into the bare refrigerator. Actually, she never buys bread. I do. I look at the back of her head. The day before, she had me bleach it blond and it looks terrible, like she is wearing a halo of straw. She was so pissed when she saw the result that she cursed in every language she knows, Russian, Italian, Spanish, German, and English, slamming around the trailer for nearly two hours. All I kept saying was, "I'm not a fucking professional," and, "You're the one who told me to leave it on for so long."

She's pissed. I'm pissed. We're even.

Yevgenia goes back to her book. The conversation is over for her. I fume in the kitchen, slamming cabinets, banging drawers. I want her attention and she won't give it to me. This is our life together. Eventually, I sit down at the dingy, chipped Formica table with her, reach into my backpack, and pull out a copy of the second Harry Potter, *Chamber of Secrets*. The book belongs to Julie. Not that she's reading it, but she carried it around long enough until she accidently left it at my house. I prop the book up so the cover is prominently displayed and begin reading.

The way some parents give their children lessons in life, or affection, or moral codes, or family history, or a sense of tradition, my mother gave me reading. Yevgenia taught me how to read at the age of four and, for many years, shaped my tastes. I am never allowed to read anything that doesn't meet with her approval. I live in fear of her chiding, "That's a baby book. Are you a baby?"

My mother swoons over the Russian writers, of course, with the exception of Nabokov. She claims he hasn't suffered enough to be a "real Russian" like Tsvetaeva or Akhmatova, and besides, Nabokov is too contemporary. When she isn't pushing the old Russians on me, she is forcing me to read other books, European "classics" that all seem to center on garden parties, prissy family feuds, social lives that are threatened to be upended by war.

I read her books dutifully, but I don't take any pleasure in them. When I was eleven I would sneak books home, the kind my mother hates, popular books that later became movies, books serving up soft-core porn and easy plotlines.

"YOU'RE *READING* THAT CRAP?" My mother sits back to light up another cigarette, eyeing the Harry Potter with contempt. "You want me to send you to school so you can continue to read baby books?"

"No, I want you to send me to school so you don't have to see me reading baby books." I give her the fakest sweet smile. I don't understand Yevgenia, how she could be such a snob. She claims she went to university back in Moscow, but it was probably some crumbling building with one professor because apparently her degree has qualified her to work only shitty jobs in America.

SINCE I'M NOT allowed at school, I spend my time in the stacks at the local library. One day I come home and at the base of the steps to the front door, I hear Steve's voice coming from inside.

"Okay I get it now. She's your *actual* daughter," he says.

Through the open window above me, the quick burst of water hitting the metal sink at full blast. I'm not sure if I am walking into a postcoital moment or a neighborly visit, but I hear a seed of irritation when Yevgenia speaks.

"If you mean, did I squeeze her out of my vagina? Then yes, she's my *actual* daughter."

"But if her dad is, what, Cuban, how come she's so . . . ?" He stops himself. I instinctively lean forward. There is a long, silent pause. I imagine my mother looking at him with her interrogator's face.

"Yes? Go on," she says.

"Well, it's just . . . I guess, I thought all Cubans were like, you know, Ricky Ricardo."

"Ricky Ricardo?" She feigns confusion.

"Yeah, like from that old TV show," he explains. "She's dark, or darker, than him."

"Dark or darker?"

I hate when Yevgenia does this. Repeating whatever she thinks is stupid so that the person speaking can see how stupid they are.

"Yeah, I mean she's, like, Black," he offers eagerly, as if Yevgenia hasn't seen this essential fact. The way he talks it's as if he is diving to help gather scattered groceries after the bag breaks.

"Oh yes, I understand," she says, adding cheerfully, "*Sei un cretino. Stronzo. Deficiente.*" When my mother is feeling especially superior to the Americans around her, she leans hard on the European side of Russia's transcontinentalism by insulting people in Italian, or sometimes French, or she'll throw out a few rude words of German.

"What's that?" Steve asks.

"Nothing," she replies. "I just noticed the time. You can take that beer with you when you leave." I hear my mother's heavy footsteps move to the door. I scramble to the other end of the carport and hide behind the front fender of the car. They wouldn't see me anyway, but I'm not taking my chances.

"Oh, I thought we were going to, you know . . ." Steve's voice trails off.

"'You know' what?" My mother must have ushered him to the door with determined swiftness because I can hear them on the landing now, Steve's already standing outside.

His voice drops to a tone that mimics an almost cartoon-ish seduction. "Well, don't you want to fool around? You seemed pretty into it."

"Naw." My mother flattens out her accent to the ugliest sound in the American diction. "I'm not interested." I hear her shut the door in his face. I wait for the shuffle of Steve's feet to move off my steps and cross the street. Sitting on the asphalt of the carport, with my back against Yevgenia's tire, I'm uncertain how to feel.

These questions of my genesis, of my race, of my father, are not new. Not to me, and certainly not to my mother. *Is she adopted?* was among the first questions asked by strangers, my mother told me. So why the ire directed at Steve? Why forgo weeks of bragging about her victory bedding him?

Under the rocky asphalt surface, my right butt cheek goes numb. Maybe Yevgenia is angry because Steve asked about me instead of her? I like this idea. Of my mother being the one who is pushed aside. Of me being desired over her. I stand and shake my legs back to life. I want to believe this, so I do, for the few seconds it takes for me to walk into my trailer.

"Hey," I say to my mother, who looks up from her seat at

the dining table when I come through the door. There is a mug of tea at her elbow; one of her notebooks is cracked open in front of her. I've interrupted her drafting a new entry on her list of edicts.

She glances up quickly and frowns. "I thought you were going to that job today?"

Shit. Yevgenia has been on me for weeks about finding part-time work. To get her off my back, I lie, saying I am looking until I have to turn the lie of looking into a lie of receiving. "Yeah," I say, "it was just orientation. I went to the library afterward." All my life, my mother has demonstrated that the skill of lying is mastered through partially telling the truth.

"What did you read at the library?" She turns her pen around in her hands. She's looking in my direction, but not at me. It could be my imagination but her eyes rest somewhere near my feet.

"A collection of poetry by Cummings." Another lie. At the library, I flip through pages of a *Time* magazine and fall asleep instead.

My mother sticks out her tongue a little to show her disgust. "Garbage. That's not poetry," she pronounces. I have her full attention now. "Next time read Khlebnikov, Mayakovsky, or even Pasternak." She goes back to her notebook, sharply underlining something.

Yevgenia drops her pen on the table and, leaning back, cups the sides of her neck with both hands. "Of all the countries in the world, and I pick the one with some of the dumbest people in it." She rolls her head from side to side before yawning loudly. "You better get paid for going in today. I'm already working doubles and I don't want to have to start cleaning shit off other people's toilets." Her dark look reminds me of our time in Las Vegas a few months ago, cleaning houses together for our so-called living.

"Okay, I'll look into it." And I am briefly convinced that I will actually try to find a job.

"Here, come sit." Yevgenia kicks a chair next to her. It bumps the leg of the table with a thump. She has that look in her eye, like she wants to lecture me from her notebook.

I groan. "Please not now."

"Sit. These are new." She flashes the notebook. I can see more than half the page is filled with her writing. "I promise, there's some important things here that you should know." My mother looks at me with a bright, hopeful smile and I know it's a trap. She just wants an audience for what will likely be a few captive hours. She'll drink and talk. The subject of Steve will come up or how she was right about Mexico or about what books I should be reading to make myself a wiser, more interesting person. A veiled insult will lead to a fight and one of us will pretend not to be hurt by the other.

"No, sorry." I feign regret. "You know, I worked today." This my mother will understand.

"Lari, *please*." Using my pet name, she knows I'll soften a little. "Just ten minutes."

I think about her and Steve, how instead of sitting here at the table with him, she'd be in her room screwing around with him. This makes me angry.

"I don't want any of your lessons right now, okay?" I turn away from her but then I can't stop myself. "I just want to be in *regular* school, with *regular* kids, who have *regular* mothers."

She closes her eyes, slowly, like she's trying to decide

if she's going to get irritated. "By *regular* you mean, what? American? Matronly? Boring women who don't embarrass you? *Please*. I'd sooner throw myself into a pit with a thousand razor-sharp stakes."

My stomach sinks. Is this the condition of being someone's child? Reflexive harm? Or is it just me? "I'm sorry," I say.

She waves her hand. "You can go," she says, focusing again on her writing.

LATER, WHEN WALKING by the dining table, I see her notebook out. I pick it up and look at the last entry written in blue ink. *Love is always labor. No one can ever tell you if it's worth it.* She underlined *always* twice.

YEVGENIA DOES IT, sort of. After eight hellish days at home, we are sitting in the parking lot of the high school when she pulls out a yellow card, curled and split at the ends.

"What's that?" I ask.

"Immunization record," she mumbles, a cigarette pressed between her lips. With the pen in her hand she writes dates in empty boxes and falsifies a doctor's signature.

"You can't do that."

"Just did. Ready?" My mother flicks her cigarette to the ground as she swings her legs out of the car. She is wearing a jean jacket with a fur collar. Her heeled boots are laced up past her ankles, skimming the ends of stretch pants meant to look like jeans. Her fake Chanel bag is pressed in her palm, the chain strap twisted around her rigid wrist a few times like she is carrying a medieval flail.

I stuff my hands in my sweatshirt, not caring if I fall behind. With a safe distance between us, there is no chance people will think we are together. Not that anyone would. We are so different from each other physically. Beyond my being Black and her white, my mother is shorter, stout with strong, solid legs. Plus, she has larger breasts than I do, a fact she always points out. The only obvious thing we share is the color of our eyes and part of my last name.

By the time I get to the principal's office my mother is already standing at reception, trying to make small talk with stone-faced Reba, the secretary whose sole function is to come to work and collect her check.

"Oh, here she is." My mother smiles in my general direction. "I was just saying to Ms."—Yevgenia stops and looks expectantly at Reba, but there is no response—"to the lady that you were eager to get back to school. I explained we had to wait for your records to be sent from abroad."

I roll my eyes. I hate when my mother lies. She leans into the counter a little harder, like it needs to support some private information. "You know, we do everything differently in Europe."

Reba doesn't look up from her papers. Her scalp and hair are the color of bricks. Her bloated white hand motions to my mother to give over the immunization record. I stand staring at them, acutely aware that these two women with bad dye jobs control my future.

"I just need to get a photocopy of this and your signature."

"Yes, of course." My mother gives me a look that tells me I owe her, like it was my idea to be born.

Reba gathers up the documents and heads for the copier at the back of the room. Through her white pants, cellulite fractures all over her ass and thighs. My mother grimaces. "*Che schifo*," she says in Italian.

My mother is an ardent antiauthoritarian. Her dislike for anyone who has any control over her is immediately activated in the strangest of circumstances. A waitress who seems to deliberately push back against a tea refill. A manager at a cinema who refuses to let her bring in her own food. And now Reba. Yevgenia rips into these lower-tier sentinels of the powers that be, commenting on their weakness or human failing. Not long ago, I was right there with her, sniping cruel observations, being part of her team, playing for her approval. And then I realized she cannot turn off these quips. Shit-talking strangers just trying to do their jobs until the insults turn into bitter conspiracies.

Yevgenia nudges me with her elbow. "What is she thinking?" She juts her chin toward Reba's backside. "It's like a hideous billboard."

"Can you shut up? Just stop talking," I say. Reba looks over at us, suspicious. My mother gives her a crinkled-nose smile as phony as her handbag.

"Oh, touchy. It's your time of the month?" Yevgenia takes my hand, squeezing it hard. I try to draw it back. She applies pressure, letting me know she's in charge. My knuckles protrude through thin skin. She says quietly, "I'll cut the tongue out of your mouth if you ever tell me to shut up again."

I don't give in to the pain. I deny her satisfaction.

"*Zanoschivy*," my mother hisses. I don't know the direct translation, but I get the gist. Yevgenia defied the immigrant-parent imperative and never bothered to formally teach me her language.

"Can I go now?" I ask when Reba hands the papers to Yevgenia.

"You'll need a hall pass," Reba says.

She writes me one and I glare at my mother as I walk to the door.

Yevgenia gives a Miss America wave. "Goodbye, dear. See you after school. I'll have your snack waiting for you." Her laugh is wicked, vampiric. We both know she will be out when I get home, likely at Rusty's or another bar, pressing her breasts against the arm of a married man, gaming for free drinks and a good time.

3

A small mind always means a small penis.

It's 4:00 p.m. and Yevgenia stumbles out of her room, naked, wearing the dull look of postpartying haze. A tumbleweed of stiff blond hair sits on her head. I'm at the dining table, gladly doing my homework, trying to avert my eyes from her. I jump when she slams the bathroom door behind her. There is a dull clatter of objects hitting vinyl flooring, cosmetics she knocks over. I hear her cursing at them like she's bullying the neighborhood children. *"Hijas de puta*, I should kick your asses. Why did you spill?" Then the sound of groaning as she bends over to pick them up. "Answer me, you little shits." Next the blast of the shower and Yevgenia sobering up while she croaks out a loud rendition of Lucio Dalla's "Balla Balla Ballerino," originally a punchy Italian song that sounds sinister coming out of my mother's mouth. I push back from the table and I see my immunization record sticking out of the corner of her fake Chanel bag.

I've never seen my health record. I glance at the handwritten notations, the years of the appointments. I study the last two entries on the card. My mother's handwriting is trim. I admire the uniformity until I notice that all the entries—not just the last two—were also written by her. From the first line to the last, all the dates of the doctor visits are within a two-month radius of her birthday. The names of doctors are mostly those of previous lovers. I think for a moment and realize I have no recollection of ever being inside a doctor's office. No white coat, no needle's jab, no tears, no soothing lollipop. Have I ever been vaccinated against anything? I wonder.

IT TAKES ME three buses and nearly two hours, but I finally get to Riverside County's free clinic just before they stop taking patients. Going in through the sliding glass doors and crossing the lobby, I know I've entered the land of the poor and underserved. Hard green plastic chairs snake around the room in long rows. Two TVs shout across from each other. On one, the news in Spanish, on the other a *Tom and Jerry* cartoon. Bodies orient themselves according to their predilections. A bank of hefty white women mostly wearing sweatpants sit pressed into seats in the left corner. A few of them angrily bounce crying babies on their laps. A long row of Black women sit along the opposite wall, speaking to one another in loud, familiar tones while watching their bored but patient children for signs of insolence. In the two middle aisles, groupings of Latinos are slumped in their seats, their hands on their chins, eyeing the sign reading NO CELLPHONES in three languages, like it might change its mind.

I crane my neck looking for an empty seat and see one next to the intake window in the multiethnic elderly section. I move to take it but an old guy, whose light brown skin is so wrinkled and timeworn it's hard to tell if he's Filipino or Mexican or African American, starts a consumptive cough that causes an Asian woman next to him to lean in the opposite direction with her hand shielding her nose and mouth.

I sigh. I go over to the Black and Latino men holding up the clinic walls with their backs and find a spot among them.

I wait.

"BORISLAVA? LARA MONTOYA-BORISLAVA?" It's twenty-five minutes past the clinic's closing time. A weary Black woman dressed in scrubs with long thick dreads tied down her back calls my name like it costs her something.

I trudge up to the window as I've watched so many people do, harassed and defensive. This woman is the state's gatekeeper. She is an obstacle to my disease-free living, which I'm sure has been greatly jeopardized by sitting around the clinic for two and a half hours.

"Says here you want youth vaccinations, you're eighteen, but you got no social security card, no driver's license, and no ID number." The woman's brown eyes lock on mine. She knows I'm lying.

From behind me, toward the back of the room, rubber sneakers screech against the floor. There is scuffling. "Dude, why you be touching me, man? You fucking crazy?" The nurse looks over my shoulder briefly and I turn to see two exhausted security guards wearing latex gloves steering a stocky Latino kid with a shaved head toward the exit.

"So, which is it?" Her upper lip curls. She folds her arms across her stomach. "I don't have time for this mess. Either you get parental consent or provide proof of age or a previous vaccination record—"

There's a loud bang by the door. The kid has kicked over a trash can on his way out. "Mara Salvatrucha, motherfuckers!" His hands twist into a gang sign and he shoves his middle finger in the air.

A peal of laughter comes from the group of Black women, drowning out the woman. "—immigration status, or you're not eligible for care," she continues. She starts to return the papers to me, her eyes already on her computer screen for the next patient.

"Wait." I read her name tag pinned to her brightly patterned scrub top. L. Morgan. I pull my crumpled evidence out of my backpack. "Ms. Morgan," I say, trying hard to sound respectful. "I need vaccinations because I think my mother forged my school records. I don't know if I've ever been vaccinated. Look, she even wrote 'Dr. Johnny Rockets.'" I point to one of the earlier entries on my record. "That's when she worked there." I hate the mewling sound in my voice as I tattle.

L. Morgan waves my words away. "How old are you?"

"Sixteen."

A forceful, annoyed sigh pushes through her nostrils.

"I'm almost seventeen?" It comes out like a question.

"Right, you're a minor. Legally, I need your mother or guardian's signature if you're still a dependent."

"What if I said she's dead?" I'm desperate.

"You really want to take it that far?"

I shrug. L. Morgan considers me for a moment. If she has an assessment of me, I can't guess what it is. She sucks her teeth but she types something into the computer anyway.

"You need to be tested for pregnancy or STDs?" She scans her eyes over me. I shake my head, embarrassed that my lack of experience leads me to fear neither.

"I'm only doing this because you're trying to do right by yourself." She turns to no one in particular and says under her breath, "I've done my good deed for the week."

She hands me a printout with an appointment. "The PA

has gone home. Come back next Tuesday at nine thirty. Better get here by eight if you want to be out by noon. Oh—you American?"

I hesitate. I am American, in that I'm not Russian or Cuban. But I'm not American in that I'm not part of what my mother calls the "provincial, uncultured, stupid mass of prudes" that make up her America. At least, I don't want to be.

I nod. "Yes. Do I need to have any ID? Birth certificate?"

"Nope. The county is just gathering statistical data."

Strangely, this information disappoints me. Though I don't know where Yevgenia keeps or if she even has my birth certificate, this is a missed opportunity to show I belong. "Thank you so much, Ms. Morgan," I say, performing a genteel poverty my mother would scorn.

"Okay, okay." She glances at the screen again, uninterested in my false manners. She's done with me and calls out to the next person, "Huang. Chun-wei Huang."

IT'S OVER AN hour since I left the clinic and I'm still waiting for the bus home. At first, I stand on the wrong side of the street. I just miss my bus by the time I realize my mistake. Then I have to pee so bad I set off for the gas station at the corner, missing another bus. I still feel good though, like I've accomplished something. I'm checking the posted bus schedule again when a silver SUV stops at the light. I look up only because the driver has the windows rolled down and the music is blaring. It's L. Morgan from the clinic. I don't wave.

She seems like a different person in her car, younger, almost happy. She feels me staring. She looks but it takes her a minute to recognize me. When she does, she turns down the music and shouts, "Why you still out here?" She squints at me as if she's trying to make out if I'm a mirage.

"I missed my bus."

She hangs her head for a few seconds. Then, almost despite herself, it seems, she calls out, "Damn it, get in. Quick."

I climb into her car as she punches the gas with a little too much force. I scramble for my seat belt, snapping it into place.

"Sorry 'bout that. There was a truck coming at us and I never trust those guys to see me. Anyway, where you headed?" She still wears her work clothes but has freed her dreads from the ponytail she had them in earlier.

"Out by seventy-four, but I'll stop anywhere really."

"Damn, you live all the way out there? There ain't nothing but rednecks and drug war fugitives out that way." She looks at me sideways, maybe to see if I'm one of them. I don't say anything. "Well, I'm not going that direction but I'll drop you at the Grapevine junction. There's a bus stop out there, I think."

"Yeah, thanks."

"Uh-huh." She turns up the music again, this time just loud enough for us to not have to talk if we don't want to.

As we drive along the stretch of the San Bernardino hills, the sun slides off the windows of the cars in front of us in long streaks of blinding light. I toy with questions I might ask her. *Nice car. What model is it? Do you have any kids? Do you like working at the clinic? How long have you been there?* I'm so busy trying to organize a conversation in my mind I don't notice we've reached the junction. I'm disappointed.

She pulls in next to the bus stop without cutting the engine. "What's your name again?" she asks.

"Lara."

"Right, Lara. My name is Leticia."

"Nice to meet you," I say.

She nods politely. "Listen, I won't be seeing you when you come to the clinic because I only work the afternoon shifts." Leticia opens her mouth to say something else but closes it again. I sense her mind warring with itself. Finally, she says hesitantly, "You know, Lara, you're a beautiful girl but, um, you gotta take care of that hair of yours. Normally I don't comment on these things. But your hair is just calling to me like it could use some product advice."

My hand goes to my head, my eyes, I'm sure, questioning. Leticia gives me a slow knowing nod, like she's breaking the news that nobody's had the heart to say until now.

"Conditioner, never shampoo, little lavender and coconut oil on the scalp, maybe some shea butter. You got yourself a bonnet?" she asks.

I shake my head no.

"I didn't think so." Leticia digs out two dollars from the pocket of her scrubs. "Get one, or wrap your hair each night. That will make a world of difference."

I take the money from her tentatively. "Thanks."

Glancing into her rearview mirror, she says, "Your bus is coming. Take care, okay?"

I can barely manage a goodbye before she turns the car back onto the road, dust and rocks kicking up under her tires.

Leticia's voice keeps playing in my mind. "You're a beautiful girl." I don't care that she followed that by saying my hair looks like shit. It's enough to be called beautiful, a first for me.

———

FOR DAYS, I hold on to Leticia's money. Touching it in my pocket until the weave of the bill's parchment is saturated with my sweat and oils and these dollars of limited value create in me a worth.

Then there comes the day when the money is no longer there. I hunt for it in my room. I tear through my jeans, rip off my sheets, bend back the spines of books. Yevgenia shouts down the hall, "*Nu!* You'll rock this house down the hill if you don't stop."

Awareness pushes out the panic as the mystery is solved. I rush into the living room. "Did you take my two dollars?" I ask, knowing she did.

"There was two dollars, yes. But is it yours? That's debatable." She sits smoking and reading on the sofa. Her fresh pack of cigarettes is likely subsidized by Leticia. I am reminded of another desecration. The price it commands.

I'm seven years old. I'm taking the garbage to the dumpsters around the back of the apartment in Anaheim. After I toss the bag into the container, I stand staring at the mountains cutting across the horizon. I can make out a bit of snow on the top of a peak. I've never seen snow up close so I'm dreaming up some way to get Yevgenia to take me there.

"What you looking at?" The voice is so friendly and so familiar, I put a name to the face without a glance. It's the dad of Patrick, a kid in my class.

"Just looking at the snow up there." I point.

"That's Mount Baldy," he says, shielding his eyes to get a better look. "You ever been?"

When I tell him I haven't but I want my mother to drive me up there, he laughs. "That's like a few hours' drive away from here."

"Oh," I say, not caring.

"Listen, walk with me this way and I'll give you five dollars." It seems like a ton of money to get for walking down the alley with him, so I figure, why not? I can buy a lot of candy with five dollars. Together we walk past the apartment complex into the parking lot of the building next to mine. It's then I realize the guy I'm walking with isn't Patrick's dad. He says he doesn't know Patrick when I ask. But I'm not alarmed. Yevgenia never lectures me like the parents on TV about talking to strangers on the street, and I'm not in the habit of being afraid of anyone but her.

"Hey, come here. I want to show you something." He ducks around the back of an empty parking garage. I'm confused at first when I see the small, wrinkly pink earthworm lying at belt level in the palm of his hand. It looks gross. "You can touch it," he says. I look up at him. Even though he's not Patrick's dad, he could be someone else's.

I hold out my hand and take the worm. It's bigger in my hand than in his. It feels cold and dead.

"Put it in your mouth," he says.

"Um, can I have my five dollars first?" I hear myself saying. For a brief moment, I'm pleased. This is a transaction. I feel smart, grown-up, even, asking for the money the way I do. I feel like my mother. And then I surprise myself. I snatch the bill just as he pulls it from his pocket and I run as fast as I can. I don't look back. I cut through apartment blocks, going around the front and then the back until I get to my building. I go inside the apartment and lock the door behind me. My mother is where I left her, back when I was a different kind of seven years old. She's sitting on the sofa reading a book and smoking a cigarette.

"Here," I say, throwing the five dollars at her. "I don't want it." I'm already stained. I can't let her know what happened. My mother has been back with me for only a few months. I worry that she would leave me again if I tell her.

Yevgenia barely looks at the money in her lap. She pushes it aside with the two fingers holding the cigarette. She asks, not really interested, "Where'd you get that?"

"Some old guy gave it to me," I say, all blasé, but my heart is thrashing in my chest. I can't look at her, so I bend down to take off my shoes. I can feel her scrutinizing me.

"Next time," she says, her eyes back on her book, "ask for twenty."

WHEN I RETURN to the clinic, I am certain Leticia has forgotten me; at least there is a part of me that hopes she has. I am ashamed for the loss of her money, ashamed of my life, which didn't allow me to think of myself as worth the gift her attention had given me. Despite all of this, stepping into the clinic, I look for her and feel sad even though I know she doesn't work the morning shift.

The waiting room is not full, though the vexation of the clientele is atmospheric, oppressive. The pent-up frustrations over money, jobs, children, housing, health, and lost opportunities are stitched into the fabric of their clothes. I move past the occupied plastic chairs, acknowledging the unity of us, the people in need of "services," too many problems too big to define. But the AC blasts and it's free, so I take an open seat in the corner.

There is a nurse, who looks Latina, standing at the intake counter. She is disinterested as an old white woman fumbles around a canvas bag she is carrying, searching for her Medicaid card. But I watch the young Black woman standing behind the old white lady. She seems agitated, like she's been standing there a long time. She taps her sandaled foot, folds and unfolds her arms in front of her. She has her hair wrapped in a bright multicolored satin scarf. I admire the beauty of her, as does, I notice, three or four men in the waiting room who watch her with wolf eyes. From behind, the young woman had the graceful body of a dancer, her legs long and strong in her spandex shorts, the curve of the small of her back, her long neck. When she turns slightly, it surprises me to see the hard, perfectly round bump of pregnancy incased in her tight hot-pink tank top.

"Why you got an attitude? I'm just asking you to change the channel," the young woman speaks over the shoulder of the old lady, directing her words at the Latina nurse. "You have two TVs and both are on the same station."

The nurse gives the young woman her best bureaucratic look of indifference. It's a steel-plated I-couldn't-give-a-fuck kind of look. She then flicks her eyes at the old woman, saying, "If you can't find your card, I'll have to reschedule you. There's an appointment at three."

The old woman looks distressed. "But that's hours from now. I know it's here someplace." She bends over the bag, stirring the contents. The items clang, like she's carrying spoons.

The young woman steps in front of the old lady, pointing at the nurse. "I'm talking to you. Why are you ignoring me?" Her voice is loud; people in the clinic start to pay attention. Even the dozing security guard by the door rouses and turns his body in the young woman's direction.

A man sitting off to the side offers his opinion to the girl, saying, "Baby, ya need to stop gettin' all worked up. Not good for the child."

"Am I talking to you?" She doesn't wait for him to reply. "Yeah, okay then." She casts her eyes at the rest of us in the room, daring us to speak. Heads turn to collectively look at the floor or glance at our empty hands. The young woman grumbles her way back to the seating area, anger emitting from her. She sits, glowering at no one in particular.

The old white woman doesn't want to surrender but has to. "Oh alright, put me down for three."

It strikes me then that poor people are always told to wait. Time was our only currency and it keeps plummeting in value.

IT'S UNCLEAR WHO caught the other looking first. Crystal, the Filipina girl from the bus stop, who lives four trailers down from me, sits as close as she can to the intake window, upright and serious. With her left hand she twirls the wooden cross held by a brown string around her neck. Her right hand rests lightly on her long denim skirt. The kids at school call Crystal "Jesus Christ Superstar" because she's a born-again fanatic, but I also suspect they call her that because there is no shorter name for a girl who looks like she's a devoted member of a polygamous cult.

I'm about to look away when she raises her hand in a quick greeting. When I wave back, she motions me over to where she's sitting. It's a casual gesture, one that I desperately want to ignore. When she removes her backpack from the plastic seat next to hers I know I'm obliged.

She smells faintly of cooked food. Garlic and peppers, not

at all unpleasant, and I realize, when I sit, we've never been this close before. In fact, we've never spoken more than a few words to each other. So, it's awkward. Crystal hugs an old, dirty light-blue JanSport close to her chest, like she is hoping the backpack will assume the shape of her body, and I wedge the sweatshirt that I had tied around my waist in the narrow space between me and the shared armrest. After what feels like several minutes, she finally speaks without looking at me.

"Hey."

"Hey," I say back, wondering how long we'll have to pretend familiarity until one of our names gets called.

"Why are you here?"

Before I answer, I steal a glance at her. Dark acne scars mix in with fresh red bumps along her high cheekbones. Her eyes are shielded by her bangs, straighter and blacker than I have ever seen hair be. "I'm here to get some shots. What about you?"

"Shots?" She looks at me, alarmed. "What do you mean, shots?"

"You know, like, vaccinations."

"Oh, okay." She sounds relieved. Crystal looks me up and down. Her eyes are deep brown and full of a skeptical envy. "Wait. Are you going someplace? Traveling or something?"

I laugh. Not at her but at the thought that my life would ever be that exciting. "I wish, but it's nothing like that. Just the standard shots you get as a kid."

"So, why are you doing it now?" she asks, and I can see it on her face, how once the words are out of her mouth, she already knows. Because even though Crystal and I aren't friends, she knows who my mother is. That's because her mother, Rhea, is as close to a female friend as my mother has at the Oasis. Crystal can already work out why I'm here.

"What about you?" I repeat as the swoosh of the intake window slides open and the nurse calls out a name.

Crystal loosens her grip on her backpack, pushing herself up. "A checkup." It's the way she says it, quick and exacting, like she's slamming a door, locking it. I don't believe her.

Then she draws a sharp breath. "What's that guy doing?" Putting her hand to her mouth, she stares out into the waiting room. She's upset, trembling, as if she's about to cry.

"Where? Who? What are you talking about?" I shift around in my seat, trying to follow her line of vision. I expect blood. Death. Something major.

She grips my arm and hisses, "There. The guy two seats in front of us, the one with the headphones."

I spot him. He has his back to us. On his lap is a portable DVD player. The screen is a dark shadow from where I'm sitting, so I squeeze over, moving Crystal with my shoulder.

For a few seconds I watch a head bob over an erect penis and lean back in my seat. "Yeah. So what?"

"But it's gross. We're in public." Crystal looks like she's going to vomit, but she's riveted. And I wonder if this is what Yevgenia sees whenever I get all high and mighty about sex.

"Well. You don't have to watch."

"I'm not," she says, but her eyes wander back to the guy.

"You are."

"It's like a car crash." Crystal smiles for the first time.

"Apparently." With my head I gesture to an old man who is so captivated by the porn that he's nearly falling out of his seat.

We giggle, stupidly, uncomfortable and maybe a bit excited. "Have you ever done something like that?" Crystal asks.

"That?" I shake my head no. And then there's the odd feeling of superiority, I'm not proud of it, but it's there. Making me more forthright and confident because Crystal is homely and shy and if either of us had any experience first, I'm certain it would be me.

"Really?" She seems surprised.

"Yes, really. I've never done any of it." I'm mentally patting myself on the back, thinking of the kind of Christian accolades I would get if I was a believer.

My name is called so I stand. "See you," I say.

Crystal nods, distracted.

I'M LEAVING THE exam room when I see Crystal getting weighed in by a heavyset nurse in tight scrubs. I linger a little. She doesn't look at me, so I call out, "Take care."

Crystal glances over. "Can my friend come with me?"

The nurse, a young white woman, picks up Crystal's chart, motioning me over with it. "Sure. Let's go take a look at this baby."

Crystal avoids my eyes.

WE STARE AT the gray wad on the black monitor while the woman in scrubs dispassionately snaps a few images. As she walks Crystal through fetal anatomy, other seeds germinate. Crystal, I imagine, feels a renewal, her body, a hungry earth, fed. She tries not to cry when the nurse points to the pulsating pixels. *That's the heart beating.*

It's involuntary, how I shift my body toward the formless mass, stealing a closer look. Crystal babbles about the wonders of her baby and I wait for my own moment of awe. What arises are pestering torments that drag my mind to the moments before this moment. I'm angry. *Someone wanted her.*

And what about me? What's so enticing about a girl like Crystal that she could choreograph sex with a man?

"Wasn't that amazing?" Crystal asks after the nurse leaves. There's the thump and tear of stiff paper towels being jerked from the metal dispenser on the wall, then the swipe and crumple of post-ultrasound cleanup. The clang of the trash can lid as it slams down is a substitute for my response.

She comes from around the privacy curtain, grinning. "Thanks for staying with me. I was scared before, so it's good to have someone here." Crystal irons the front of her T-shirt down with her hand, stopping briefly on her belly. The maternal gesture seems, under the circumstances, deceitful.

"Are you keeping it?"

She flinches. Her eyes blink and her body stiffens as if I have just thrown ice-cold water on her. "Yes," she says.

"But why? You have options, you know." Later, I regret my attempt to forcibly enter her entire life, but just then, I couldn't give a shit. For one irrational moment, I imagine that Steve is the father of her baby. Why not? It seemed like the next logical step. Wasn't Crystal able to achieve something I could not?

She shakes her head at me, sad and disappointed. Swinging her backpack over her shoulder, she pushes past me to the door.

◆

Absolutely no Sylvia Plath. Save "tormented melancholy" for the "decadent poetesses."

There is a spot on the floor illuminated by the October light coming in from the tiny living room window. As the sun rises the spot goes from a watery gray to a faint yellow. I'm lying on Steve's sofa. Another "I'll be back in a couple of hours" has turned into overnight babysitting.

As usual, Brody eventually crashed out in front of the TV and I dragged him to his room. In the dark I move through the trailer, snooping around, looking at old photos, reading past-due notices, fingering clothes hanging in the closet, smelling worn T-shirts. One time, I lay on Steve and Terri's bed, trying, maybe, to figure the two of them out by osmosis. I accidently fell asleep and later awoke as Terri tumbled in, fully clothed next to me. "You scared me," she mumbled into her pillow. Soon the air was filled with the fermented and distilled fumes of her body. I said nothing and slipped out of her room. I wouldn't lie on their bed again.

This morning, I hear Steve's bike riding the saddle of the mountain, cutting through the pass. The engine's muffled whine, trapped by the valley walls, echoes for miles. I'm fully awake. My heart is beating fast. There is vulnerability at this early hour. Do I stay on the sofa? Stand at the door? Indecision immobilizes me. I lie still, feigning sleep.

He comes in quietly and sets his helmet down on the table near the door. I hold my breath as his footsteps approach the sofa.

He stands over me. "Lara?" he whispers. "Hey, Lara." His voice is clear, but he's been drinking.

I rouse slightly, drawing my knees up in a fetal position, but don't open my eyes. I'm not sure what I'm doing, but Steve is looking at me and I don't want that to end. I feel the sofa sag a little under his weight as he sits next to me. His hip at my waist. With the exception of my mother, this is the first time in years I've been so close to another person.

Steve puts his hand on my arm. I nearly jump out of my skin. "Lara. I'm back."

I open my eyes. That's when I know I am going to kiss him. I reach up and pull him toward me. I've never kissed anyone before, nor have I ever been suffocated, but that's what it feels like. Steve's tongue punches into my mouth, a blind man swinging in the dark. His mouth tastes of salt and stale wheat. Because he's drunk, I feel powerful, in control. This, I imagine, is what makes Yevgenia such an enthusiast. And for a moment I parrot what I think she would do to Steve. So, I press into him, moving my mouth quickly; our kiss is sloppy, too wet, too urgent. More the performance of kissing than actual kissing. But I press on by lifting my shirt over my head and put one of his hands on my breast. He kneads at my flimsy bra. It's too rough but I don't say so. Instead, I grab at his lower back, guiding him on top of me. His knee bangs into my shin. With his full weight on me, I struggle to unpin one of my arms and I pull my bra cup down to expose my breast. It cuts painfully into the tender underside of my skin and I place Steve's hand over my nipple. And then the name *Ricky Ricardo* slips itself, gummy and formless, inside my mind.

That's when the sofa is like a leaking canoe, slowly folding in around our weight. I feel like I am about to drown. With two hands on Steve's chest I create enough space to get out from underneath him. He sits up. "Here," I say, pulling him. He staggers a bit to his feet. I think we are heading to the bedroom but Steve starts tugging at his own pants, unbuttoning them quickly, pushing them down to his knees. He then tries to pull my jeans down without unzipping them.

"Dad?" Brody's voice comes from down the hallway. I freeze.

Steve turns his head. "Go back to bed."

There's the soft thud of Brody's feet on the hallway floor. The light snaps on. He stands watching us as I scramble to put my shirt on.

"No, don't stop," Steve says. His arm shoots out, yanking at my T-shirt, pulling some of my hair.

"Ouch," I say, rubbing my head. Brody is still in the hallway.

"I'll be one minute. Go back to bed," Steve shouts in Brody's direction. Then he turns back to me, smiling. It's like he's trying to convince me to take my medicine. "Keep going. Ignore him, he'll leave," he whispers. He moves back to the sofa. His breath is more animal than human. I fight the feeling of nausea. I no longer know what I am doing. "Here," he says, "suck me off." He grabs my wrists and I am next to him. He palms the back of my head with one hand and pushes my shoulder down with the other.

My head hovers at Steve's lap. I stare at the heavy testicles nesting in a bed of light brown pubic hair.

"What about Brody?"

"Never mind him." Steve's preoccupied by his dick. He begins rubbing the tip of his penis with urgency. "Quick, I'm losing this." He spits in his hand and strokes vigorously.

I cast my eyes up toward the door. I always think of Brody as a little kid concerned only with what's right in front of him. But leaning against the wall as he is, stoically, his eyes slightly dimmed, I understand that his loneliness is a lot like mine, carefully pruned like a prizewinning bonsai, gifted to us by people who are adults in name only. I have stood exactly as he stands now, watching my parent become a beggar to her bodily desires and in doing so choosing to turn me into a nobody.

I move out of Steve's grip and sit up. "I don't think I can do this."

"What? Why?" Steve looks at me, confused.

"I'm gonna go," I say, trying to adjust my clothes quickly.

Steve runs his hands through his hair. "Man, I get it now. You two are fucking teases." He sits with his hands at his side, not pulling up his pants. "I know chicks like you. Fuck, I married one. You all string dudes along until you get yours, then you'll fuck any Tom, Dick, or Harry."

"It's not like that. I just . . ." I can't explain myself to him, much less to myself. But I know that I am not like my mother, or Terri, for that matter. "I've never done this before."

Steve's laugh is cynical. "You're a virgin? Don't give me that shit. Girls like you are out here having sex the first chance you get."

"I'm not like that," I say, not understanding what I'm defending—the abstract value of my virginity or the callow idea I can name myself. Maybe that's why my voice breaks a little.

Steve looks at me, screwing his brows together, seeing me. "How old are you? No, don't answer that." He stretches his T-shirt down to cover himself. "Sorry, I'm drunk. You should go."

I wring my hands and a nervous, sick feeling roils in my stomach. "Uh, it was really . . . nice," I say to his silent, avoiding eyes. "Thank you," I add for reasons unknown.

He gets off the sofa, pulling up his pants. Turning his back, he says to Brody, "What's the matter, B.? You thirsty?" He goes to the kitchen, ruffling Brody's hair as he passes. Brody fusses on the heels of his father, but not before casting a glance in my direction, quickly, like he hopes I'm just part of a bad dream.

A fog of embarrassment creeps over my body and an empty, hollow feeling expands painfully at the back of my throat and moves up to my eyes. I leave their trailer, wondering how to shed myself. Outside, the sun grazes the crags in the backside of the San Gabriel Mountains to the north. To the south, the thin line of gray-brown smog is rising darkly over the San Bernardinos. It's a matter of an hour or two before the valley is filled with the heat and exhaust from the morning commute. And I think about that encyclopedia in Mexico. How, despite its thousands of pages, the ancient Greeks had no words for a girl like me.

GIRLS LIKE ME end up being girls like my mother. Isn't that what Steve means? And there is a rage inside me that I point in her direction. She has ruined this for me. The thing I want is the thing I can't do. After I slam the door to my trailer, tense and wild, my hands move quickly around the dishes and glasses cluttering the countertop, and there it is, my mother's tumbler, the glass she uses for all her booze. Flinging open cabinets, I try to find where she keeps her drink and I see a half-full bottle of something brown. I fill her cup with it. I cough and gag at the first gulp, but I want to drink it fast, as if it's acid, hoping that by some miracle, my insides will burn as hot and sharp as my own humiliation. I finish the glass, banging it roughly on the counter. My head and stomach both feel like they're making slow somersaults. Sliding to the floor I sit against the cabinets, pressing my nails into the cool vinyl. Death. There was a small part of me that wants it, or maybe just a darkness that I won't wake up from. And I think of Yevgenia, and what she would say if she found me dead, here, on our kitchen floor. How would she eulogize me, if she would at all? Would she use her own words or those of someone else?

IT WAS YEARS AGO, after my mother returned from her time away from me, that she started reading almost daily from her shitty notebooks. Page after page of dictums that all had cautionary backstories she would elaborate on. Let no person or book misuse my body or my mind, and all that shit. But what had she taught me about death? Her stories about souls being "howled back" by the grieving living, like the time I cried over the death of the neighbor's cat found dead in the street. And later, her admiration for women who took matters into their own hands by murdering an abusive ex or her incessant reciting of one or two poems by Danielle Collobert:

> a body there—practicing pain—as if it hadn't had
>> enough
> of this suffering

All I knew was that Collobert had killed herself, as my mother would tell me, "But not over some fucking man, like that whimpering American simpleton, Plath." I am a simpleton. This is what she would make of me now. Because I feel like I'm dying and she would think it was over Steve. But it's because of her, her endless rules and ceaseless drilling of her fucked-up treatises on sex and men.

———

UNDERNEATH ME THE floor tips and tilts, like I'm a dinghy trapped in a storm. Unable to stand, I push myself to my knees and that's when I feel the vomit rise and I am uncertain if the splat I hear is my inside coming out or my body hitting the floor before I black out.

◆

Don't fake an orgasm, ever. It's okay to fake love or interest or kindness, but don't fake your orgasm. You rob not only yourself of pleasure but the pleasure of other unfortunates who bed the awful lover.

I'm lying on the sofa with the TV on mute, trying to do homework, but really, I'm staring at the wall, ashamed and stupid and hating myself. I don't remember much of my attempt to drink myself into the afterlife, but I woke up feeling worse than I had before, only covered in my own vomit and with a smashing headache. My mother said nothing, stepping over me, it seems, on her way to her bedroom.

"Who reads and watches TV together? What? You have money to pay the electric bill?" The floor of our mobile home thunders under Yevgenia's angry feet. She turns off the TV. A heavy fog of White Shoulders has followed her out of the bathroom. It fills the trailer with a powdery sweet smell that's part cleaning solution, part bug repellent. My mother always complains that the scent is a cheap, watered-down replacement for her old Krasnaya Moskva perfume. I think I'm going to vomit again.

But the fierce look from my mother, as she stands in front of the TV, hands on her hips, keeps me in my place. It would be a perfectly matronly pose, except for the white fuck-me pumps and the savagely short, tight black dress. It's 1:00 p.m. on a Saturday. She could be heading to the library for all I know.

"You want to grow up *dryannoya*?" She motions again to the TV. But I know she's really talking about my sloppy drinking.

And even when she asks stupid questions like this, if I want to be "trashy," it takes me too long to come up with a smart-ass response. On this day in particular, I'm feeling empty of comebacks. I don't want to tell my mother about Steve, what I almost did, what I couldn't do. But she knows. I can sense it. She hovers, like she's about to dispense an unsolicited version of her motherly "advice."

Yevgenia takes her fake Chanel and hangs it on the armrest of the Russian imperial chair and sits next to me.

We are close enough that I'm not sure if the drink from last night I smell is hers or mine. Even with makeup, the thin skin under my mother's eyes is slightly purple, smudged with black eyeliner. At first, we stare silently at each other, the imprecise shadow of familial debt between us.

My mother sighs. "Let me ask you something."

"No, please don't." How do I explain to my mother that I am undone, weakened by my ruinous attempt because I can't be more like her?

"Did Steve hurt you? Touch you in any way that you didn't want?"

"No. Please, just stop. I don't want to talk about this." And these words come back to me by rote. How many times has my mother asked me this and how many times have I answered in the same way? A male teacher when I was in the sixth grade. The guy who lived next door to us in El Paso. The twin brothers who came to the library every Sunday. Each and every one of her boyfriends I had ever met: Nate, Jacques, Mario, Igor, Sam, Axel, Dan, Tom, Victor, Ken, Ivan, Roger, and Diego, and the many whose names neither one of us remembers.

She rubs her hands together. "When it comes to men, what do I always say?"

"What?" I ask. Her question catches me off guard. She says too many things about men or writes them down in her notebooks. I start guessing. "Always use a condom? Don't date a guy who talks too much? Never sleep with someone who's too nice to you?" I could go on, probably for months, but I stop, seeing that Yevgenia is nodding her head to all of it. She leans forward to snatch the pack of cigarettes off the table in front of me, now desperate for a smoke.

"Yes," she says, sitting back down next to me. "All true. But don't forget that I also say, 'Stay away from men who fuss over their hair.' Really. There's nothing to be gained when a man's grooming goes beyond a bit of cologne and toothpaste." Her lighter clicks up a flame. She brings it to the cigarette held between her lips.

"But here's what's most important," she continues. "You need to ask yourself what you know about love."

With the word *love*, I move my eyes from her face to the uneven burn of the cigarette's cherry. "I don't love Steve. I never said that."

She rolls her eyes. "Fine, but you're sixteen, so in a way, you think you do."

"I'm going to my room." I start to stand up.

"No, sit." Her foot kicks the leg of the coffee table, commanding my attention. "Look, I get it. Steve is good-looking. He smiles at you. He's the pedestrian fantasy. But it's not love or anything, okay?"

"Can we just drop it?" I slide back to the farthest corner on the sofa, pretending I can put an ocean between us.

"Fine, but you know, it's easy to call something love when it isn't. People do it all the time."

"But not you, right?" I ask. My mother is always the exception to every rule.

"Me?" She chokes back a laugh. "Yes, me most of all." This surprises me. I try not to react. She has my full attention.

"What I do know, too well, is how men are. And this guy Steve—" Her thumb jerks in the direction of his trailer. "You can do better than him if you're looking for someone to be your first. There must be a cute virgin at school who will worship you for changing their life. Maybe a girl? You know, the first time I had sex was with Elena Aleksandrovna Komaeva. Women are too emotionally complicated for me, but the sex is gorgeous."

And there it is. Sex.

She doesn't get it. I wonder if she ever will. I don't want sex talk. What I'm seeking, she doesn't have the answer to. There is no way my mother will ever know how *girls like me* are already seen as embodying depravities so crude that sex is a shackle, not freedom. "Will you drop it?" I say. "It's not about sex or love. I just fucking babysit his kid, okay?"

"Don't get your panties twisted." Yevgenia leans over to flick her ash on a plate in front of her. "I'm just saying, there's love and then there's lust. They're different, so don't confuse them. That's all."

"Bye." I head off to my room.

"You should stay. I'll do your cards."

I wave her off. Not too long ago I would have begged my mother to tell my fortune with her cards. It's the only time I'm allowed in her room. She lights candles. We sit on her bed, the cards spread between us. It wasn't until I was thirteen that I stopped entertaining her. I grew tired of every reading ending with *There's an impressive, towering figure, a female, who knows what's best for you even when you disagree.*

"Your loss," she says.

◆

Pay careful attention to the men who withhold compliments, or who compliment you only when you dress a certain way. They are controlling and hiding a tendency for violence.

Outside, from the trailer behind mine, a screen door screeches open. The neighbor's kids spill out into their carport. They're screaming at each other again. From inside, a female voice yells, "Shut the fuck up!" But they don't.

Their noise brings me out of my stupor. It's dusk. After roaming the mall in Riverside, alone, half-heartedly looking for work, collecting applications so I can leave them around whenever my mother gets on my back, I go home, fall asleep on the sofa. Now the kids are throwing rocks at each other in my yard. The crackling blast ricocheting off the metal siding brings me to the front door. They're so locked in their fight they can't see me. A little boy, younger than Brody, stands over his sister, kicking at her.

"Yo, get up, ya nigga-ass bitch!" he shouts at her.

"Hey, hey!" I yell at the boy from my steps. "Why you saying that shit?"

The kids look up at me and for a brief moment, recognition passes through us. We don't know one another, but in a way, we *are* one another. We are three ocher-hued Black kids, with our curly, knotted, lopsided hair. The kids wear torn clothing that's too small for them. They will be in those clothes for months before anyone really cares or can afford to do anything about it.

"I'll say whatever the fuck I want, lady." The little boy sticks out his chest.

His sister scrambles to her feet, chiming in, "Yeah, you ole nasty ass."

"You two hate yourself so much that you want to kill each other out here? Define yourselves by the words of white supremacy?" I can hear Charles in my voice, in my questions that are statements, with vocabulary I barely know the meaning of and they surely do not.

"Yo, don't be talking to my kids that way," a voice comes from behind me. A broad-shouldered white woman in yellow leggings and an oversize black Raiders T-shirt stands at the back corner of my tiny lot. "Guys, get the fuck out of her yard." She motions to the kids.

"Do you have to talk to them like that?" Yevgenia would ask the same thing, but stronger, with more force. My mother is the type to mind her own business until it's brought, as is the case, to her doorstep. Then she's ruthless, like the time I watched her drown a pillowcase of day-old kittens who had the bad luck of being born in our garage.

"Are you paying my rent?" The mother raises her finger in the air, pointing at me, her face dotted with pink and red

splotches. Her blond topknot convulses with rage. "You help-
ing me raise my kids?" I watch the children skirt by her, anx-
ious, and I regret saying anything. I know how this works. The
more cornered she feels, the more judged and shat on by life,
the more she'll take it out on them.

I stay silent.

"Yeah, you pussy, I didn't think so." She turns her back
on me, gratified. I stay, one, two, three breaths, then hear
the sounds of the mother shouting at her kids: *Stupid shits.
You dumb assholes.* And up past the trailer rooftops, the bald
mountains peek, silent observers.

In my trailer, I rage. I hate the Oasis, the people who live
here, our lives mutilated by endless wasted hours. I hate the
fucking obstacles, the barriers that we put up, the ones that
we don't. When I hang out with Charles, he talks about how
"the system" is against us. I only nod my head, like I can see
the figure of the system lurking outside my window, slipping money from my neighbors' wallets while they sleep,
disappearing their jobs, baiting them into fistfights or DUIs
or drug convictions. But my imagination is incomplete. The
system may start outside, but it gets in. It's a parasite, and we,
the people of the Oasis, are its hosts. The system is in the cel-
lular makeup of our bodies. It's part of our psychology, our
inherited traits, our human origins. We, the prostrate people
of the Oasis, excel in the work of the system. We domesticate
our suffering, neuter our aspirations. We detonate our fury
so often at one another that we are depleted by the time we
even think to look at the system. And yet, in small, fleeting
moments, we may find the way back to our gaunt and ragged
selves. We make grand declarations, vow to change the lives we
think we steer. Then when we aren't looking, we're defeated.

And for a few moments we'll be stunned. How did we forget? Defeat always comes. In the drink we promise we won't touch. The child we say we won't beat. The job we vow to show up for.

The night air claps cool against my face when I step out. A barrage of music plays from multiple trailers. Hip-hop, heavy metal, and mariachi compete against one another from cheap sound systems or from car speakers so expensive and elaborate they probably put the local radio station's equipment to shame. It's a Friday night. People are mostly paid, mostly happy. But I am agitated. I want more. I go down my steps and walk the dark street. The yard dogs bark at me when I pass their trailers. I know where I'm heading. Deep in the vein of the Oasis is a cul-de-sac where the only double-wide rests. The home of Charles and his aunt Eunice is the original Oasis trailer, the progenitor. As I approach, the Destiny's Child song "Say My Name" beats its way out of the metal walls, onto the dirt lawn.

Motion lights snap on aggressively when my foot skims the walkway's slab of pavement. Then the snap of blinds as a hand peeks through to see who's come this far. I reach out to open the gate and stop when I see a sign hanging off the chain link. It reads, WARNING! ELECTRIC FENCE! and ¡ATENCIÓN! ¡CERCA ELÉCTRICA!, with a drawing of a hand being shocked in case of illiteracy. I contemplate turning back. Then the music cuts. The door opens and a lazy, warm yellow light illuminates the figure of Charles in his doorway. I can't see his face, but I can hear the smile when he asks, "Black, did you walk all the way over here just so I could shame that unironic Afro you're sporting?"

———

ON A LATE Saturday afternoon, we're sitting on my cramped steps. With my mother working or out, my place becomes a refuge for both Charles and Julie. Only, Julie has to lie to her parents, saying she's joined the "cosmetology club" at school so she can escape them on weekends. Sometimes I wish I had that problem. Had another place to go, a real job instead of the one I lie about to keep Yevgenia at bay. But I don't. It's either inside or outside. Today it's the heat that's pushed us outside. Either Papa Bear or the shitty municipality or the county or some stoned jackass at the electric company has cut the power at the Oasis. We're sitting in my living room when it happens. Julie is about to tell us about her night with some guy named Miguel when a loud click turns everything dark. We shuffle around in the dim light, grabbing the last of whatever is cold in the refrigerator.

Julie holds a Corona up to her face. "Can I have this?" she asks.

"Oh, split that with me," Charles says eagerly.

"Sure," I say, moving the milk to the freezer.

Outside, Julie and Charles pass the last beer between them and soon the stagnant hot air is suffocating us. Julie starts her story over again from the top. "When I stopped to get gas, I notice someone was staring at me. The guy was beautiful." She breaks down the syllables so that it comes out *be-you-tee-full*. "I mean seriously tasty. He kept giving me these dark eyes and long lashes for days."

"You met at the gas station?" Charles asks, leaning forward in encouragement. "That's fucking hot."

"Isn't that dangerous?" I ask. I give Charles a hard look. *Poseur.* He's a virgin too. This is something I discovered weeks ago when I asked him if he'd ever had sex. He swore me to silence.

Julie shrugs and says, "Isn't that the point? It's like the surprise at the bottom of the cereal box." She seems too cavalier. But she's got courage I don't have. It's a type of currency.

"I know, right?" Charles chimes in all too eagerly, rolling his eyes at my inexperience, my modesty.

Julie cracks her hand against my thigh playfully. "If we don't find you a viable lay soon, you'll turn into an old woman."

"Nothing wrong with that." My voice is chipper. "At least I'll die in my own bed instead of out in a ditch somewhere. But then again, they look for girls like you." I want to stop talking but I can't. *Girls like you*, Steve's phrase, is a weapon I also want to use. "Girls like me? We are left to rot. Another name on a missing person's list."

Julie's body goes rigid. Disgust passes over Charles's face. "Sorry," I say. "Really, I didn't mean it."

"Well, yeah, you kind of did." Julie doesn't look at me. Instead she shields her eyes with her hand, staring out onto the cloudless sky. "It's fucking hotter than balls out here and we're sitting in the sun." She stands up, brushing the butt of her low-slung jean shorts. The entirety of her midriff is showing. She's right. I do mean it and I feel like an asshole for it.

"Talk to you later," she says, without turning to either of us.

"What the fuck, Lara?" Charles is pissed as he watches Julie drive off. I brace for the tirade.

"You have to stop with all this Mother Superior shit. Just because you're all squeamish about sex doesn't mean the rest of us have to be too." He stands up like he's going to leave. I'm not sure if it's the heat or some other source of exhaustion that makes me not care.

"I'm not squeamish," I say.

Charles stretches, crossing his arms in front of his chest.

If I didn't know him, I would think he's warming up for some sport. He's casually dressed in loose-fitting gray-and-white basketball shorts and a white T-shirt with a photo of Albert Einstein on it.

"You try to act like sex is something you're curious about, but you're not," he says.

I shake my head. "Not true."

"Like, I'm a virgin by circumstance only. You are by choice."

"That doesn't mean anything." I bite the side of my tongue. I will not tell Charles about Steve. That I tried and failed. And he'd want to know why and I'm not sure I can go into all that—the years of my mother's preoccupation with my sexual initiation, her countless lessons, and her warnings.

"Listen, all I'm saying is that maybe you're asexual. You know, like Emily Brontë or Isaac Newton. So just be cool about it, okay? Don't make the rest of us feel like shit."

"People aren't asexual," I say. "Only plants are." I think of my biology class and correct myself. "Some plants."

Charles sighs. "Well, whatever you are, just own that shit. And you better not act all condescending when I start talking about all the sex I'm having some day. Soon. I hope. Because I *will* be singing it from the rooftops. Every damn detail. Okay?"

"Yeah, okay," I say. "But be aware that if you're looking for the heavens to rejoice, your news won't be carried very far from these rooftops."

"Damn," he says with slow confusion, "does *everything* have to be an issue with you? Keep on like this and you'll never know if you're asexual by choice."

"Sorry." And I am, and I know he's right about my attitude. But asexual? I don't know. How do I tell him that I'm not sure if I ever have a choice when it comes to sex? That I worry that if I do it, or have any interest at all, my mother will be there shoving her instructions down my throat. She'll hover, making sure that I'm not compromised. That I can pretend to be in control, which is better than the more likely scenario of turning it all into a sport.

I look out just over his shoulder, where the gravel road seems to tumble off the planet into one big drain. I yearn for the Oasis to ooze right into the sewer along with the street and the stones and the dirt and the crunchy, yellowed grass.

"Oh God," Charles says. I turn my head to see what he sees.

Crystal's making her way toward my trailer, looking like she stepped out of a Stephen King novel. After the clinic, I regard her differently. She's a shape-shifter. Her body, a sensual container clothed in the chaste, ugly uniform of a long skirt and a church charity-box button-up shirt with flowers barfed all over it. She walks stoically, at a pace that might have been similar to Joan of Arc's death march.

Charles grunts dissatisfaction, hissing, "That girl is horror-movie creepy."

"Don't," I say, ignoring how he looks at me, like I've lost my mind. And maybe I have. Since our last meeting Crystal has managed to get an even bigger wooden cross necklace. But it's her shoes. Her impossibly white puffy shoes. How she can go up and down these dusty roads and not get her shoes dirty is unsettling.

"Hey," I call out.

Charles sucks his teeth. "Come on."

Under my breath I inform him, "At least she's not a virgin. She's got that on us."

Charles's mouth hangs open to say something but Crystal

now stands at the base of the steps. Her face is shiny with sweat.

"Hi." She looks shyly at Charles, who just nods his head in greeting. "Aren't you guys hot sitting out here?"

"Fan's dead. Power's out," I say. "What about you? Where are you headed?" Charles turns toward me, his eyes wide like he's about to murder someone, anyone. He's moving like he's about to call it a day. I get it. Charles has no interest in Crystal. Hell, I barely have an interest in her. And yet, where Charles might want to dig foxholes for each of us, tiny unrelated islands dotting the crumbly, worthless soil of the Oasis, we are the same. To each other. And especially to the world ready to forget people like us, useless scraps. Landfill fodder.

"I'm going to the store. Do you want anything? Or you want to come with me?" Crystal pats her pocket hidden in the fabric of her skirt so we don't misunderstand her. I wonder how she got her money and if she's trying to buy our friendship.

Charles's face lights up. He's not one to turn down a free anything. He pushes off the rickety wooden railing. "Sure. Let's go."

I watch the two of them turn out of my dusty lot, onto the road. The sun burns the top of my head, leaving me feverish. When I stand, the pooling blood in my veins floods to my feet.

Shielding her eyes, Crystal peers up at me. "Are you coming?"

4

Steer clear of ugly men, for obvious reasons. On the other hand, men who are better-looking than you will make you feel that they are an unpaid debt. They will hang it over your head.

Brody is becoming a regular fixture around my place, even before my disastrous encounter with Steve. It starts slowly, with him standing on the sidewalk outside my house. I sit out on the front step looking at him until we both get bored and I tell him to go home.

"I can't. They locked the door." Brody looks like he's going to cry. "I need to take a poop." That day, and the days that follow, he ends up staying over at my house until late in the evening. Usually he falls asleep and then I hear his mother's voice or her car across the street. The first night, I half drag, half carry him to his house. It's still the time of year when the heat seems to evaporate slowly and the crickets chirp like mechanical fiddles until dawn. Brody is crashed out against me, his head hanging limply against my neck. Carrying him like this dislodges something within me. I am a protector, capable, and in charge. An unfamiliar sense of owning myself.

So when Brody is sitting at my front door again when I come home from school, I'm not annoyed.

"Dude," I say to Brody, "I showed you where the key is. Why aren't you inside? It's freaking hot out here."

He sits shredding paper into little balls. He looks rougher than usual. His face is streaked with dirt. He's been crying.

"What's up?" I don't want to know, but I ask anyway.

He ignores me and tries to hide his face.

"Okay, whatever. You know you're going to have to clean that up," I say, motioning to the mess of paper.

I go into the kitchen and pull the last box of mac and cheese from the cupboard. This is supposed to be my dinner, but I'll share. Brody is always hungry. Eventually he comes in, drags a chair to the dining table, and sits.

I peer out of the kitchen. He's bent over, head down. I clear my throat. He doesn't look up.

Walking to the edge of the table, I speak to him in a voice that tries to sound older and reassuring but it comes off fake. "I see that you're going through something." These are the same words a guidance counselor from three schools ago used with me. That guy was an overly caring, splotchy-faced white man in a wrinkle-free button-up and baggy jeans.

"It's okay if you don't want to tell me about it, but if—" I stop abruptly. Brody is grimy. His arms are mottled with dirt rings. Under his fingernails are half-moon crescents of black mud. "Hey," I say. "You're going to have to wash those hands of yours. Look at them. Man, they're filthy." I move closer. The scent of fetid boiled spinach comes from him. "On second thought, you really need to take a bath." I pull the bowl of food away from him and Brody starts crying.

"Why can't people fucking leave me alone?" His voice is ragged, his face bright red. "I hate it. I hate everyone." His voice grows louder; his body begins shaking. "I hate everything. Fucking school. My fucking parents." He bangs on the table; the spoon in the bowl jumps. "I wish they would all just die."

"Okay, first," I shout over him, "stop hitting the fucking furniture. Just tell me what the fuck is going on." I want to think he's reacting to bullying at school, by teachers, by other kids. I know what it's like to wear the impoverished absence of anyone's care. It inspires fear and a cruel license for others to hurt you, shame you, blame you. I'm scared to offer him real comfort. I'm still driven by the misunderstanding that an extension of empathy will cause me to collapse too.

"Look, your dad is cool. You can't hate him." I avoid saying anything about Terri.

"What do you know?" he says. "You did *it* with him. But he's gonna leave. It's just like last time."

"I didn't do *it* with him. And what do you mean, 'He's going to leave'?" I'm unable to conceal my alarm. "Wait a sec, are your parents going to get a divorce?" For a moment, I want a big enough place in Steve's life to break up his marriage.

Brody is on to me. "You wish."

"No, I don't."

"Whatever." Brody pushes back from the table and goes to the door.

"Don't you want to eat your mac and cheese?"

"Forget it," he says, the back of his hair matted, like it hasn't been brushed for days.

TERRI SEEMS TO be home a lot more, which means that whenever Steve is around, we can hear them fighting. One night, Yevgenia and I stand by our door, listening to shouting that's mostly incoherent. My mother mutters bullshit like, "Can you see he's a real bastard? Both of them total waste cases. If he hits her, I'm going to fucking break down that door. Just watch me." Then she and I will argue like sportscasters defending our team, with me saying things like, "She's more likely to hit him. Listen to how crazy she is." This will go on for hours until Papa Bear limps over to their trailer, a baseball bat in hand, threatening to evict them if they don't shut the fuck up.

"BLEH," YEVGENIA SAYS with a genuine shudder. "I could never have something like that in bed. It's like bestiality." She's standing by our front door, looking out across the street, watching Terri lean into a guy who is obviously her new boyfriend. My mother never shies away from disgusting men, so I peer over her shoulder, intrigued.

Everybody calls him "Big Mike" like he's a cuddly teddy bear, but he isn't. Big Mike is a biker, or at least he dresses like one: jeans, motorcycle boots, wallet chain, a leather vest covered with patches of skulls, a Confederate flag, and the name of the chapter of a motorcycle club. All I've ever seen him drive is Terri's Honda. In the beginning Charles, Julie, and I don't know enough about Big Mike to really be scared of him, so we spend whole afternoons stealing furtive glances, shit talking. Charles goes on and on about how fat Big Mike is. *I bet a bike wouldn't hold his weight.* Julie is inspired to use words she normally doesn't. *Oh my God, the dude is so foul.* And it's true, Big Mike's gray hair hangs past his shoulders in thin, oily strips. He has so many tattoos that they muddy his arms.

Terri starts to bring Big Mike around whenever Steve is away, and sometimes even when he's there. The whole arrangement seems to offend everyone at the Oasis.

"Steve doesn't need to have a woman who does that to him," Rhea, Crystal's mother, says, leaning on the kitchen sink as my mother fixes them both another drink. "I mean, my God, look at him, this is tearing him up."

Rhea, who usually is an unapologetic party girl who can't resist a dirty joke or my mother's gin and tonic, seems distressed by the whole thing.

I sit on the sofa, pretending to read.

"Yeah, the dude ain't supposed to be living there, he's not authorized by me, but they're paid up for the next three months since he got there, so, not good business to kick him out," Papa Bear offers while packing a bong at the kitchen table.

Papa Bear has the habit of threatening eviction on a whim. Both Rhea and my mother ignore him. "These American women are crazy," my mother says, cutting into an old lime. "But I have to give my hat to her, Terri is getting it. I mean, *I* wouldn't take these guys, but a boyfriend and a lover, why not?"

Rhea, who works as a nurse's aide at an old folks' home, is still wearing her dark blue scrub pants and plain T-shirt. She passes the bottle of gin to Yevgenia, nodding her head like she's considering it. "Yeah, but did you see the titties?" Rhea smiles slyly at my mother before they both erupt in a drunken, uninhibited laugh.

After a few moments, Yevgenia switches to an inebriated moralism like she's auditioning for a spot as a TV evangelical. "Well, it takes two to tango, they say, and he brought some of this on himself." My mother pauses, handing Rhea her drink.

"But I agree. Terri shouldn't flaunt it." Yevgenia catches my eye, warning, *Don't go near Steve.*

Papa Bear bends over the bong between his knees, choking down a stoner's cough. "Man, that poor kid though. To be in the mix of all that shit. It ain't right."

Rhea and Yevgenia sit down at the table with him. My mother is not a pot smoker, but she doesn't mind it in the house. Papa Bear holds out the bong to Rhea, who clutches it with both hands. "Yeah, it ain't right," she repeats, like she's singing the chorus to a song.

BRODY STARTS SLEEPING on our sofa every night. His blond hair peeks out from underneath the mint green blanket Julie gave me after I mentioned that it's my favorite color. I hope he doesn't pee or wipe his snot on it. I try to peer over the top of the blanket to get a look at him. Brody's face typically carries a mixture of anger and sadness but not now. At rest, I can see that he's a cute kid, might even grow up to be a good-looking guy. Will that save him the way it saves his dad? Whatever his path is from here, it's not off to a great start.

I look around our shitty little trailer and wonder how much longer Yevgenia will want to live this life. Her work is steady; I have friends and school is okay. But it doesn't take much for her to change directions—a passing conversation about a pretty town, a brochure for another state, a traffic violation, a man, a notice of past-due rent, boredom. The only certainty in my life is that my mother and I will leave the Oasis, and when we do, Brody isn't coming with us.

"Why are you looking at me?" Brody pulls the blanket below his eyes.

"Because that's mine," I say, pointing to the cover.

He's quiet for a moment. He pulls the blanket down to his waist as he sits up. "Sorry. I was cold."

Brody never apologizes. Lately he never says much beyond a string of curse words mixed with complaints and demands. Then I see it. On the side of his cheek, just below his eye, is a bright red mark. I step a little closer.

"What happened?" I ask. "Did that guy, Big Mike, did he hit you?" It's not outside the realm of possibilities. Brody told me and Yevgenia that Big Mike was just home from prison. With a look of admiration, he said that Big Mike's official sentence was for "torture and mayhem" because he cut the fingertips off two guys who owed him money for drugs. I thought Brody was joking until I saw Big Mike shouting at Terri as they were getting out of her car one day. He was spitting his words. His enormous hands were in her face, using his index finger like a drill. Big Mike kicked the wall next to where Terri cowered, busting a hole in the trailer's plastic skirt. I was grateful that my mother wasn't home. She doesn't stand for that kind of violence, men threatening or hitting women.

Brody sighs. "Nothing. I did it myself. I fell off a skateboard."

"Are you sure?"

"Yes. Your mom already asked me a thousand times." His words come out sharp, annoyed.

I stare at him, uncertain.

"Okay," I finally say. "What do you want for breakfast?" I spend the rest of the morning watching him carefully, trying to decide if he's lying.

AS SOON AS I cross the street, it starts raining, an emaciated California rain. Thin and inefficient at first, evaporating nearly the second it hits the ground. Then the rain decides to fully commit to the task and comes down harder. Eucalyptus trees line the road for about a half mile, offering me cover. I inhale the smell of the crushed leaves under my feet. But then there are no more trees. It's as if the city planners ran out of seeds or maybe they looked out on the scrubby brown landscape and decided no worthy person would venture farther. I cross over the gravel road, rounding fields of water-logged, yellowed, knee-high weeds listing over to one side, as if the relief of the rain is too much for them. I approach the Oasis by the back way, passing a trailer that Papa Bear had the sheriff slap an eviction notice on a couple of weeks ago. An older Black man, Mr. Dionne, used to live there. After he tripped going up the trailer steps, he stopped paying rent and his sisters came in a procession of pastel suits one Sunday morning with a U-Haul trailer hitch and that was that. Turnover is the nature of the Oasis. It's been nearly four months since our arrival. People come and go. Sometimes the leavers slowly roll out of the park in triumph, their belongings jammed into the backs of trucks in broad daylight, waving like they're participants in the Rose Bowl parade. Others pack up under the cover of night, escaping back-due rent, the court-ordered eviction, and, maybe, the shame of hitting rock bottom, again. Those of us who stay look on in envy or relief and wonder if our departures will be by day or night.

A young white family lives in Mr. Dionne's place now. I hear Papa Bear tell my mother that the new guy used to work at some government lab as a scientist but he lost his job.

"Dude's working as an entry-level prison guard now," Papa Bear says, all matter-of-fact. "Ain't that shitty? All that education and he's working some crap-pay job that any of us could get."

Yevgenia doesn't believe it. She's leaning against the kitchen cabinet, cigarette hanging between her fingers. "No. That can't be right," she says, her voice turning up in volume at Papa Bear's insistence. "That guy's got a drug problem, or maybe he got busted for kiddie porn or something like that."

"Kiddie porn? Man, Evie, that's fucked-up." Papa Bear hacks, his lungs getting the best of him. "He's got a wife and kid, man. Why go dark like that?"

"Wife and kid?" Yevgenia snorts, skeptical. "Have you seen him? Never trust a man who puts gel in his hair. *And* he wears undershirts. If that doesn't scream creep, then you know nothing about life. I'm telling you, he's up to no good." Again, a collection of my mother's many decrees. I doubt Papa Bear knows that she writes these things down, these laws she lives by, and that he, as a relatively normal guy, is certainly verboten.

"Well, whatever," Papa Bear says, backing down from my mother like he always does, maybe hoping his conciliatory nature will pave a path to her bed. "Dude's paying on time so I've got no complaints."

I SCAN THE prison guard's trailer as I go by. Nothing sinister about the place. It looks like all the others around here. A faded, dusty, gray tin box with a carport roof sagging under the weight of lowered expectations. The only difference is the green-and-yellow swing set with a slide next to his trailer.

As I approach home, I see Brody leaning against his mother's car like he's waiting to go someplace. His hair is cut and he wears a clean white T-shirt. I walk to the edge of his drive and stand under the cover of the carport, wiping rain from my nose. "I like your buzz cut," I say. "They finally sending you to military school?"

Brody looks at me, stricken.

"I'm just joking, B." I walk toward him. "Seriously, where are you going? You're all dressed up."

"I don't know," he says. "But you should go. My dad's not here. I haven't seen him in a while." Brody glances at his front door like he's afraid it might open.

Sometimes when Brody speaks, a part of my mind goes elsewhere. I hurry him along with all my "uh-huhs" and "sounds goods" and "reallys." I've become an adult. But he seems nervous. I lean in and lower my voice. "Are you okay? Is that—"

"I'm fine. Please, Lara, you have to go." He seems scared.

"What's going on?"

He puts his fingers to his lips and mouths, "Go home."

I don't know if I should leave him but feel myself start to back away.

The front door scrapes open. The drag of metal on metal sounds as loud as scaffolding twisting away from a building just before it collapses. I stop briefly and then turn quickly toward my trailer.

"Son." I don't have to look in the direction of the voice. It's Big Mike. "What's she doing over here?" I make it to the middle of the street. Brody grumbles an answer that I can't hear.

"Hey! Hey you! Let me ask you something!" Big Mike shouts at my back. His colossal voice is tinged with curiosity.

Perhaps it's out of fear, but I turn and face him. He stands on the top step of the trailer. The door is open behind him. Big Mike looks ready for his version of church with his salt-and-pepper hair pulled back into a ponytail, a tucked-in black button-up shirt stretching taut against his pregnant belly. His long, slow gaze penetrates beneath my sweatshirt.

Big Mike raises a fleshy, corn-fed hand to his chin, stroking it, acting like he's some philosopher. He asks, "With you being muddled race and all, do you like white dick or Black dick better?"

PART II

MONUMENTS TO A SCHOLARLY ERROR

Two rabbits on a road during the Stalinist terror of 1937.

FIRST RABBIT: "Where are you going in such a hurry?"

SECOND RABBIT: "Haven't you heard? There's a rumor going around that all camels are to be castrated."

FIRST RABBIT: "But you're not a camel."

SECOND RABBIT: "After they catch you and castrate you, try proving you're not a camel."

—YEVGENIA BORISLAVA, original author unknown

5

There is no such thing as "friendship." There are people who know you and people who pretend to know you.

"Listen to this," Charles says to no one in particular, but I know he's speaking to me. "'From the viewpoint of racism, there is no exterior, there are no people on the outside. There are only people who should be like us and whose crime it is not to be.'" He looks more mature than Julie and me. Sitting with his feet up on the coffee table and wearing a pair of fake black plastic-rimmed glasses, like he's a vacationing scholar. He holds a thick book in one hand and a pencil in the other.

"What are you reading?" Julie asks.

Charles doesn't answer her. He pauses to underline something in his book and continues, "'The dividing line is not between inside and outside but rather is internal to simultaneous signifying chains and successive subjective choices. Racism never detects the particles of the other; it propagates waves of sameness.'" Charles looks up at the ceiling, like he's swirling the idea around in his mind. "It propagates waves of sameness," he repeats, nodding.

Julie sits up from her spot on the sofa. She leans forward, determined not to be ignored. "I asked, what are you reading?" There is an edge to her voice.

"Yeah, what's the book?" I chime in, trying to keep the mood light. Lately, this is my role, keeping the peace. Not that anyone is fighting, really. But our exhaustion with one another is kindling. The three of us are in it deep. Seeing one another every day, making grand declarations about our future selves. Shit like, we're moving to New York together after we graduate, becoming roommates. We'll go to London, Julie working at Harrods while Charles and I study at Oxford or something. As it happens, the more we talk about it, the further out of reach those dreams seem.

"*A Thousand Plateaus* by Deleuze and Guattari," Charles replies, flipping the cover of the book over to display the title. "Bruno lent it to me."

"Bruno. It figures. That guy is boring as shit." Julie pouts and looks toward the door. Bruno is Charles's new grad student friend he's crushing on. Though I'm not sure why. Bruno's a lanky, pale kid from Toronto with a high forehead and pointy nose; there's nothing cute about him. But Julie and I have seen him only once, briefly, when we dropped Charles off at UC Riverside. Charles wouldn't let us get out of the car because he thought we'd blow his lie about being in college.

I agree with Julie about Bruno, even if we've never met him. Lately all Charles does is pelt Bruno's words and ideas at us. "Huh," I grunt. "'Particles of the other.' That has the makings of a poem."

Julie rolls her eyes.

"Maybe." Charles thinks about it. "But not really." Julie starts to open her mouth, but I jump in before she can start an argument.

"Check this out," I say, waving a book that our teacher Ms. Kim gave me the week before. I clear my throat. My voice wavers with insecurity. Reading out loud is as painful for me as sitting behind the bus driver, my face visible in his wide rearview mirror.

"'I lost my soul over an ocean,'" I start, looking up at Charles to make sure he's listening. "'I am a scrap of difference that makes fools angry. My steps in the streets raise the barrier walls higher and reinforce the stones of indifference.'" I swallow and look over at Julie, who is biting her nails. "'I am the immigrant, the exiled star, and I go forward with my head turned back.'" I close the book.

Charles sticks out his hand. "Here. Let me see that." I'm sitting on the floor next to the sofa and toss the book in his direction.

"It's a good book," I say as Charles thumbs through it. For once I feel adjacent to his superiority.

"*Loukoum*," Charles says, reading the book's title. "What's this? African?"

He tosses the book back to me.

"Sort of. I mean yes, but the character lives in Paris."

Charles's eyes light up. "Paris? Okay. I might—"

"Oh my God, guys," Julie groans. "Fucking-a, shut up already." She looks pissed off enough to tear out her hair. "You're both torturing me. If I wanted to sit around talking about books, I'd join a book club." She stands up and starts pacing the room. "Can't we go out and do something? I mean, I have to be home in less than two hours."

Charles looks at her, annoyed. "Damn. Just relax. Why does it always have to be about you?"

"Oh, that's a good one," Julie huffs. "All we ever do is what you want."

I get up and start for the bathroom. "Now where are *you* going?" Charles calls after me. "You can't walk away when shit gets uncomfortable."

"I'm not in this. You two figure it out."

"What, you afraid to tell Julie what you're really thinking?" he asks, his voice heavy with accusation. Julie is looking at me now as if I'm about to drop a big reveal. But she isn't about to be cornered.

"Oh no, Lara. Tell him he's a self-centered asshole. You said it yourself a few weeks ago."

"I'm not doing this," I say. "If the two of you want to fight, do it. But I'm out." I go into the bathroom. Standing in front of the mirror, I listen to Julie and Charles go at each other.

"You're just using me for my car."

"You're just using us to piss off your parents."

"You treat everyone like shit. You think we're stupid."

"You act like I owe you something."

This goes on for a while and I begin to wonder if life without friends might be easier. No expectations. No pretending to like the same music or books or movies. No having to commiserate over invisible problems like parents or drops in GPAs.

But I don't want to go back to being alone.

There's a break in their bickering. I leave the bathroom. Julie's hair, in a high white-blond ponytail, shudders as she bends over to gather up her stuff. The heavy chain with a padlock around her neck swings side to side. Charles doesn't look up from his book.

"Are you leaving?" I ask.

"Fuck, I might as well. There's nothing going on here." She stands by the door, her backpack slung over one shoulder. Her thighs show through manufactured rips in her jeans. Her lips are slashed in a bright blue shade.

"Charles, come on," I say, trying to get him to apologize. He looks up from his book, the fake glasses on the tip of his nose. I get it then, what they already know about the three of us. We more than compromise to be around one another. Together, we're biding time.

"Whatever. I'm out." Julie slams the door behind her. I watch it for a few moments, waiting for her to come back.

"Fuck it," Charles says after several minutes, "her parents will get her a new phone or something. She'll get over it." He leans over the chair, reaching into his backpack. He's on to the next diversion. "Can I show you these?" He's holding up a folder.

I glance at it, not sure I want to know what's inside.

"Poems," he says, handing it to me.

"Now?" I ask, fingering the thick stack.

Charles nods. "Sure."

I'm not eager to read his poems. I already sit through drafts that he reads out loud and even went to one of his readings. On every occasion, I throw out perfunctory accolades. Maybe this is the price of friendship, so I sigh and give in to the task. "Okay, can I start anywhere or do I start from page one?"

"Anywhere is fine," he says, settling back in his seat. I read and then reread lines, feeling self-conscious under his gaze.

"Can you not watch me?" I ask.

"Oh, okay. Sorry." He looks back down at his book. I don't understand poetry. It's like walking into the middle of a dinner party and sitting off to the side, eating cold food. Some of Charles's poetry is connected to the books we read for Ms. Kim's class. Those are the boring and derivative poems. They show effort. As if Charles is impressed with the sound of things, not their substance. "The life of the mind," he calls it—a special ecosystem that apparently feeds off obscure European philosophers. This is what kills much of his poetry for me. It's only when he releases himself from the burden to be a different kind of Black boy, to be seen as smart in a way that many people value, that his poems seem incandescent. Poems about confusion, about how Charles feels about himself, about who he loves and about his place in the world. These are the poems that rattle me. It's not that they're beautifully rendered—I wouldn't know how to determine that. It's the quality of his disorientation. All the things that he questions, I question too. I recognize this in the scribbled notes in the margins of his papers. The way he crosses his name out and writes and rewrites it, *Charles Quincy Bell; C. Q. Bell; C. Quincy Bell; Charles Bell; Quincy Bell; Charles Quincy; CQB.* Charles is looking to name himself, to have a hand in shaping the noise around him, interrupt it, redirect it, have it all bend to his will.

"So?" he asks. He is cautious and, I recognize, slightly regretful. A feeling of inadequacy overwhelms me. I speak but am afraid of being discovered. I'm not as smart as him.

"I think these are really good. Has Ms. Kim seen them?" I hand the folder back to him, wanting to free myself from the obligation of critique. As I do this, I hear a car round the corner coming toward the trailer. Snatches from Mashina Vremeni, classic Soviet rock that's equal parts bard, pirate song, and symphonic polka, cut through our conversation.

"Shit," I say. "My mom is home." Charles hasn't met Yevgenia yet.

"Does that mean I have to leave?"

"No, no. It's cool. Believe me, she doesn't care." I listen and watch the door intently, trying to determine the type of mood she may be in. "My mom can be a bit, uh, out there and her friends are whack jobs," I add in case she has someone with her.

"I get it. I have some of those in my family too." Charles is trying to make me feel better, ease the discomfort of exposure. His need to control his own narrative runs deeper than mine. Julie and I have never been inside Charles's trailer. We know only what he wants us to see.

YEVGENIA'S HEELS SCATTER pebbles across the yard. The bang of the first step and then the second reverberates throughout the trailer.

"*Shlyuxa vokzal'naya!*" Her keys clang as they hit the porch.

Train station whore? I give Charles a worried look.

He whispers hoarsely, "Listen, it has to be better than when I went over to Julie's house for the first and last time. Her mother was so scared to be around a Black man that she kept dropping shit."

We wait for a moment, staring at the door expectantly. Nothing.

"You should have seen it," Charles continues. "It was fucking crazy. This prim-ass white woman standing in the middle of her living room with, like, broken plates at her feet, saying through clenched teeth, 'We're so happy to welcome you. Our family is friends with everyone no matter if they are Black, white, or purple.'" Charles's voice goes high and excitable imitating Julie's mother. "Anyway, I didn't want to be part of Julie's little diversity training, so I got the fuck out."

I nod, half listening, wondering what's taking my mother so long. Then I hear her key ring jangle at the door, turning the lock.

"Hello," Yevgenia says, not really looking at us, but at a letter she's holding. Then her male radar comes to full attention. She peels her face away from the note in her hand, flinging it on the dining table. "Oh, hello, company," she says with interest, eyeing Charles like he's a juicy steak.

Charles looks at me cautiously and then at my mother. "Hi," he says. On his face, a parade of judgments. My mother is wearing a skintight, floral-patterned dress trimmed with lace that's more boudoir than work wear. My mother's clothes and the way she fits into them always bring her attention. She's into sparkles, cleavage-exposing glittered tops that say things like "porn star" or "trashy," shiny plastic skirts and leggings, dominatrix shoes and boots. She calls me "priggish," saying I'm "straightjacketed by puritanical values" whenever I complain about her outfits.

"Lari." Yevgenia uses my pet name. She's either drunk and in a voluble mood or about to ask me for something I'm not going to give. "You didn't tell me you'd be bringing someone over." My mother speaks to me but her eyes are on Charles. "Did she offer you anything to eat? To drink? She probably didn't. It's a very American habit, that. People come over to visit a person living in the richest country in the world and they make their guests starve." My mother marches to the kitchen. The hollow explosion of her patent plastic heels against the elevated floors of our wheeled existence rattles me. She bangs around the kitchen, slamming cabinet doors, chopping stuff, throwing things into bowls. When Yevgenia sets down plates of meats, boiled potatoes, and pickled condiments, I know she has just reenacted the miracle of five loaves and two fish.

My mother doesn't sit with us. Instead, she apologizes to Charles and asks me to follow her. "I need to show you something," she explains, pulling me into the dark bathroom, flicking on the light.

"Can't this wait?" I shift from foot to foot, sighing heavily.

My mother studies me for the briefest of moments, like she's forgotten what she's supposed to do and is reading my face for the next set of instructions. "Oh, right," she says, pulling off her shirt, exposing her braless chest.

A *tsk* escapes from my mouth out of habit. Yevgenia rolls her eyes at me. I scan her body. "Well, what am I looking for?"

"Right here." She cups her breast in her hand. "See that? Underneath?"

I bend closer. The light isn't good. Our bathroom is cramped. On the underside of her breast, right on what would be her bra line if she wore one, is a red bumpy patch. "It's a rash," I say, feeling like an efficient doctor. "You probably got it from something you wore. Or sweating."

She folds her breast up tight to her chest, turns to the mirror. The skin is so white it's almost translucent. Squinting at it in the mirror, Yevgenia finally shrugs. "Yeah, I guess so." She grabs her shirt, bunches it in one fist, her other hand on the door knob.

"Nope. No way." I step in front of her. "There's no way in hell you're going out to talk to my friend naked."

Her smile is deviant. "Prude," she says, laughing. "Who is that kid, anyway? He's cute, has a sweet face. Long fingers. He'll make someone a nice curio."

"Yeah, someone, but not you." I open the bathroom door and let myself out.

"No, no, not me." She says it in an exaggerated way so I don't believe her.

"He won't be interested in you," I hiss, blocking her in the narrow hallway in case she decides to go toward the living room. "He's gay," I say proudly, like I've won an argument.

Her eyes brighten. "That's perfect. Gays are masterful with toys. Get him to teach you something." She closes her bedroom door behind her.

CHARLES LOOKS LIKE he can't decide if he should get up and run. His knee is bouncing frantically. He's eyeing the door.

"You heard all of that, didn't you?" I ask.

"Yeah," he says. "It's cool. Kind of funny." He pulls out another book from his backpack, wanting to quickly change the subject. "Have you read this?" He shows me the cover: Wittgenstein's *Philosophical Investigations*, third edition. The book is old and looks boring.

I shake my head. "Do you have as much homework as I do? We have that paper for Kim's class plus the math test coming up," I say, wanting to keep us on firmer ground. I know how conversations can go with Charles. He puzzles out ideas on you, regardless of your interest or willingness. This exasperates Julie. I only tolerate it from time to time.

We both look up when Yevgenia makes her way down the hall again.

"I'm pulling a double," she announces. "Don't wait up for me." She has changed into skintight jeans with rhinestones spattered down the front. Her breasts are aggressively pushed up like she's offering them on a tray. Her tank top reads SEXY in the unlikely event one of her bar patrons finds her outfit too nuanced.

"But you just got home." It's knee-jerk, my need to keep tabs on her.

"Somebody's got to make the rent. Like the song says, 'It's all about the Benjamins, baby.'" My mother grins at Charles like she's sharing a joke with him.

I cringe. This is my version of Julie's mother. I glance at Charles. He presses his lips in a tight, polite smile. I know the look, feel it deeply. The gentle surrender of your humanity in favor of moving peacefully through a moment that aims to displace you from it.

My mother will not notice. While Yevgenia never lets anyone forget that she's Russian, her take on Blackness is all American. She marvels at what she calls the ingenuity of, say, Black music or the rhythmic abilities of Black bodies, but when talk turns to racist practices in hiring or the need for more Black teachers, she'll complain that it's all *politically correct nonsense*, declaring with warped know-it-all pride, "The Bolsheviks invented political correctness."

"Alright, bye." There's no use arguing with her. I want to push her out the door, salvage what I can of my friendship with Charles, our dignity.

"Don't worry, I'm leaving," she says, grabbing her purse off the table. She pauses. "What's that you have there?" Yevgenia nods at the book in Charles's hand.

He turns the book over and reads the title: "*Philosophical Investigations*." Yevgenia goes closer to the sofa.

"Yes, I know Wittgenstein's work." She reaches out for the text. Charles passes it to her and she starts thumbing through the pages. "I'm not familiar with this translation. I have only read his work in the German."

"Really?" Charles is impressed. He stares at her with curiosity, but perhaps a little skepticism.

"Yes, I mean, it was years ago, at university," she muses, mostly to herself. "I always found him strange. For example, in *Logik*—have you read it?" Yevgenia asks Charles quickly, not waiting for an answer. "There is that line, 'All the propositions of logic are generalizations of tautologies and all generalizations of tautologies are propositions of logic.' How can a man so uncertain of himself be so certain, fanatical even, when it comes to the mess of something being true or false?"

Charles nods slowly, listening. "Yes, I see what you mean." Though it isn't clear to me if he does, because I'm completely lost.

Yevgenia sits down on the sofa next to him, fishing out a cigarette from her purse. "Would you like?" She holds up the pack to him.

To my surprise, Charles delicately removes a cigarette, his face aglow when he leans in to the lighter.

"I mean, when you have lived as I have, Soviet, Russian, here and there, you understand, like Wittgenstein did too, eventually"—she holds up a finger—"how the world bleeds. You see that there are no lines. There are only circles that overlie circles." Yevgenia raises her eyebrows, showing that she is dead serious in her analysis. "Right?"

I sit across from them in the Russian chair as they talk. None of this makes sense to me. A half an hour, then an hour, and so on, time ticks. The house grows darker with the evening and their nonstop chatter. I get up, walk around, then sit again. I wonder how to insert myself. Perhaps it's all the philosophical talk that has me seeing this conflict, this inability on my part to stick my foot in and make my presence known, as an existential crisis. I am nobody in the world, of no significance, with nothing to offer. I try out this line of thinking until I throw my head back and huff my annoyance. Yevgenia and Charles look over at me, their faces in shadows.

"Aren't you going to work?" I ask, feeling like the parent who pulls the plug on a raucous party.

Yevgenia waves her hand. "I'll leave soon." She stands and turns to Charles. "Like a drink? I have the best vodka and maybe one or two beers."

"I'll try the vodka." Charles also stands, smiling at me like he's just been offered a free ride in a limousine.

My mother calls from the kitchen, "Lari, I know you don't want any alcohol, my little Victorian."

My face burns. "Yeah, I think there's a law against it. It's called underage drinking," I remind her.

My mother has a sad half smile on her face when she appears from around the kitchen. Cupping my elbow, she gently pulls me toward her, whispering so Charles can't hear, "Be softer, *zaya*. The world is full of ugly. Don't let it drown you."

I step back from my mother and search her face for signs of too much drink. Her smile is tender, slow, like she knows what I am up to.

"I'm not drunk," she says, patting my arm. "I'm just your mother."

YEVGENIA FINALLY LEAVES for work, but not before she loans Charles a stack of her stolen library books, gives him a few notes on his poetry, and pulls three cards for him.

Her car isn't out of the driveway before Charles turns to me and says, "Your mom is incredible. She's dope as fuck. I mean, she's read everything. She's so—" He searches for the perfect word.

Overbearing? Full of shit? Base? Narcissistic?

Charles snaps his fingers when he finds it. "Cosmopolitan."

MY EYES LAND on the envelope she tossed on the table earlier. Later, I will see the official-looking seal and DSH-Atascadero with a name and address in the upper right corner. But the letter is gone and I know she's hiding something from me.

✦

Never trust a man who talks too much. Men who jabber on are men who don't read. They are needy men. Men who can't, or won't, satisfy in bed.

"That you don't have a father is the Blackest thing about you," Charles says to me. "And your obsession and longing for him is the whitest."

"Charles." Crystal's tone is scolding, parental. "That's mean. You can't say that."

"Hush, Mother Mary. It's a joke." Charles's head rolls loose on his neck as he gives me an evil side-eye. He doesn't want to have to explain to her that as a fatherless Black child himself, he has every right.

"And I wish you would stop calling me that." I am sitting on the floor between Crystal's knees as she tugs my hair into cornrows, which will, once she is done, coil into five braids that rest over my right shoulder. I can't see her face but I imagine she's pouting. Charles calls her "Mother Mary" now that she's started to show and refuses to say who the father is.

It's an empty Saturday at my house and our shit talking fills time. Like prisoners on the yard, I imagine, Charles and I pluck at nearly healed scabs, pouring light mirth in each, the pleasure in pain. I'm getting good at this, playing at being cruel. Hurling bubble-wrapped insults for laughs.

"Please." I direct my words to Charles, scrambling to find my comeback. "The Blackest thing about you is your longing to be white."

"There you go again"—Charles slaps his thigh, shaking his head like he's disappointed—"tryin' to make everything about you."

"Fuck you."

Charles leans forward to admire Crystal's work. "My, my," he says in a southern falsetto. "A Black child is born. Now you go on out there and claim your culture, sis."

"But isn't she part, what, white or Spanish or I don't know?" Crystal asks.

"Black," I say, thinking about how the world makes sense to me, or maybe how I make sense to the world. "Actually, an Afro-Cuban American Slav," I try out.

"Oh no, that's terrible," Charles says, leaning over to laugh. "You sound like a fucking sandwich or a French art collector we'd call Cubic-Slave."

"You're so corny." I laugh with him, feeling myself bloom.

Crystal yanks my hair. "Can you both stop?"

"Easy," I say, rubbing my scalp, screwing my brows together at Charles, like *the fuck?*

"What's wrong, Rosemary, the baby eating at you?" Charles winks at me, then casts a fake sympathetic glance at Crystal. He's not thrilled to have her hanging around, but Julie is in Hawaii with her parents for ten days and Crystal's been sharing her seemingly endless stream of cash with us for weeks now, so he tolerates her.

I feel her hands go limp against my head. She turns her

body away from me, standing up. "You two make fun of everything. You're supposed to be friends." She starts crying, full-blown sobs, and I bite my lip to stop myself from smiling. Charles is sitting in the Russian chair. He bends at the waist to look down at his feet. Anything to not catch my eye. We don't mean to be shitty people, but we've not learned yet the alternatives to kicking when someone is down.

"Why would you make fun of Lara for not having a dad?"

Charles and I cast a quick glance at each other, trying to remember which of our many disses didn't involve the lack of our fathers.

Crystal is towering between us, the top point of the triangle, forcing us to look at her. And we do. She's wearing a billowy yellow skirt and a tented black T-shirt. In pregnancy, there's a coarse beauty to her. Her features seem more pronounced, her nose wider, her cheekbones stretched flat across her face. Her brown eyes, deeper set but bright. If anyone noticed Crystal before, it wasn't because of her middling appearance. But in pregnancy she's something remarkable. Nothing about her is contained. She is on the verge of herself. Her body pulses even when she's still. Veins rise out of her skin like flooded rivers.

"None of us have fathers, not even your baby." I say this out loud without meaning to. But then, it's there.

"My baby has a father." Crystal wipes her eyes, defiant.

"Of course, we all do technically," Charles says, not ready to let the jokes go. Raising my hand, I gesture for him to stop.

"*My* baby has a father." It's as if the more she says it the truer it will be. It annoys me.

"Well, where is he then?" I challenge. "Because all I see is you getting bigger."

"Hey, Lara, come on." Charles's voice chides me from

moralizing, reminds me that I am not making conversation anymore but am out for blood.

"I'm sorry, Crystal. Really. Let's forget about it." I can't tell her what I have been thinking for weeks. How the envy I had over her desirability turned to pity once her growing belly became a time bomb. That she would have the baby before she even graduated or had a job or took a split second to pretend that she could have a future made me dismiss her. I didn't understand her appetite for keeping a kid under these shitty circumstances. But then, so many of the girls around us do. And she would join them. Those women whose haunted shouts leak from the trailers with screaming, crying kids, stacks of unpaid bills, and the unhappy men they try to keep happy.

I cross the room to give Crystal a quick hug. I feel Charles's eyes on me. He's gauging my sincerity. I drop my voice lower, so that only she can hear. "I shouldn't have said anything. You're going to be a great mom." Somehow my words don't offer comfort. A fat tear slips from the well of her eye.

"Hey, it's going to be okay," I say, and this makes it worse.

Crystal is on the brink; everything from her neck up seems to be spilling over. A moan springs up from the base of her throat. She grabs on to me, sobbing.

I glance at Charles to rescue me. A show of compassion is not second nature for me and the intensity with which I am called to be a swift-thinking, kind human is more than what I am built for.

Charles jumps up from the chair and approaches her slowly with his hands out in front of him. Later he will try to make it sound like it was something beautiful, this act. *She was a bird with broken wings.* Or some such bullshit. But I describe it more like the approach you would take when coming across a rattlesnake.

"You don't understand!" She's yelling, two jugular bands pushing out from both sides of her neck. "He doesn't want the baby. That's why he keeps giving me money. He wants me to kill it." Charles reaches for her as her knees buckle slightly. As he walks Crystal to my sofa, I can't help thinking of what Yevgenia would make of all this drama. But even as I stand back and observe Charles tending to Crystal, literally offering his shoulder to cry on as she presses in next to him, I know my mother would be better than me, quick with a tissue, a kind word, a hand to hold.

"I'll get some water," I say, totally useless.

"I THINK I took Dale's virginity tonight," Yevgenia announces when she comes home from work at 2:00 a.m.

"Lari," she says as she slides onto the sofa as I sit up, "you should have seen that guy's face." My mother is exuberant, smelling like she just swam out of an empty vodka bottle. "I said, 'I need your help with some screaming in the bathroom.' And God, did I make him scream." She giggles as she bends to unlace her knee-high boots. She kicks them off, sighing. "Ah . . . the perks of my job, Lari. You need to get one."

"Yep," I say, low enough so she can't hear me. "Rusty's is all about the endless supply of liquor and sloppy old guys instead of overtime and healthcare." I move to the kitchen to get her a glass of water. I am full up on sex. What really interests me is romance. Now *that* is something I've only seen on TV.

"I told him we really *washed* that stall." Yevgenia keeps talking to me from the sofa like I care. "Are you getting me water? I'd rather have tea."

"Okay," I say, unperturbed. I don't mind when Yevgenia is drunk. She seems less eviscerating and scheming. In fact, in the space between inebriation and passed-out drunk, my mother is a benevolent sage.

"Anyway"—her voice drops like she's looking down—"I think I hurt my elbow when we moved to the floor."

I grimace at the faucet. I don't understand how my mother and I could be related. It's not surprising, I guess, that this is a myth that she helped create. My mother would have me believe that I'm a mental emanation. Sprung from the glory of God's countenance. That I'm the sweat of trees, a particle of light, alluvium. And yet, my mother is not religious, nor does she care especially for the natural world. For Yevgenia, it's all about parthenogenesis. Reproduction without fertilization. Immaculate conception. To hear her, my seed is dew. Dropped from a needle of a spruce tree. Carried by the sideways glance of God. Or she says I began as an afterthought, a footprint left in the sand, impregnating her as she walked. Even as a little kid, I recognized these hypnotic tales for what they are: lore shaped by my mother's clumsy hands to mock my origins. I know I'm from the same stuff as any other child. Biological matter created not in the eye of God but in the collision of flesh and blood. I have a father. Some days, I have more than one.

YURI STEPANOV IS my first father. Despite being a little Black girl with a mass of dry curly hair that Yevgenia, out of lack of interest and frustration, cut periodically into a sadly misshapen and lopsided Afro, it makes sense. Yuri is Russian, my mother is too, and, therefore, so am I. It's a tidy narrative of a nuclear family. Any explaining, if it had to be done, was summed up in the phrase *latent genes*—a term I learned from my third-grade teacher, Mrs. Gunderson, when she commented on my family drawing of Yuri, Yevgenia, and me.

But Yuri's Russianness isn't the only reason he was my first father. That Yevgenia has actual photocopies of a few newspaper articles about him means that he exists. This opens the possibility that my mother's many stories might be at least partially true. So yes, Yuri is real, according to *The New York Times*, *The Washington Post*, and the *Detroit Weekly*. And also, I like that Yuri is a player on the world scene in a way my mother and I never can be. My favorite article on him is from *The New York Times* from March 13, 1981, three whole years before my birth, titled "Russians Seize Ballet Dancer Who Fled and Returned." When I was a kid, before I could read, I thought my mother kept these articles because she loved Yuri. But after I could piece together the words, it all made sense. Why he couldn't come back and claim me. Why my mother never said he was my father. It was just too dangerous for Yuri. He was wanted by the KGB.

YEVGENIA IS CURLED into a fetal position on the sofa. I think she's sleeping, so I watch, absorbing her quiet. When she is free from burden, my mother is beautiful. I lean slightly to study her features. In her flat, round face, high forehead, and almond eyes are bands of Slavic, Romani, and Tatar people. There is wildness in my mother's beauty. Born somewhere between the Ural Mountains and the Volga basin, carved by wind and snow. Hers is a face that holds much of the world without effort, and for that, it's regrettable that I don't look like her.

Yevgenia startles me by sitting up, stretching. She points to her purse on the chair. "Pass me my cigarettes."

"Tell me about Yuri," I blurt out. It's all the paternity talk with Charles and Crystal that has fathers on my mind.

"What?" my mother asks, her voice wavering with drunken exhaustion.

"You know, Yuri."

Yevgenia eyes me suspiciously. I can see she's weighing the request. "Why do you want to know about him?"

I deflect her question. "Wasn't he the guy who brought you to New York?" I know this isn't the case. And I know she will correct me.

"That's garbage. I don't know who told you that." She pats the sofa. I move to sit. The air seems heavy around her.

"Let's forget about it," I offer.

"No, I'll tell you," she says, yawning loudly. "Then I am going to bed. I go back to work in a few hours."

YURI IS CENTRAL to my mother's origin story. She will talk about him when people ask how she came to America and she will talk about him when people ask why she left the Soviet Union. Like all tellers of origin stories, Yevgenia has hers down pat.

She pulls out a smoke, lighting up. "I'm not sure why I followed Yuri Stepanov. He wasn't much to look at. You know, he had such a funny head. It always made me think that he was stepped on as a baby. The top was flat and smooth. His bangs"—she gestures with a hand, cigarette ash falling—"were cut bluntly against his brow. You know, a real Frankenstein."

I watch my mother in profile, how the light from the table lamp next to the armrest warms her skin, making it slightly golden. Her hair, which she has tried to take from black to blond to brown, is less calico and more even. I can smell the essence of her under the dimming astringent of alcohol. She smells of salty air, an empty beach at dawn, like that winter when I was ten and we lived in a camper van on the Texas Gulf Coast, huddling together in a single bed. That scent of hers cuts through burning tobacco, through booze.

In these moments, it's impossible not to love her. She's chasing a memory down, bringing me along. I'm in. There's no jostling, no games, no score keeping. Just the past, a past that isn't mine, but that somehow, I also belong to.

"You know, I was a few years older than you are now and had never been outside of Russia." Yevgenia takes a long, slow drag. Her mind is already on that night in 1980 when the shape of her future was far from her thoughts, when she saw Yuri Stepanov quietly sneak out the side door of the hotel. They were on tour in Rome. Out of sheer professional hierarchy Yevgenia had no business following Yuri. He was a dancer, a principal. She was also a trained dancer but not good enough for a company, so she became a junior costumer, a glorified seamstress who found herself on the plane with the Moscow Classical Ballet, thanks to Olga Ivanova's surprise late-term pregnancy.

Yevgenia leans to flick her ash on a plate on the coffee table in front of her. "I stood watching the back of Yuri's head as he dashed across Via Cavour. I mean, maybe I knew what he was doing then, you know, the significance of it." She looks at me, smiling. "I remember him nearly getting hit by two boys on a Vespa. *A Vespa.* Those are fun." Yevgenia explains that she wanted to call out after Yuri, but she lost him in the traffic.

"You know," my mother says, sounding contemplative, as if still questioning herself after all these years, "I almost turned back to the hotel. In fact," she says, extending her hand in front of her, "I had reached out to grab the door, and bam!" She claps her hands together. "It hit me. I realized that I was free. I mean, sure, the company handlers would go looking for Yuri. But not me, not for several hours, anyway."

At first Yevgenia figured she had until morning, so she decided she would walk around Rome that night, maybe find a bar, make out with a stranger. "I would be the first of my friends to say I had a real Italian man." Then she'd sneak back to the hotel.

But as she wandered away from the hotel, she asked herself a question that she hadn't considered before. "I thought about the chaos that Yuri's disappearance would cause and in comparison, I wondered, 'Who am I?' I was seamstress number fifteen, on the road only thanks to some fluke. I mean, who cares about the girl who sits in the dark corner, mending sleeves or zippers or beads on the costumes that those bitchy dancers carelessly tore out of?" Yevgenia's voice is clotted with resentment. If she went back to the hotel, her life would always be the needle and thread, and worse, the obscurity, the business of making something beautiful for someone else's body. She wasn't having any of that. "So I said, fuck it." And she headed out onto the Roman streets.

"So then you caught up with Yuri?" I push her to say more.

"No, never saw him, any of them, after." Yevgenia closes her eyes, leans her head back on the sofa. "I need to go to bed." She talks through her yawn.

"Yeah, but Rome? You loved it, right?"

"Love? An overused American word, love." My mother raises her eyebrows at my naivete. "A broke foreign girl?" Yevgenia's memories are shoring up her sobriety. I instantly regret asking.

"You remember reading *Lolita*?" she asks, and I wonder if she recalls the fights we had when I was twelve, trying to sneak a thin volume of Agatha Christie between the pages of *Lolita*.

"Think of *Lolita*, but without the trappings of a middle-class American existence. She's an urchin, one among many, and there are hundreds of Humbert Humberts, each more destructive than the last." Yevgenia leans forward, forcefully crushing out her cigarette. "So, no. I wouldn't say love. I would say an education." Her eyes go dark. This is a memory she won't share.

"Still"—she stands and stretches, signaling that she's off to bed—"I don't know why I followed Yuri. He wasn't a beauty from the neck up. But in his unitard"—her eyes grow mischievous—"with his muscular legs and the nice-sized bulge under his dance belt, well, that was something."

Yevgenia's yawn catches in her throat. Air scraping along tunnel walls. Serenity lays itself out over our trailer in thin muslin. I feel her eyes taking me in. Yevgenia's hand reaches down, hovering just above my cheek, and I move my face slightly, my skin tingling where I hope she will caress. She plucks one of my braids, holding it between two fingers, inspecting it. For a moment, I open my mouth and then close it, weighing the reception of my newly defined self, Afro-Cuban American Slav.

"What are you now? An African Queen?" Her voice is slick, mocking. "Get rid of it. It's too ghetto."

◆

Wealthy men are pointless bloodsuckers looking for a maid or a mother.

There are moments that you can't walk back from. I used to think these moments happened suddenly, by surprise. Like if you look up and a car is already crushing you. But then there are those moments when you watch the edges fray, strand by strand, and do nothing, not because there's no action to be taken, but because the cloth before you is an endless bolt of fabric and you haven't yet asked, *What is the cost of a single thread?*

It starts with Steve.

He shuns me. So I become a voyeur, like the mountains surrounding us. Whenever he's home I eavesdrop on the music he's blasting. I come to associate Santana, Sam Cooke, and Paul McCartney with him. I watch strange people come and go. Withering men and women with cagey gaits, pockets concealing what they hold in their hands. After them, Steve emerges from his trailer, a little less shiny than when he entered. Despite all of this, I don't stop pining for him, but I do stop blaming myself for not getting past our first and last night together. Julie helps me with that.

We're sitting outside my house, and Julie's going on and on about how great Charles thinks his poetry is now that he's invited to read at some college coffee shop in Riverside. Charles doesn't want us there because he's worried we'll act like "kids in high school." But Julie is scheming anyway.

"He's become such an asshole." She makes a big deal about heading home, but thirty minutes have passed and here she still is, leaning against her car. "You notice how he hardly hangs out with either one of us? We should just show up there. Sit right in the front row. And I bet he wears that fucking Hugo Boss jacket I got him."

I just let her complain. Staring out at the thick layer of haze that rings Mount San Jacinto, I don't notice Steve coming out of his trailer until he's halfway across the street. He is barefoot, jeans slung low on his hips, a streak of brownish-yellow on his rumpled white T-shirt.

"'Sup?" he calls out, raising his chin in greeting as he approaches, bouncing from foot to foot as he crosses the road. "I know. I'm a total loser for coming out in bare feet." He continues to step lightly until he's at arm's length.

"How you doing?" He gives me a grin that on another day would have me commit it to memory, but not today. Maybe because when Steve leans in for a hug, he smells of moldy shoes.

"Hey, I was wondering if either of you had a couple of bucks you could lend me," he says, looking pointedly at the purse that hangs across Julie's body.

Julie's eyes grow wide. I know she's thinking, *What the fuck?*

"My bike is in the shop." Steve gestures toward his empty carport with his head. "I haven't gone to the bank yet."

Julie sighs, pulling out her wallet. She tries to shield it from Steve, who inches closer, glimpsing what he wants.

"I'll take that ten spot," he says eagerly. "Pay you back tomorrow."

Between Steve and Terri, I am probably owed over a thousand dollars for babysitting. I doubt that he will ever pay Julie back and from the way she reluctantly hands over the money, I can see she has her misgivings too.

"Thanks," he says, tipping an imaginary hat before hobbling back to his trailer. It's corny. I'm embarrassed for him.

"Dude's not right," Julie says.

"Yeah." I nod. "I think he's been drinking too much."

"Or something," Julie adds. "He'd be off limits in my book, if I were you." Then she puts her hands on my shoulders, turning me toward her. "Tell me that the two of you haven't hooked up again since, you know, the last time. He's officially a walking STD."

"What? No." I shrug out of her grip.

"Good," she says, repeating: "Dude's not right."

As we watch Steve scramble up his stairs and disappear into his trailer, I can't argue with her.

AFTER THAT, if Steve's home, he rarely leaves his room, but when he does, he asks me for stuff—a beer, a cigarette, a few dollars. I never have any of those things. With Terri gone again, Brody is alone mostly, so I end up pretending to watch him, but really, I'm waiting on Steve. Hoping he'll come walking through his front door or emerge from his room as the person who once kissed me.

"Don't you ever have any homework?" I ask Brody. He's sitting in front of the TV, craning his neck, his mouth half open.

"Nope," he says without tearing his eyes from the screen.

"What about friends? Don't you ever go play with some kids? You know, do something other than this shit?" I add under my breath. I'm leaning against the entrance door, figuring out the phone Julie gave me when her parents bought her a new Nokia. There's no service plan on it, but I don't care.

I hear my mother's voice outside Brody's house. She's in a huff, yelling through the windows. "Hey, Terri! Steve is on my front steps." She bangs on the screen door until Brody and I show our faces.

"Oh," she says, and for a moment she seems disoriented, her eyes scanning the trailer for people other than us. "Come." She beckons us with an angry finger, turning sharply away from the door.

We race after her.

"There." She points like she's on the witness stand. "Get your *boyfriend* off my steps."

Yevgenia's enraged stride kicks up the decorative white stones that landscape every yard at the Oasis.

"Fucking druggie," she shouts at the heap of denim on the ground, blocking her door. "I saw you move, asshole. You're still alive. But if you come around here again I'll kill you myself." My mother may be a champion drinker but she doesn't tolerate hard drugs. Yevgenia steps over him and storms into the house. She slams the door so hard I think the trailer will rock off its foundation.

Brody and I move in to get a closer look. The motorcycle boots and blond hair poking out from the jean jacket definitely belong to Steve.

"Is he alive?" I have to ask. The body that lies before us is unnaturally coiled, the arms coming from a place somewhere in the middle of the torso. The legs seem to sprout from the shoulders.

Brody is oddly practical. "Get his arms," he says as he grabs Steve's legs. He pulls in one direction and I in the other, not knowing which way to go. Brody's face turns red with the strain. Our feet stumble over the stones, scattering them. I fall. Steve's neck and upper back smash into my knee.

"Help me," I grunt. Brody drops Steve's legs and comes around to my side. Without speaking, we drag him to the curb like the weekly garbage. We push and rock until Steve grumbles a little, rolling onto his stomach. His cheek is pressed hard into the ground. He doesn't move. Brody goes around the side of my trailer and comes back with the hose. Water splatters against the white rocks, turning them gray.

The hose doesn't reach Steve so Brody blasts the water at him by pressing his thumb over the nozzle.

"Hey man, stop," Steve mumbles, moving his hands slowly and ineffectively to his face. He doesn't get up.

"Brody, that's enough," I say. I notice I'm shaking when I put my hand on Brody's arm to take away the hose. Brody goes to sit on my front steps, looking out at Steve. I sit down next to him. We're sweating and defeated but afraid to say so. I don't realize I'm crying until Brody shouts, "Why are you crying for him? He's a fucking loser just like the rest of them!" He jumps up and runs over to Steve. He starts kicking him in the ass and the backs of his legs. "I hate you!" Brody screams, his voice high, ragged, a shirt torn on an exposed nail.

"Stop it. You'll hurt him. Just stop."

"Good. I want to." Brody starts pacing like he isn't sure what he wants to do next. "I wish you were dead." Brody spits at Steve. "I hate you." He's crying and I remember that he's a little kid. A screech breaks through his sobbing, like an animal unleashing long-held grief. "Asshole! I fucking hate you!" Brody says, backing out of my yard.

There are so many reasons to sit on the steps that day and worry, and so I do. For Brody, and myself too, maybe even a little for Steve, though it's too late. All that I've been too afraid to think is now confirmed. That for people like Brody and me, other kids from the Oasis, our parents, there can be no stars among us, no bright shiny people who are immune to the abject realities of our lives. I worry because I'm certain that Brody will never make it out, and what about me? What if I've miscalculated my smarts, my strength, my prospects? Hadn't everyone at the Oasis already done that? After all, the distance between me and the lump of human crumpled and wasted in my yard is only the narrow strip of asphalt between his trailer and mine.

It's too hot outside. The sun is falling directly on Steve. He's going to burn and blister. I surprise myself with a feeling of satisfaction. I want him to fry, to feel pain. Still, I go into my house in search of a towel to cover his face. I find only a washcloth. I'm too exhausted to try to move him into the shade. I kneel down. Steve's breathing is steady, like he's in a deep sleep. I arrange the tiny square on his face. Yevgenia comes to the door, watching me. "Come on. There's nothing you can do for him. He's made his own bed."

Yevgenia's face is soft but her jaw is set. I know this look and I want no part of it. "I don't need any of your pearls of wisdom. So spare me, okay?" I brush past her as I go in. I'm not angry at Yevgenia. I'm just not up for all the smart-ass comments she'll lob at me. Dropping onto my bed, I decide not to come out until Yevgenia leaves for work.

"Hey." She's knocking on my door, poking her head in. "I am sorry, you know. It's a terrible way to live." I look up at her from my mattress. Her hair is pulled up to a thin high pony-tail at the center of her head. She's dressed for work in a tight neon pink tank top and low-slung jeans.

"Are you sorry for Steve, Brody, or us?"

"Of course for Steve, but yes, maybe all of us." She moves into the doorway a little and leans against the wall. There's a part of me that wants to tell her to leave, to tell her she's uninvited, but the other part misses her, the part of her that was never her but my idea of her. The person I could grab on to and hold.

I forget how small my mother is, petite. But her presence takes up the entire room. She looks around my windowless space. I hold my breath and wait for her to start with the insults, but she says nothing. I follow her eyes, take in what she sees. The blank walls—except for a postcard of Josephine Baker that Charles gave me because he said I would look like her if I ever smiled—yesterday's clothes piled in the corner, my library books in a stack next to my bed. Her eyes move around the room but she doesn't look at me.

"You know, you look younger without makeup." I blurt this out, wanting to grab her attention.

"Ha." My mother pretends not to care, but she's pleased. Pushing off the wall, she inches back into the doorframe, ready to leave. Finally, her eyes rest on my face. "Get those books off the floor. You'll end up ruining them."

AND LIKE ALL the other moments between us, this too gets lost in the inevitable ways we disappoint each other.

6

*Never bed married men. They will be grateful at first, then
you will become a handmaiden to their guilt.*

We walk the length of the mall before Julie decides where she
wants to stop.

"Oh God, that is so cute. We have to go in."

I never have any money, so I follow Julie in and out of
stores, becoming part of her shoplifting routine.

This is how it's done: Julie picks up several matching outfits in both our sizes. Before heading to a changing room,
we linger to look at the jewelry or sunglasses or shoes. We
go into separate dressing rooms. Soon I can hear Julie rustling around. She starts swooning or complaining about
the fit. "This is so amazing, Lara. You have to see it. Are you
dressed?"

Julie pops out of the changing room. "Come out. Show me."

Then I stand in front of her, saying stupid stuff like,
"That's super cute, but way too baggy."

We start swapping clothes back and forth until the eyes of
the kid who works the dressing room glaze over. With a tool
she bought off eBay, Julie swiftly removes security tags. "Well,
I'm done," she says through the thin walls.

Together we dump a pile of clothes on the returns table.
Sometimes Julie will take one or two items up to the register
to buy and return later. Mostly, she will stand in line—I think

this is her favorite part—and start whining out loud about whatever she holds in her hand. "Does this look good on me?"

My response is always a tentative "It's okay." And then she starts with the "I don't know" and "Maybe I should think about it." Then she asks the cashier to put it on hold and we leave the store. We stick to the script every time, but on this day, Julie wants to linger, so maybe that's why we get caught.

"Let me grab something to drink." Julie goes to the Starbucks next to the mall's exit.

We're standing in line when two guys come up next to us. One is short and beefy. He's in all black—pants, leather jacket, T-shirt—and is wearing a thick silver chain around his neck. The other is taller, in a blue polo and jeans.

"Excuse me, ma'am," says the shorter guy. Julie turns to me, rolling her eyes. We aren't strangers to gross old guys trying to talk to us. We ignore them. It's a few seconds before his words register.

Mall Security. A couple of questions. Come with us. Julie and I blink a few times at the identification they hold under our noses.

The walk to the brightly lit office is interminable. I am uncomfortably hot. Blood rushes in my ears. My mouth is dry. I keep my head down to avoid what I'm sure are the judgmental glares of self-righteous law-abiding citizens. When I do look up, I see Julie talking in an easy way with the guy in black leather. She touches his arms lightly, smiling big at him. She's working her charm double time without success.

Eddie and Manuel are their names. The four of us sit down at a small table with our folding chairs in a half circle. We're looking at security footage rolling on the screen. Julie and I sit in silence. It seems they have nothing on us but their suspicions. Julie starts speaking first.

"I don't know why you're showing us this tape. We're just walking around the store. I chose not to buy anything. Is that a crime?" Her voice is shrill but authoritative, dripping with entitlement, the advantage of her birthright.

Manuel is in all blue. He has established himself as the good cop, nicely asking us to take a seat, wondering if he can get us some water. He nods his head in agreement. "You're right. We don't want to waste your time. It's just that the store manager asked us to have a quick look in your bags." He smiles at us. "Then we can send you on your way." He sounds reasonable. I think about taking the bag and throwing it on the table, confessing to all of it. I glance at Julie.

Her cheeks are red and she's all huffy. I've never seen her this way before. Her hands shaking, she points at the guys. "Listen, my father is a lawyer. I know my rights. You can't make me open my bag."

Eddie, dressed in black, turns to his partner. "Don't waste your time. You're just trying to do your job. These girls don't give a shit about that." There's a sour taste in my mouth.

Julie jumps in, seeing an open window. "Yeah, listen to him. You're wasting your time. We haven't done anything wrong. So we're going to leave."

Eddie throws up his hands and walks out of the office.

"Hey, wait. Hold on," says Manuel. His eyes drift to the door and then back at us. "You don't want to go down this road. We have a reliable claim and if you won't agree to cooperate then further action will be taken."

Further action will be taken. Now I'm really ready to turn us in. I start to speak, "Alright, we—"

"What are you doing? Don't say another word." Julie looks like she wants to kill me.

"You should listen to her," Manuel says to Julie, pointing at me.

She rolls her eyes. "Right."

We all just sit there, a faint buzz of electricity coming from the lights overhead. I want to vomit.

Eventually Eddie comes back into the room. "Still no bag?"

His partner shakes his head.

Julie looks at her phone, checking the time. "We're leaving. You can't hold us. False imprisonment. We're being held against our will. This is kidnapping." She is seventeen and sounds so certain. I admire her for having no fear. I almost start to believe that we're innocent. When she stands, I stand. Eddie is blocking the door.

"Our friends from the sheriff's office are on their way over. If you want a slap on the wrist, I suggest you stay here. But if you want to take the chance of getting a strike against you, by all means, walk out the door." He moves gracefully, stepping aside.

My knees go a little wobbly then. My ears are pounding. "Come on," I say to Julie. "Just give him the bag."

Her face is red. Tears are welling up in her eyes. "No. Fucking. Way. I don't consent to a search by these assholes." Julie is furious. "Call the cops. I don't give a shit. I know my rights."

That's what troubles me. Julie might know her rights, but I don't know mine. I don't have a bag. No actual stolen property is on me, but I benefit from Julie's pilfering. How innocent or guilty am I? What will the cops do to me? I fall back in my chair. I look over at Julie. She's arguing with the security guys. "You have no evidence. It's all conjecture." She sounds like a TV lawyer.

"If you're so innocent, then open your bag and be on your way," the guy in black taunts.

I could be home reading or watching TV or arguing with my mother. But then I might not have a friend, and in some ways, that's far worse than getting arrested. Police radios are popping off a strange, crackling, unintelligible language echoing in the hallway. Julie looks at me. For the first time, she's scared. She shrugs slowly. A huge sigh releases itself from her body. Her gesture says a few things: one, sorry; two, she didn't actually think they were going to call the cops; and three, she's going to find a way to get us out of this. I sigh back at her, *Whatever.*

The police materialize in the room, making it feel as small as a bathroom stall. Eddie and Manuel fist-bump the deputies, a man and a woman in stiff khaki shirts and tight Army green pants. They yuk it up, and then the lady says, "Okay, girls, come with us." I feel almost too heavy to drag myself up from the plastic chair. But I do.

It's dark when we get outside but I can still see the peaks of the San Bernardinos in silhouette. Julie and I are silent. The belt on the female cop jiggles and bobs with each step. Their car is parked in the fire lane at the front entrance. The guy is talking to us, but I can hear only my heart pumping blood. He opens the door. And I think, *No one has ever held a car door open for me before.*

JULIE'S PARENTS COME to the police station within an hour of our arrest. The cops bring us both out to the reception area, mostly because Julie begs them to not leave me behind. I spot who I'm sure is Julie's dad first thing. He's the only white man not in a police uniform and he still looks like he owns the place. He's rocking back on his heeled brown loafers, his arms across his chest like he's waiting for someone to bring him a cup of coffee.

"Daddy!" Julie is so relieved to see him that she nearly knocks him over with her hug. "I'm so, so sorry," she says into his collar, like she might cry. Julie's mother, a painfully thin woman with a benign expression, clears her throat. Since they ignore her, so do I.

Julie's dad pats her back, glancing over at me. He isn't exactly friendly but he isn't angry either. He presses his lips together in a tight smile. "They found eighty dollars' worth of merchandise and a garment tag remover. The store could press charges, but I've called in a favor." He rubs the back of Julie's head. "I trust that this was all just a misunderstanding that won't happen again. I would hate to think that you would ruin your future over something stupid." He looks at me, raising one eyebrow. There is a quiet hostility. I understand girls like me are supposed to be the seed of bad influence on girls like Julie. Isn't that why she chooses to be my friend?

Julie's mom folds her thin arms around herself as an officer tells her that Julie won't be issued a ticket or pay a fine, this time. "It was just a mistake," she says, three gold bangles on her wrist chiming with dissatisfaction. As they sign Julie out, her mother points to me and says to the officers, "This young lady's mother will be here any minute. Please see that she's comfortable." Then she comes up to me and pats my hand. "Don't worry, dear. Your mother will be here soon. Call Julie tomorrow and let us know you're alright."

Julie's mother speaks with some clipped black-and-white-movie accent. It's supposed to be proper New England upper-class but it sounds super fake. Even so, I appreciate her kindness, no matter how weird she is. I keep looking over her shoulder because I don't want them to run into Yevgenia, if she even decides to come. It's nice to pretend for a few minutes that I have a life equivalent to Julie's, to get close to the kind of family I see on TV. I like thinking that I might come from people who take charge, get indignant on behalf of their kid, that I might have parents who even offer a hug when the kid screws up.

"Thank you, Mrs. Harrison," I say. It's all a sham. I know it. They probably do too. Julie leaves the building holding tightly to her father. Her mother walks beside them, her shoulders curving inward.

IT'S AFTER NINE at night when Yevgenia strolls into the police station wearing some getup that causes the officer on duty to think she's a prostitute who lost her way to booking. My mother sashays her hips so widely it makes me think she's trying to dislodge coins stuck up her crotch. I'm sitting at the desk that belongs to Sergeant Hammond, according to the nameplate. Through the glass doors Yevgenia and I lock eyes, though her face shows no recognition.

She sits in one of the blue plastic seats in the reception area. Bright fluorescent splashes down on her, unforgiving. Yevgenia looks like shit, but I know it's not due to my situation. She stares at me blankly, like I'm a bagger at the checkout. She smooths her recently dyed black hair with her hands and then fluffs it up again. Lighting up a Camel, she pretends that it's 1960 instead of 2000.

"Excuse me, ma'am. There's no smoking in here."

My mother acts like she doesn't hear the short white woman standing behind the intake desk.

"Hey, I said no smoking," the woman says more forcefully, more police-like. "Go outside."

Yevgenia fakes concern, looking at the cigarette with confusion, as if someone put it in her hand when she wasn't looking. Then she asks in her typical Russian way, blunt and without shame, "How much will it take to get a prisoner out?"

The officer twists up her face, perplexed.

I don't think to move from the desk, to go out to my mother, get us out of there. I'm used to being summoned by her. Following her by invitation only. And it has not been extended.

Yevgenia rummages in her tiny purse and pulls out a crumpled bill. "You take twenty dollars?" The way she rocks slightly in her chair is almost imperceptible. My mother is an excellent drunk, really high functioning.

The officer looks around the waiting room like she's trying to get a witness. When her eyes fall on me in the office, I gesture, letting her know that my mother belongs to me.

The officer gives me a thumbs-up and a slow, knowing nod, like there's some understanding between us. I head to the office door, preparing to leave. She turns to Yevgenia. "She's free to go." The cop points in my direction. "There are no charges, hon, so we can't hold her." She's speaking to my mother in the tone and volume Americans use with foreigners. "Just sign her out"—she holds up a clipboard—"and she can go home, understand? She can go." The cop motions to the door with both hands. "You know, *salida*. Um, *dejar*," the cop says in Spanish.

My mother turns her head sluggishly. A look of *What the*

fuck did you just say to me? is written all over her face. My mother doesn't tolerate even the mere hint of being patronized, something she feels Americans are especially good at.

Yevgenia stands, tugging the edges of her short spandex skirt. I move in closer, just in case I have to tear my mother off the cop. She tosses her cigarette on the floor. Throwing her shoulders back, she pulverizes the butt with her foot. She walks calmly out of the station, her red purse smacking against her hip, her key ring keeping time. She doesn't bother to acknowledge me. The fact that I'm at the police station inconveniences her and, worse, forces her to deal with what she calls the special variety of Americans—the bureaucrats, the "fucking American Americans," she calls them.

I resist the urge to run after her. But then, Yevgenia leaves me so often that I'm prepared for it, and I know she always comes back.

"Was that your mother?" The lady cop is leaning against the intake desk.

I nod, watching the sliding doors.

"She's a firecracker, huh?" The cop hikes her pants up. "A real piece of work."

Looking away, tilting my head toward the ceiling, I tell myself Yevgenia will be back. She's just going out for a smoke.

"Is there anyone else you can call? Grandmother? An aunt?"

"No."

"Right, well, you can't stay in here all night." She pans the nearly empty lobby. "If that mother of yours doesn't come back for you, we'll have to charge her with desertion of a minor, got it?"

"Yeah, I get it. I speak English."

"Did I say you didn't? All I'm saying is that we'll get

the county out to your mother's and then next thing you know, there's a CPS docket with your name on it. You know what that is?" Her fat bushy eyebrows conspire into a self-important arch. "Child Protective Services. I'd be calling her and telling her to get her ass back over here if you don't want to rot in foster care."

My eyes drop from her face. Coffee stains are spattered dots across her wide chest. "Yeah, okay."

It's between shifts. I think they've forgotten about me when I fall asleep in the plastic chairs. But they don't. Some-time after midnight they put me in a single cell when one becomes free. That's when I hear two cops passing in the cor-ridor. "Hey, de Souza, did you see that crazy Russian chick in the parking lot chatting up Murphy? Great tits, right?" The sound of their laughter drip, drip, drips like a leaky faucet.

❖

Never trust a man who is silent while fucking. They are either repressed or control freaks. No good.

"Yo, Mon-toy-ya, let's go." A lazy voice cuts through the shuf-fling of feet against concrete, the coughs, the babbling, and the clanging. I blink my eyes. The stainless-steel bed I'm rest-ing on confuses me until I see "Shit for brains" underneath "Crips," both shakily carved in the thick yellow paint cover-ing the jail's cinder block walls.

An officer who looks like he's twelve stands in front of my cell. "Montoya?" He looks at the paper he's holding with his skinny fingers and adds, "Borislava." He swills my last name.

"Yep." My reply is rigid. Until a few years ago, I never gave much thought to my name. I spent an entire afternoon filling a piece of paper with "Lara Montoya," but it didn't feel right. Then I tried "Lara Borislava" and that proved to be no better. So I kept "Montoya-Borislava." Still, when I see my name written or a teacher calls attendance on the first day of school, there's a brief moment of surprise when I realize, that's me. It's a mystery why my mother decided to give me both her name and my father's. But just like my parents, their combined surnames don't share any poetry. He's Cuban. And she's Russian. He's Black. She's white. In history's roulette, they are representatives of many failed alliances. And in the U.S. context, my parents, their names, seem to bump into each other, just foreign enough to sound like mouths stuffed with marbles and just ordinary enough to not warrant a second glance. Immigrants. The visible invisible. The wallpaper in a crowded room.

The question of compatibility isn't just about my parents or their last names. The schism between who I am and what I am called, the genesis of this conflict I associate with the book *Doctor Zhivago*. The year before she left me the first time, my mother read *Doctor Zhivago* to me every night at bedtime. We were living in Truckee, California, then, a small mountain town famous for being the final resting place of many in the Donner Party. Yevgenia wanted to try out Truckee's winter. She ended up waiting and hoping for snow that wouldn't come. We were in a tiny studio apartment above a veterinarian's office. It was so hot at night that we'd sit out on the balcony rocking together on the squeaky porch swing; the yelps and cries of caged dogs frayed my mother's nerves. To drive out her frustration, my mother turned to those of Yuri Zhivago. Her reading voice rose clear over the mountain hemlocks, over the Douglas firs, and even, it seemed, over the distant sequoias. I don't remember it, but she once told me we read Pasternak as an incantation for winter and to drown out the dogs below. What I do recall is hearing my name pass through my mother's lips over and over again as she read about Lara Antipova and how much I grew to hate Lara for her poor tragic timing and bad luck.

When we finished the book, I asked my mother, "Why did you name me after her?"

She looked at me confused. "What's wrong with Lara? She's the heartbeat of longing and its death."

I wasn't convinced and Yevgenia knew it. She smacked the book down in the space between us and stood up abruptly. "You have a name. Be grateful."

MY FEET TINGLE when I jump down from the metal bed. I wait for the guard to open the door.

"You're going home," he says, moving aside so I can walk in front of him. He appears to be wearing two or three bullet-proof vests under his uniform. His head is an apple on top of his shoulders. "You're lucky." His tone is thick with do-gooder congeniality that reminds me of a church service I went to once. "We were just about to hand you over to Protective Services."

It's almost as if he's too relieved for me. I know the officer has not yet seen Yevgenia, because if he had, he would conclude I'd be better off as a ward of the state than with her. The clock on the wall reads 5:30. Over the heads of the four or five people waiting in the station lobby, I see my mother sitting at Sergeant Hammond's desk in the same chair I was in a few hours earlier. An older Asian cop with a stern face sits in front of her. He's talking to my mother. I stand by the wall pretending I'm not there, reading a laminated Drug Free Workplace poster issuing health warnings with too many exclamation points. I can't hear what he's saying but from the way Yevgenia's jaw clenches, he's laying into her. He issues her a ticket she has to pay within sixty days or she goes to court. I get a warning.

"One hundred ninety dollars you owe me." Her kitten heels are slapping against her feet as we walk through the covered parking lot. Her dusty blue Toyota sits alone in the corner. The driver's-side windows are rolled down. She opens her door and gets in. I pull my door handle. It snaps back, refusing to give. I rap on the closed window, pointing to the locked door. Yevgenia, who is applying lipstick, sighs and reluctantly unlocks it. There's a mountain of books stacked high on my seat. I bend to move them.

"*Nyet.* Not on the floor."

Wordlessly, I restack the books on the back seat. I don't look at the titles. These days, she tends toward the German philosophers, Schopenhauer and Nietzsche if she can't get her hands on a "classic" book.

"I'd rather read depressive misogynists than contemporary fiction in English," she will say. For her, "contemporary" started with the Victorians.

◆

Mothers are the sacrificial lamb. Why stick your neck out for the blade if you can get an abortion?

When I realize we're pulling into Rusty's, I groan. The rectangular building, too close to the edge of Route 74, looks like a prefab house fell off the back of a flatbed. It's only 6:30 in the morning, so I can't understand how the parking lot is already full with dusty vans, mud-spattered pickup trucks, and a couple of road-worn semis.

Yevgenia turns to me. "I'm fine with the silent treatment. But you are no political prisoner, okay? You owe me a hundred ninety dollars and you pay today."

"What, you want me to work the bar? Isn't that illegal?"

"You're not working the bar. Jamie quit. You're the new busboy."

"But . . . can't I do something else? I'll get a job, promise." It sounds weak even to my ears. For months, the lengths I have gone to avoid employment should qualify me for the Olympics.

My mother hacks a loud, fake laugh as she gets out of the car, saying, "Life is no chocolate box, princess." Her heels sink into the gravel as she marches up to the white aluminum door. Placards covering the only window read, NO SHOES, NO SHIRT, NO SERVICE, MUST BE 21 TO ENTER, and a large blue *A* from the health inspector.

Working with Yevgenia at Rusty's isn't like working with my mother at all. Not only because I'm to keep quiet about our kinship ties, but because, on the job, it's like a stranger is in possession of my mother's body. She walks into Rusty's and switches into "Evie," an overly attentive barmaid who is as ready with a beer as she is with a quip or an unoriginal aphorism. It's like Yevgenia is trying to be American among Americans and she's using the Midwest as her model.

"Hey there, Evie, how ya doin'?" old guys with baseball caps and young guys playing pool call out to her. To which she replies, "I'm good, honey buns. Happy as a clam."

Two women, one white and one Black, who I come to

know as Desi and Sherri, nearly always greet her in unison, something like, "Hey girl, cute shoes you got on."

And she returns with, "Thanks, ladies. Everything has beauty but not everyone sees it." Then she greets other regulars with, "Hey there, sweeties." Or struts up to a guy saying, "While the cat's away the mice will play, huh?"

She dances with whoever is on the "dance floor," a piece of linoleum where the carpet doesn't reach. She twirls and dips, pulling out her ancient ballet moves, the ones I watched her do when I was five. Then she's back behind the bar, passing out bottles of Bud, reminding Russ, Rusty, the owner, who usually sits hunched in the far corner, that the tap is out again. She winks her way past a newcomer who sits down uneasily, eyes darting across the room, sizing up the place, wearing the scared look of a man or woman desperate for a drink and nothing else. "Just a minute, hon. I'll be with you in a jiff," Yevgenia, as Evie, says. I'm left wondering when the word *jiff* became part of her vocabulary.

She goes on like this until it gets dark and the regulars start deteriorating with each drink. Then, sometime after ten, in a patch of quiet, my mother reaches under the bar and pulls out a bottle of vodka and a jar of pickles. She takes out a whiskey glass, quickly downs three shots, takes a bite of pickle. Then she stands for a moment and looks around to see who she needs to lift off the floor, designate a driver for, or sit and listen to. Once, when I've been working off my debt for a few weeks, I come out from the back to see my mother sitting with a man weeping into his beer.

"Bob, you gotta be a man about this. Sometimes, if you want something to come back to you, you have to set it free. There are plenty of fish in the ocean." My mother rubs her hand up and down his back, giving him comfort that he can't get elsewhere. For as long as it takes me to gather glasses, carry them back to the kitchen, put plastic bowls on the shelves, and take out the garbage, my mother sits with him, listening. I stop and watch her face, trying to read what's behind all her whispering. "There, there, sweetheart. I know it hurts." But there is nothing, none of the games she plays, none of the score keeping, no empty hand ready to snatch what it can get. I understand why she's loved at Rusty's. She never forgets a birthday, that a grandchild's ill, the wife's name. There is never "You Americans this or that." She gives to the patrons without overwhelming them with too many details about her life, including introducing me as her daughter.

NOT LONG AFTER I start at Rusty's, the old man himself seems to finally look up from his beer. I feel his eyes on me as I carry the gray tub of clean glasses out to the bar where my mother is leaning into a story being told by two new patrons.

"Evie." Russ motions her over. Since Russ is cheap, the establishment's soundtrack is provided by an old stereo hanging off a single shelf mounted behind the bar. Russ, who must have used his last dollar to open the place because he didn't like drinking alone, keeps the radio on a Central Valley station that plays generic rock whenever they aren't broadcasting a Dodgers game.

"Be right back, boys," my mother says, tapping the bar top twice and flitting over to Russ. "What is it, love?"

Heading to the back, I stand by the door, trying to listen through the noise and clatter of the place.

"Who's the new girl?" is his question, I think, somewhat

obscured by an extended guitar riff playing over the speaker. But my mother's answer is loud and clear.

"Oh, her?" she asks, her voice going high. "She's my room-mate. It's just temporary." After, she comes in and says to me, "You have to put some muscle into it. Russ is noticing that the glasses aren't as clean as before." She holds out a glass for me to inspect. There's lipstick on it. "Russ is the big boss," she explains, as if I didn't know.

"Fuck the big boss. Tell him he needs to fix the dish-washer." I don't care if Russ hears me. My mother's been at this for weeks with me, having me come in before or after her by twenty or thirty minutes. *Don't want too many questions*, she says. *Don't want to give people the wrong idea.*

"Hey," my mother says sternly.

"It's just temporary, right, roommate?"

"Get over it." She lowers her voice, speaking to me harshly. "I can't lose this job."

We glare at each other before she slaps a wide smile on her face and goes out to tend to her customers.

She'll claim that this is a work permit issue, that I can't even be in the bar because of my age. But there is another meaning to this, there always is. I remember, because she won't let me forget, what happened three summers before, when she had me sit in the lobby of the private club in Mal-ibu where she worked in housekeeping. They fired her when they found out that I was her daughter. They said it was be-cause she couldn't bring a kid to work, but she knew Mandy brought her kid to work, *nursed him and everything in the lounge and didn't get fired*. On the night she was terminated, Yevgenia made me go sit out in the car as she clogged the club's main toilets and keyed "KKK" on the manager's car.

I **TRY TO** let go of the whole "roommate" thing, but I'm pissed off. I know how my mother operates. There's actually a part of her that believes that she's protecting me and not in fact protecting herself. So one night, after she calls a taxi for the always-troubled Bob and starts to close up the place, I'm ready to call her out, only, I don't know where to start. So I end up asking, "Why are you so nice to these people? I mean, they barely know you." It's nearly 2:00 a.m. I'm sitting at the bar eating stale pretzels and drinking a Coke for dinner again. My mother is at the cash register, counting money, putting it in three separate piles. She holds up a finger, telling me to wait. I can make out the tally of the soft, hypnotic Russian numbers on her lips. The money goes into a blue bag with an industrial zipper that she places in a lockbox, storing it in a safe under the black plastic mat on the floor.

She stuffs another pile of cash into a white money belt that she has worn since before I was born. Then she shoves twelve one-dollar bills toward me. "Tips," she says. I look carefully at the stack of bills in front of me. I've been working my ass off for weeks, coming in after school and every other week-end. For a time, it was every weekend until I threatened to call the Labor Department. This is the first money I've seen. I don't care that it's only twelve dollars. I feel rich. More importantly, it means that I no longer owe my mother, so I'm rich and debt free.

"What were you asking?" My mother comes to stand in front of me.

"Oh." The money draws my eyes. *Do I have to come back and wash any more dishes at Rusty's?* That's the question I should ask but instead I blurt out, "I was just wondering why you're always so nice to everyone. They're, like, strangers."

My mother smiles. "It's my job."

"Really? Rusty pays you to call everyone sweetie, to comfort them when they get dumped, and bring them food when they're sick?"

I haven't noticed before how the skin around my mother's eyes sag, how I exhaust her. She sighs. "These people are *semya*. I take care of them and they take care of me."

"Family? Really? They don't know you. I mean, half of them actually think your name is Evie. The other half think you're Italian. I bet most of them don't even know how to read."

"So this is a problem?"

"Yes, yes, it is."

Yevgenia shakes her head. "I don't expect you to understand. You think loyalty is given away like sex with drug whores? Cheaply? Easily?" She moves away from me, closing the discussion.

"I'm not stupid. Just say what you mean," I say.

"You started this." My mother crosses her arms over her chest. "*You* say what you mean."

"Okay." I hesitate. "I think it's fucked-up that you made me sleep in jail even after they told you I could go home. If one of these 'family members' were in jail, it seems like you would sell the shirt off your back to get them out. But not me? I'm your fucking daughter." I watch her closely.

Yevgenia comes around the bar and stands next to me as I sit on the stool. Her face is red, twisted in rage. I think she's going to hit me. "Let me tell you," she says, pointing to the ground like she's claiming her territory. "These people, they may be many things, but they would never, ever be in jail.

Why? Because they're not stupid." As she grabs her ring of keys, words heave out of her chest. "You want to be better than me? Then do better than me."

"I'm your fucking daughter," I repeat, watching her move to the door. She wants to put an end to the conversation, maybe put an end to us. "Why did you lie and say I was your roommate? Are you too ashamed of me to introduce me to your *semya*? Why not a fucking cousin or niece? Too close? Or would you rather I pretend that I'm some neighborhood brat you're babysitting? Ride on the floor of the car, so no one sees your Black kid?"

Yevgenia blinks at me, one, two times. Her voice is so quiet, it's barely audible. "Do you ever think about how it must be for me? I walk into a room and start talking. Everyone around me immediately thinks, *Natasha. Sex worker. Slut.* And then I have a kid who looks like you, in this country crazy with their racism? It's not easy. It makes people think I am a certain kind of woman. Get a hand on my ass or up my skirt. I lose jobs. Get kicked out of apartments. Is it me? Is it you?" She shrugs. "Listen, it's not fair to either of us. And yeah, I wish I was a better person, I wish this fucking country was a better place. But it's not, okay?" My mother opens the door, holds it wide. But it's a closure. There is nothing more to say, for now.

7

Don't go in search of love. That's not how you find it. It finds you in the form of one smoldering person, say an Irishman on holiday who you lost in the crowd or the Moroccan whose wife interrupts. Outside of books, these are the purest forms of love. The loves rooted in a singular moment of hope and then it's gone.

Since my night in jail and working with my mother at Rusty's, she starts waking me up at the crack of dawn, standing over me, eating a piece of toast or drinking a milky cup of tea. Every morning.

"You can stop policing me," I say when I have had enough. It's 5:00 a.m., two whole hours before I need to even think about waking up.

She ignores me. "Chip-chop. We have an appointment."

"But I have a science test today and a quiz in English."

Yevgenia huffs. "Get your ass up. This won't take long. I'll get you back in time to take your precious exams."

I eye her suspiciously. We hardly go anywhere together anymore but I know better than to ask where we're headed, mostly because I might not like the answer. Her clothes offer no clues. She is what she considers "fully dressed," wearing a black strapless tube of fabric the size of a dish towel.

"You're wearing that?" I ask as I pull a sweatshirt over my head and jam on a pair of jeans.

"Are you wearing that?" she counters. "It's too hot."

"Well, if we're not going to the beach then I'll wear real clothes," I say, eyeing her getup.

"Okay, okay." Yevgenia signals that she's done conversing.

She's right. Though it's nearly winter, the weather in the California desert is a trickster. I know the sweatshirt will be too hot by the afternoon. On second thought, I yank on a tank top and tie the sweatshirt around my waist. I hunt around for my shoes.

"Let's go." Her keys jangle.

OUTSIDE IT'S STILL dark but the sun is rising slowly. A slim strand of orange is crawling up and over the ridge line of the mountains. We speed toward it on the highway. Quietly, my mother and I watch as orange light saturates and expands in the sky.

Yevgenia leans back in her seat, a single hand on the wheel. She steers comfortably. In the other hand, her cigarette is a maestro's baton, directing Viktor Tsoi singing a somber rendition of "Pachka Sigaret." This is my mother's road music. She sings and I listen, the strange lyrics, the soft consonants rounding. I'll never tell her, but I find the hollow recordings of her Soviet rock comforting. The music is just far-flung enough to create a detachment in me. When we get to what I recognize as one of my mother's favorite Kino songs, "A Star Called the Sun," which she once translated for me, I close my eyes and hum quietly.

I FALL ASLEEP and wake only when my mother slows the car at a stoplight. I see clusters of people sitting on overturned milk crates pushed up against squat buildings. A few tents are pitched on the sidewalk. A guy in a wheelchair smokes dejectedly, while two other men sit on the curb, one of them holding a broken blue-and-white-striped beach umbrella.

"Where are we?" I ask.

"Almost there." Her head ducks slightly under the visor, her eyes darting back and forth, looking for an address.

"Ah," she says when she sees it. She turns the car slowly into a narrow lane. I catch a glimpse of a green sign on the building: COMMUNITY HEALTH CLINIC.

I groan. "You dragged me all the way out here to take me to a doctor? We could have gone to Riverside."

"*Zatknis.*" Shut up. My mother's temper flares. Given our fight at Rusty's, I don't say another word.

In the parking lot, cars face the clinic. But Yevgenia parks away from the building, in the direction of a chain-link fence. A vagrant homestead is spread under the trees in a shaded back corner of the parking lot. A big blue tarp is tied to the top of the fence, forming a tent roof that extends down over three shopping carts. Next to the tent is another shopping cart piled high with gathered plastic bottles and cans. Three stuffed black trash bags are bungeed to the sides of the cart. It's hard to look away from the loaded bags and not imagine how long it takes to gather up what will likely be marginal profits.

"Get out, but stay by the door. We'll go inside in just a minute." Yevgenia bends over her purse and starts rooting around for something.

I hesitate, waiting to see if she will turn off the car and put her keys away. She doesn't. If she wants, she can drive off at any moment, leaving me.

"Go on," she says. She's still rummaging around in that bag of hers. I sigh and pop open the door.

Leaning against the car, I try to keep my gaze from turning to the homeless encampment. The air holds the stink of heated garbage, tar, and exhaust. Light reflects off the asphalt, burning my eyes. The rattling sounds of buses pulling away from their stops and cars going too fast come from behind the clinic. *What is taking her so long?* I knock on the window. "Can we go now?" I peek into the car. Yevgenia is slowly rubbing lotion up and down her arms like she's luxuriating at the spa.

"Come on, it's hot out here." Sweat blooms at my hairline. I can't hear her, but I see Yevgenia tense up, like she's annoyed at the interruption. She reapplies lipstick, spreads her bangs out across her forehead. Finally, she gets out of the car.

"Stay there," she says, coming around to my side. Her hands are on my shoulders; she's turning me around slowly like I'm a pig on a spit.

"What are you doing?"

"Okay," she says, brushing her hands together, completing her task. "Let's go." She walks quickly toward the clinic door. I stand frozen.

"What's going on? Why'd you do that?" I call after her. My mind runs with a dozen scenarios. Showing the hit man his mark? I look up on the flat roofs of buildings and see nothing. Selling me off to some old guy? I squint, trying to peer through the windows of the parked cars around us. They all seem empty.

YEVGENIA IS CHATTING cordially in Spanish with the receptionist when I catch up to her. It's clear that my mother has
been to this clinic before. Maybe if I weren't sixteen, I might
find this and my mother's other little mysteries strange, but
I don't.

I can't understand all that they're saying, but Yevgenia
makes a comment about a "snake in the pants" and both she
and the receptionist throw their heads back laughing. My
mother adjusts her body slightly, like she's inviting me into
the conversation. "*Es mi hija*, Lara."

The receptionist smiles. "*Ah, la famosa, famosa. ¿Cómo
estás, cariña?*"

Her words land in my ears, and I register them, fully com-
prehending. My mouth opens but my mind seizes, unable to
pull out the sounds that spin in my head. I sputter.

"No worries, Gloria," my mother says. "She doesn't speak
Spanish."

"Well, that's too bad. You should teach her."

My mother shrugs. "You know how these kids are."

"So true. You know my son, the older one, Hector . . ."

I'm furious at my mother. My face burns from the lies
she tells. As if she ever offers to teach me Russian or Spanish.
And as if I'm the one who rejects another way to know her, be
closer to her. Didn't she choose to make me the tourist, the
outsider in her life?

Yevgenia motions for me to go sit down, but I'm way ahead
of her, looking for an open chair in the narrow, crowded
waiting room. Thinking about how I can strangle my mother,
I step over the feet of some grandpa and plunk down next to
him. Across from me sits an older woman wearing a faded
black dress and sensible shoes. Her hair is swept up in a chi-

gnon and a black sweater is draped over her shoulders. She holds her purse tightly against her lap like it might fly away. Her eyes are on my mother; in fact, all eyes are on my mother. Most are stares of neutrality, a "wonder who that is" sort of look. Others are lurid, stares that seem to lick my mother's legs and bare shoulders. But the woman across from me, her stare is one of fierce disgust. Any other day, the bonds of filial loyalty would kick in, but my mother has embarrassed me, made me look stupid because I don't speak her languages.

The old woman's judgment elevates me. Vindicated, I too sit in hatred of my mother. Her clothes, her dirty jokes, her easy laugh. The fact that Yevgenia can't just sit down and be quiet like the rest of us. No. My mother stands and chats until a nurse, an impressively tall Black woman in pink scrubs, calls her in to see the doctor.

I sit for a while, picking at my nails, contemplating getting up and leaving. The waiting room is filling with all kinds of calamities. A scared-looking kid holding his arm sitting next to a woman playing a Gameboy. Another woman sitting with one shoe on and holding her other foot out in front of her like it might bite, but it looks normal to me. There are a few pregnant girls, either sleeping or looking bored. My eyes lock on a Black man wearing a white shirt. The shirt is too big on him. We stare at each other for a few seconds. His eyes are a deep brown; he wears his hair in a short Afro of loose black curls. He has a mole above his lip, the kind that seems painted on. His smile is so tentative, I'm not sure he's doing it until he raises his hand off his leg in what seems to be a quick hello.

"Lara?" The nurse in pink scrubs jerks her head in a gesture that says to follow her. I stand and look at the guy one last time, trying to decide if he's a pervert or trying to be nice. He sits up a little in his seat, like he wants to say something, probably ask for money or my phone number, so I look away, heading toward the nurse.

"Your mom wants to try and get you back there before the doctor moves on to another patient." Her Adam's apple bobs when she speaks. "You're the Lara we keep hearing about, huh?"

"Oh God. I can only imagine what crap my mother has said," I mumble.

"Only good things."

"Yeah, right. You must have her mistaken for someone else then."

The nurse turns. At first, she looks confused, then a short flash of anger in her eyes. She sets her jaw in that way adults do when they're going to launch into a long diatribe about how much they do for you, how hard they work, how they gave up their dreams so you can have everything and whatnot. Since Yevgenia never says that to me, I guess this nurse is about to say it for her. But she doesn't.

"Has anyone ever told you that you have a booty attitude?" she asks, her voice dropping to a harsh, low whisper. She's looking down at me, her hairline bordered by dusted foundation.

Actually, I want to be brave enough to say, you're now the third person, after my mother and my mother's ex-lover Tito, who I suspect tore the arm off a stuffed bear he had given to me when he thought there was still a chance of being friends. But I feel fragile. The nurse's words sting.

"Look, I get it. Life isn't perfect. But try to go easy on your mom."

I nod. There is no way to explain all the years of dysfunction. Besides, she's already on Yevgenia's side. So I walk quietly through the door that she holds open.

A mousy-looking woman in a white coat with stringy brown hair is bent over a chart. My mother is leaning against the examination table, tightening the straps of her shoes.

"Here she is, Dr. J.," my mother says.

The doctor doesn't look up. "Okay, hop onto the table there. Let's fit you for an IUD." She puts her pen down and flashes a professional smile that's supposed to be reassuring. "Evie, you gave her an Advil beforehand, right?" The doctor starts washing her hands in the sink.

An IUD? I shake my head. "No, she didn't. But I don't need an IUD. I don't want one."

The doctor considers me for the first time. "Oh, well, uh, it only hurts for a split second, like a pinch, and then it's over. No reason to be afraid."

"I'm not afraid," I lie. "It's just that I don't need it."

"Yes," my mother says. "You're a virgin today, but who knows about tomorrow?"

I glare at her. "I do. I don't need one today or tomorrow or even next week." Do I care if I have a "booty attitude"? Right now, not really. "You can't force me."

"Well, it's a really effective long-term method of birth control. I think that you'll find that once it's in, um, Lara, you won't notice it." I hate the way the doctor says my name, like there's an *e* in it, as in "Lera." I distrust her immediately. I believe mispronouncing names is a sign of deep narcissism and laziness. That's why I hate when Yevgenia lets people call her "Evie."

"Still," I say, "I don't want one."

"*Otvali.*" Piss off. Yevgenia throws her hands up in the air. She is done with me.

The doctor shrugs as if to say, well, we gave it a good try. She snaps some papers onto a clipboard and walks to the door. "Just come back whenever you're ready. And Evie, I'll see you in a few weeks. Just let the girls up front know."

"What the hell?" I ask when the doctor leaves.

"You have to think of these things," my mother says, slipping her purse over her shoulder. "You won't stay a virgin forever."

My mind goes to that night with Steve. I'm not sure I want to repeat that anytime soon. "Listen, it's my body. I'll tell you when I need it."

"Better not come running to me if you turn up pregnant. I thought you'd be smarter than this." She fumes. We walk shoulder to shoulder down the corridor.

Yevgenia pushes impatiently through the health center doors. The sun is at the highest point by the time we leave. We shield our eyes. It's good to be outside even if the air is dank. At least it doesn't smell of rubbing alcohol and air conditioner coolant.

"Why'd you bring me all the way out here? We drove for like, what, two hours?" I ask. It makes no sense. "This can't be the only place to get an IUD."

My mother walks to her side of the car and unlocks the doors. I get in. She pulls a cigarette out of the pack, looks once in her rearview mirror as if making sure no one is watching. Then she lights up, inhaling deeply, exhaling slowly in relief. It's funny, because in school they always try to teach you that smoking doesn't make you look cool, but Yevgenia proves that it does.

IT'S WHEN WE'RE speeding south down San Pedro Street under the Route 10 overpass when she asks, "So, did you see him?"

"See who?" I look out the window, trying to spot whoever she's talking about.

She sucks another drag off her cigarette, savoring the tobacco, holding it in her mouth. "Your father."

PART III

БЕДНЫЕ ЛЮДИ, OR WHO CAN BE HAPPY
AND FREE IN AMERICA?

Some days, honey, I wish I could turn myself
into one big fist and grind this miserable
country to powder.

—JAMES BALDWIN, *Another Country*

8

Never immortalize the mother. For that matter the father too. People on pedestals are just people you can't reach.

If it weren't for dear Elián González, the Cuban boy found a year ago tied to an inner tube off the Florida coast, my second father would have no place in my imagination.

When Elián first arrived on Florida's shores, he was on hot rotation for the twenty-four-hour news. They'd replay footage of him being wheeled into some hospital in Miami on a stretcher, talking about how the kid lost his parents during a "tragedy at sea." I recall Yevgenia, who usually insisted that I turn off the TV when she's around, standing next to me watching the coverage.

"Two days at sea and he looks like that?" Her voice ripe with cynicism, but she nodded an admiring approval.

"What's that supposed to mean?" I didn't have any reason to defend the kid, but still, I found her reaction unnecessary.

"I mean look at him, he's a poster child for *los gusanos staroy gvardii*. He's clean, he's cute, he's the right complexion." She scowled at the screen.

Staroy gvardii. The old guard. I have heard her use this term most of my life without ever really knowing what it means. Yevgenia always seemed to complain about "feeding the old guard" when it came to taxes, speeding tickets, and voting. I'm not sure how this applied to Elián González but I was certain she's winding up to tell me.

"Antisocialist pigs, every last one of them. Fucking exiles. They all come to America to bleed red, white, and blue. Join the fascists. I know"—she pointed to herself—"give him two or three years tops, he loses the accent and the whites embrace him with open arms. They do that with some immigrants, you know, the Russians, the Irish, the Jews, the Italians, the light Hispanics, they go to the other side." She waved her hand at the TV. "This whole thing is probably staged to embarrass Castro at the WTO. The capitalists are nervous." She turned to me, her eyebrows raised. "You know, people are threatening to march in the streets. Perhaps now these American pussies will finally read their Lenin."

I don't remember remarking on her racial analysis, it's just too close, but Castro and the WTO? I interjected, "*Please.* How is that even connected? They fished this kid out of the water. His parents just died, probably right in front of him." Images flashed on the screen of Elián leaving the hospital, limply holding the hands of two adults, looking scared out of his mind. His clothes were so crisp that I could almost smell their newness. Someone thought to place a baseball cap on his head, jauntily flipped to the side. Okay, maybe not the best choice for a grieving child, and for a second, I considered my mother's conspiracy theory. The kid was too telegenic. His appeal too manufactured.

"Conservative porn." Yevgenia grunted her disapproval. "People in Miami are collectively creaming their pants right now." She grabbed her purse from the dining table and looped her large warden's ring of keys around her wrist. They rattled and clanged like many excited yapping dogs about to go outside.

"By the way, they're lying," she said smugly before walking out the door. "*Both* his parents didn't die. That boy's father is in Cuba and he wants him back."

That boy's father is in Cuba and he wants him back.

I'm not aware then how my mother's words will leave me festering a noxious resentment toward Elián that would suppurate even after he's long gone. Is it taboo to fantasize lines of kinship? Because I imagine I'm Elián's sister. His evil sister. The unacknowledged dark child. The baby left swaddled next to the toilet in a public bathroom, like at an airport or a McDonald's. So as the TV erupted over the months with questions and debates around Elián González's patria and paternity—who wants him and who gets to keep him—I sink further into orphaned statelessness.

My father, my actual father, is Cuban. My mother let it slip out one day, years ago. Of course, she had been drinking. I was eight or maybe eleven, so my memory is as unreliable as any of Yevgenia's stories—drunk or sober.

If Elián González is the right kind of Cuban, I was raised on the knowledge that my father, Vladimiro, was not. Vladimiro Larenzo Fidel Montoya, who everyone called "Miro," is a Black schizophrenic. There's no sympathy in my father's migration, nothing the media might cry over. Nothing like Elián. According to my mother, after months of boiling his leather belts hoping for a taste of meat during the first wave of food shortages in Cuba, my father, Miro, boarded a rickety sea vessel called the *Evelyn* during the 1980 Mariel boatlift. He was a young man around twenty, hungry and confused. Like Elián, my father may have had a vague sense of what going to "La Yuma" was all about. But America was only solidified for him after he arrived in Miami and began his diet of candy bars and discrimination.

When I was old enough to understand that my real father was Cuban, I tried to find him in books. I began reading everything I could by Cuban authors—well, everything written in English. My Spanish was marginal and I learned to be okay with that, although Mr. Collado, my fourth-grade Spanish teacher, got angry with me. Sometimes he would say, "Ay, come on, Lara, you should know better. Your accent is perfect but you have the grammar of a three-year-old." Sure, it stung when he said that, and the giggles of my classmates clung. But I was more hurt by the possibility that I would never be native, even though I had no clue what that meant. It left a window open for me. That I "sounded" like I could come from someplace put Cuba in my mind in the way that Russia never was—though I recognize that the Cuba of my father is not the Cuba of my fantasies. In my Cuba, I want men in white suits, black-and-white wing tips, a Panama hat. I want the women in tight red cha-cha dresses, the sound of a vibrant danzón streaming down the street from the open balcony of an immaculate Spanish colonial building dripping with bright pink bougainvillea. I want the sun to be filtered through gauzy cotton clouds and cradled against the rounded bodies of 1950s Cadillacs all parked in a line of rainbow colors along the streets. I want the cry of ¡Hola, amiga!, sly dirty-word puns, and the uproar of laughter that comes from full, content bellies and the possibilities of dreams. I want people who look like me, with brown skin in a range of hues. I want no questions asked.

Russia, on the other hand, belongs to my mother. In certain specific ways, it's off limits. It's harder to imagine the kind of warmth and laughter and acceptance from Russia that I imagine for Cuba. Russia seems cold, limiting, fallow.

It seems to be a country of ferine, insatiate hunger, cruel insider jokes, irrational superstition—my mother through and through.

Elián González jolts me out of the safe perch of my armchair. If both his father and his country want him, then surely, my thinking goes, mine will want me too.

AFTER OUR MORNING at the clinic, I have questions. I want my mother to arrange a meeting. But Yevgenia acts like she works in customer service for the *Exxon Valdez* and takes an attitude of stubborn, frustrating deflection. All she'll say on the matter is, "Look, I did what was asked. He wanted to see you and so he did." She's right, of course. Through her crude tactics, by putting me on display in the parking lot that day, leaving me to stand outside the car, making me sit in the waiting room even after the appointment was over, he saw me.

"Yeah, but when did you talk to him? Why didn't you tell me?" Not that I would have known what to say to the lonely-looking Black man who said hello to me at the doctor's office, but that was my decision to make, not hers.

"I didn't 'talk' to him." Yevgenia uses air quotes, and I can't help feel like she is dismissing me. "They sent me a letter from the state hospital. He was in the psych ward, okay?"

I think back to the letter she had the night she met Charles. All this time and she didn't tell me.

She's watching my face carefully. "Don't get involved. When it comes to your father it's very complicated, very difficult, and I can't handle it right now."

"That's fine," I say, too tired to keep pushing against the walls she throws up. "I'll figure it out on my own." The room

is filled with the intoxicating haze of many cigarettes. I latch
tight to the back of the Russian chair. Across the small coffee table strewn with empty glasses, half-drunk mugs of tea,
a cake plate buried under a mound of crushed butts, my
mother is at rest on the sofa.

She's lying on her back. Her limbs flung over her head
draping the sofa's armrest. Yevgenia's between colors. Dark
roots. Orange-yellow tips. Her eyes are closed. Since she's in a
plain washed-out navy blue T-shirt and cutoffs, I know she's
not going to work. Inaudible Russian wisps from her lips; the
rise and fall of her stomach makes me think she's wishing
me dead.

"What's that?" I say, loud and tormenting. I would love to
lure her into a fight.

She opens one eye. "I wish you would figure out getting a
fucking job. I work two shifts to cover your ass and you worry
about an ancient pair of cock and balls? Miro is your father
in name only."

"Name. Skin. Hair." I speak loud and slow, as if her hearing is impaired. "I know you don't forget, so why should I?"
My mind is on her denial of me at Rusty's, and other times.

"God. That's what this is about?" Both eyes are open and
she's sitting up, her hands curled as if they're ready for my
neck. She accidently kicks the coffee table. The cups clatter,
interrupting the gathering storm. She freezes. Her eyes are
trained on the mess of the table in front of her, but really, I
know she's looking inward. Outside, in the fishbowl of the
Oasis, a car beats heavy bass above the shouts and laughter of
young men reenacting plays of yesterday's Lakers game as if
they were there.

Yevgenia's matted hair flares in a stiff peacock tail. She
tries to brush it down with her fingers. "Lara, let this go."

She's drained and, I assume, weakened by the endless chain of time spent at her job. I move away from the chair.

"No." I walk toward her so that I am next to the sofa.

She stands. Though Yevgenia is shorter than I am, I can't rid myself of the trace of fear. The constant nag that shadowed me in childhood. I knew what my mother could do, how the flat of the palm could burn the skin, how quick a plate, a book, or a shoe could turn into a weapon. I knew how ordinary words were molded into sharpened objects in her mouth and how any combination of these things held in the grip of her rage could drop me to my knees and leave me clawing the floor. But that was years ago.

The smell of wet tobacco and yeast sail off her skin. Her nostrils swell, exasperated. Before I see it coming, Yevgenia pins my arm to her chest, her nails digging between tendons until I am numb from fingertips to elbow.

"You think your father will save you? That he's your ticket into what? The Black Panther Party? This American race bullshit? How Pavlovian." She looks at me with eyes that see no way out. She shakes her head, releases my arm. "Go," she challenges. "Go be their Black American, fight for your right to commodification. Go earn your place on a bar of soap, a box of cereal. Join the imperialists. Isn't that the dream? Freedom." She taunts me with a chipper know-it-all tone and I hate her for it. I step away from her but she is already heading toward her bedroom.

"Why, you jealous? You wish your American dream gave you more than a discounted pass into whiteness? All for the low price of sitting down and shutting up when they go out to murder people of color."

She pauses at her door. "*People of color?* My God, you are ignorant." The wood-paneled walls dim her frame, turning her into a dark statue. "Just remember one thing, I kept you. Me. No one else."

◆

Sometimes you have to play nice to get what you want. But always carry a knife in your back pocket. Importantly, be ready to use it.

It's true. My mother kept me, but she also tried passing me on to others, and that I won't forget, despite her coming back. But when I needed her to let me go, begged her even, she wouldn't. Not because she loved me, but because she needed company on her self-guided journey to misery. Diego, the third among my so-called fathers, taught me this.

Yevgenia met Diego when he was leaving a hotel restaurant, a nice one, I imagine, because he's rich. And my mother, therefore, determined. From one week to the next we were sleeping in a rented single room a few steps away from the Church of Guadalupe in Mérida, and the next, we are in a taxi pulling up to the wrought iron gates of a sprawling hacienda. I was skeptical. Diego was tall and in good enough shape to camouflage his real age. Maybe he was sixty-five, maybe seventy-five. He carried himself as a handsome man, had a full head of neat black and silver hair combed back in a way that made him look like a politician. The first time I saw him, he and his housekeeper, Magda, were both dressed in powder blue, he in a suit and she in a uniform. They had a level of formality I wasn't used to. So obviously, when we arrived at the house, I thought Diego was the butler and that my mother would be joining the staff.

But I should have known from the way Yevgenia softened

her consonants or tilted her head or blinked slowly at Diego whenever she spoke that she had made him her lover. And no lover this old would be without some promise of a payday. Normally I wouldn't have minded, but the last time my mother landed a fish this big, she left me. So, I was concerned, at first, only for myself and then for Diego. He was so accommodating to my mother, taking her hand as they walked, pulling chairs out for her. He'd take Yevgenia to Mexico City for shopping, leaving me behind with Magda, a plain, skinny woman whose judgmental silence was, I imagined, as close to a convent as I would ever get. I grew lonely and wanted us to move on. But Yevgenia liked her spot next to the pool, with Magda on incessant rotation carrying out vodka gimlets, fresh ashtrays, cut limes, and books from Diego's library. Whenever I would start my campaign to leave, she would look over the tops of her white plastic sunglasses and say, "What's not to enjoy? Okay, the sex, but we have everything here. Think of it as a vacation."

Diego, who was not a big drinker nor did he like tanning, must have been lonely too, even with my mother's presence. We had this in common. Soon we became something like friends and found a predictability in our days together. Mornings in the courtyard reading, lunch with Yevgenia in the pool house, a siesta for all but Magda—who my mother was convinced was watering down the vodka and snooping through her things—followed by more reading: Diego and me in the library, my mother by the pool. Then I'd walk the grounds with Diego, who might tell me stories about his life in Portugal, where, as an architect, he set off all over the world to design buildings for people. In Paris, where he created a luxury apartment building that housed the artwork of a famous painter, or the outskirts of Shanghai, where he planned the new modern wing of a university. And I told him about the places I'd lived: the apartment in Culver City that caught on fire after the family five doors down hoarded gasoline in twenty-gallon trash cans when the prices went up and the small two-bedroom house in Orange that had the front porch taken out when a drunk driver crashed into it. I didn't think of these stories as sad but Diego would say things like: *What an awful experience*, or, *I'm so sorry*, always with genuine concern for me. And though I know I shouldn't have, I felt acknowledged by his pity. Like he cared for me, like a parent should. Mostly, though, we talked about books. "*Minha querida*," he would say, taking hold of my hand while we walked, "I'll teach you Portuguese. Then you can read Florbela Espanca and José Saramago in the original." I knew that this was a promise that would likely never come to pass, but he seemed to believe it and I wanted to, so we were both happy. And I stopped begging Yevgenia to leave and began making plans to stay. There was talk of a private tutor in Spanish and other preparations for school, eventually leading to courses at the university in Mexico City where I told Diego that I would study architecture.

But after five months, one night, I caught Yevgenia stealing whole bottles of liquor from the bar outside the formal dining room.

"What are you doing?"

My mother brought her fingers to her lips. "Quiet. Don't alert the spy. She could be anywhere right now."

"She's already in her room. Can you answer me, where are you taking those?" I asked, but I already knew. I'd seen the signs. The long day trips by herself. The drinking more than usual. The uptick in petty arguments with Magda.

"Pack your bags. We're done with golden cages."

"No. I'm staying." I was scared of my mother but I figured this is what she had wanted all along. To be rid of me.

"Bullshit. We go tomorrow." My mother turned away from me, two bottles knocking together in her arms.

"No. I'm not." My voice was louder than I had expected, smacking against the stucco walls and sliding down to the tile floors. "I am happy here. I want to stay."

Yevgenia turned to face me. "This isn't reality," she said, stepping closer to whisper. "Can't you see this place is making you soft? Besides, I am not leaving you here so you can become some child bride."

"It's not like that," I said, afraid that I might start crying. "Why do you always have to be like that? He's like a father."

"*Please.*" Yevgenia rolled her eyes at me. "Don't be stupid. There's nothing innocent here." She moved closer, putting her cheek next to my neck, and I was grateful her hands were full of bottles because she was angry enough to grab me, dig her nails into my skin. "You wouldn't want a father, believe me." Her voice was bitter. "I'm doing this for you. So be ready in the morning; don't make things difficult."

The next day, our bags were packed and the taxi waited just inside the gate, and Diego stood by the car as we were leaving. He leaned down and kissed both my cheeks. "Read Saramago; even in translation he's very good." With his thumb, he wiped a tear from my face.

"It's okay, Lara." Diego attempted to smile but I could see how sad he was. "This is your home. When you come back, you can tell me about everything you've read."

I nodded, unable to speak. Diego's face seemed to break with the realization that we were actually leaving and there was nothing he could do about it.

Yevgenia pressed her palm against my back, pushing me toward the taxi. "Get in," she said. I never had a father, but I did have a mother, so I listened.

"Evie," Diego said, nearly collapsing at my mother's feet, "please, I'll marry you. Give you both the best of everything. Think of Lara." It was the only time I had seen a man weep. Yevgenia freed her legs from his grasp with a shake and slipped into the taxi. Magda scooped Diego up, cursing Yevgenia with a quiet enraged stare. Together, they slowly ambled into the house. I looked back at Diego and the yellow hacienda, feeling sorry for him and already missing our still-born hours of reading in the courtyard.

"*Vzyat' sibya v ruki*," my mother uttered, disgusted. And I tried to pull myself together, turning my face away so she wouldn't see me cry.

"Come on." She snapped her fingers twice. "It was getting to be too much *nuclear family*." Yevgenia pulled a pack of cigarettes from her purse. "Now we get back to our adventure." She held her lighter up like it was a trophy. And within ten minutes, my life went back to the way it had been before Diego. My mother had the driver drop us off at a cheap salon on the edge of town where she bleached her hair blond, while I sat flipping through old issues of *Vanidades* and watching my mother sneak sips from a bottle of Diego's vodka when she thought no one was looking.

◆

Stay away from stupid men. Their sexual imagination is limited to the missionary position.

My original plan is that Julie, Charles, and I are skipping school Wednesday to look for my dad in Los Angeles, near the clinic. I prepare a few days ahead of time, mapping out likely spots where homeless men might congregate. I steal some money from Yevgenia's stash. I practice my long-lost-daughter speech. When Wednesday comes, I'm waiting at the entrance of the school parking lot, ready. The first bell rings. I start to look around frantically. I already sent Julie two text messages that go unanswered.

When the warning bell sounds, I start kicking at the ground, contemplating my options. There is no telling how many buses it will take to get to LA and I really don't want to go on my own. I look at my phone again. Nothing. "Fuck it," I say, and head off to the bus stop. I'm not sure if I'm going home or setting out to find my dad.

Then Julie's car pulls up next to me. A screechy guitar riff slams through the open window. Rather than turning it down she shouts over it, "Where the hell are you going?"

"Where do you think?" I hope I look at her like she's out of her mind. I'm agitated, angrier than I need to be. "I'm going to the fucking bus stop."

"Okay, but why?" Julie asks, turning the music down finally.

"To go find my dad, remember?"

Julie slaps her hand to her forehead. "Oh fuck, was that today? I am so sorry. I totally forgot."

"Yeah, no shit." I look up the street to see if there's a bus heading in my direction. I decide I'm going home. I'll let the search go for another day when my mood is better.

"Come on. Get in," Julie says. "Let's go find this guy."

"No. I'm going home." The truth is, I've lost my nerve.

"Don't be an idiot. Get in."

I never like that Julie throws around insults. Yevgenia does the same. Calling people stupid or dummies or idiots, like undermining a person's intelligence is acceptable among friends or family.

"Should we wait for Charles?"

"Just get in the damn car. Jeez, I'm burning up all my gas just sitting here."

"Fine." I walk around to the passenger side. "Where's Charles?"

"How the fuck do I know? You know more about him now than I do." Julie's voice is flat.

She's right, sort of. Their friendship isn't the same after their fight at my house. Besides, if Charles isn't faking being a college student in Riverside trying to get with some guy he likes, then he's hanging out at my house with my mother. I press my lips together and say nothing.

"Your seat belt," Julie reminds me. She puts the car in drive only when I snap it into place.

A **FEELING OF** dread settles in as visions of me and Julie traipsing around Skid Row seep into my imagination. We haven't even hit the highway and we're already out of place. Julie, with her expertly cut anarchy T-shirt, hair ratted into two high-perched pigtails, epitomizes studied rebellion. And me with my blue-and-white-striped T-shirt and jeans, looking like I've been hired to swab the deck at a yacht club. I'm not sure why I think we need Charles to join the fray. Especially since he's likely to come wearing one of his stupid scarves and the glasses that he thinks make him look so smart.

Julie has turned up her music again. Beating out the tune on the steering wheel, she sings along, shaking her head in an exaggerated, performative way, like I imagine professional singers do.

"What?" she asks when she sees me staring. "It's the fucking Red Hot Chili Peppers."

"Yeah, I know," I say, which is kind of a lie because I've never heard of them and she knows it. I'm still mad at her for getting us arrested and at myself for allowing that to happen. I feel like I can't trust Julie, like something has broken, finally, that cannot be repaired.

"Let's just get this over with, okay? Thank God my dad is out of town," she mutters, shuffling the same song two more times before we get on the freeway, heading south.

"TURN LEFT IN THERE," I say, pointing to a desolate strip mall, a stain on a side street off the freeway exit. We're making a detour to Hobo Depot, a spot five or six miles south of Skid Row. After a few wrong turns, Julie slows down as we come to the building, still pockmarked, scorched, and boarded up nearly ten years after Rodney King.

"Pull up to the front of that liquor store," I say. "I think this is the one the guy meant." We've been at this for hours. This is our fourth liquor store and Julie's pissed off and ready to head home. She tells me this is our last try. I have to agree with her. My head is hurting from the bald dejection of the streets we drive down.

Julie parks right under the *L* that's hanging dangerously off the facade of the store. I'm tempted to ask her to move to another spot, worried that a strong wind might bring it crashing down. Splayed underneath the sign, swollen-faced men sun themselves on the sidewalk in their vomit and piss-stained clothes like bloated lizards. I don't look at Julie, who hesitates before turning off the engine. There's nothing to say to each other. We're both scared for ourselves, in different ways. She, in that way that centers *her*. Her safety, her body, her property. I'm more focused on the forces outside myself. I'm scared that the fabric of my life is made from the same material as these men in front of us. That when and if I fall, there'll be nothing but the pavement to catch me too.

"Wait here," I say. "I'll be right back,"

"But I . . ." I can hear Julie's mind assessing the risk. I understand our friendship has an expiration date. Maybe all friendships do.

BUT HERE'S THE REALITY.

Sometimes I catch Julie looking at me with a combination of guilt and relief. It's fleeting, this look. But I know, in the way she gives me her old clothes or leaves uneaten food at my house, that she feels sorry for me. Up until that very moment, I haven't considered the burdens of our crooked placement in the world, how our pretending compatibility will lead to the slow death of our friendship, because we will never be equal.

"What? Are you scared? Get over it. These guys are so loaded they'll think you're a mirage." I am furious at Julie's obvious weakness, which I don't want to acknowledge is similar to mine, so I attempt to act the way my mother would. Tough. Pragmatic. Unstoppable.

Julie sweeps her eyes across the windshield at the slumped-over men, their grubby hands jammed protectively in their crotches. Heavy black makeup rims her lids like she's leaking tar. Her jaw starts to move. I figure she's about to ask to come with me, so I slam the door. I move across the parking lot on shaky legs, hoping that Julie can't see that I am actually a coward.

Mounds of wool blankets and dirty coats seem to rupture out of the concrete like pimples. It's hard to tell which hump is human. The smell of urine, shit, and pus from sores that won't heal all mixed up with booze is so strong that I cover my nose.

I walk to the edge of a dirty gray blanket and bend over slightly. "Hey man. Hey." I'm not going to reach out and touch it. I get no response. I see two men sitting with their backs against the building. They look older, like fifty or something, but it's hard to tell. One is Black and the other, I guess, is white. The Black guy sits on a plastic milk crate. His dirty blue "Cal" hoodie is fraying at the sleeves. His legs are out in front of him, showing me feet that looked like they're encased in seven or eight pairs of filthy socks.

I take two or three steps closer to them. The white guy's face is red and splotchy. Broken capillaries cross his nose and cheeks. He's sitting on a piece of oily cardboard box. His T-shirt is splashed with brown stains. It takes me a moment to realize it's blood.

"Listen, do you guys know Miro? A Cuban dude? Black." This is the full extent of my knowledge about my father.

"You a cop? 'Cause I ain't no snitch," the white guy says. He blinks at me, confused, with unsteady eyes.

"No, no, not a cop."

"You from LAHSA then? Did you bring something?" the Black man asks.

"Bring you something?" I'm not sure what LAHSA is. I start dipping my hand into my pocket.

The Black man's gaze holds, unmoving, around my knees as he speaks. "Yeah, like a present."

I can't tell if he is messing with me or if I have stepped into his delusion. In my pocket, I feel the crushed paper of dollar bills. I decide to go along.

"Yeah, I have a present for you." It's a low moment, lying to the guy. "So, where is he?"

"No, ma'am. You can't play me like that. Present first." He holds out his swollen fingers. The skin of his palm is thick, as if the whole underside of his hand is a callous.

I don't mean to, but I step back. I look toward Julie's white Lexus gleaming in the sun. I can't see through the windows but I know she's freaking out. I hope she doesn't drive off and leave me. I sigh, leaning forward and pulling some cash from my pocket.

"Here. There you go." I let three dollars fall before the guy touches them. His hands scramble for them in midair.

He brings the money up to his face, examining it. "That's it?"

"Miro?" I clap my hands, trying to keep his focus.

"Try the underpass," the guy says, sucking his teeth in disgust.

I turn, trying to locate an underpass on the horizon. I spot one two blocks away from where I stand.

"Cheap-ass bitch," he mutters.

"Fucking ungrateful drunk." It's an odd sensation, being so taken over by the kind of emotions I tamp down every day. I want to be mean, hateful, even. It bothers me but I can't deny the feeling of power I get by being an asshole to this guy. I know that power like this is a complete sham, but there's a liberation to not caring or worrying if anyone has heard me. Still, my heart is racing as I walk away. I try to calm myself, knowing the chances are slim that he'll come after me.

Julie's horn honks behind me. I can hear exasperation in it. I turn slightly, motioning for her to flip a U and park on the street. She pulls out of the parking lot and stops the car dead in my path.

She lowers her window, and the top of her head pokes out of it. "Come on, Lara. I need to go."

"Stay here. I'll be back in a sec." I tap the hood of her car lightly. *I'm in control.*

"Where are you going?" she asks.

I point to the concrete bridge brightly adorned in spray paint. Whole treatises of disrespect and turf battles play out in tags defaced by other tags.

"Um, I think I should come with you. It could be dangerous." Julie's forehead wrinkles in concern.

This is when I wish I had come alone. I look up at the freeway underpass. I can't see any movement. I'm not sure who I'll find up there or what's around the corners of the overgrown bushes. All I know is this moment I don't want to share with Julie.

"No. Stay here. You should be with the car. You know, just in case." I'm not sure what I mean by "just in case" so I leave it open to her interpretation.

I jog across the street as she yells out, "This is it, Lara. I'm giving you ten minutes and then I'm gone."

So far, the hours that Julie and I have spent looking for my dad have been filled with dead ends. This could be another. Trying to find Miro is like looking for a stray cat.

Everybody's seen him, but nobody knows where he is. I reach the edge of the concrete embankment. I stop before climbing up. The air is heavy with the sounds of semis and their exhaust. Someplace off in the distance, the beeping of a truck in reverse.

I am exposed as I climb up the embankment of the underpass. Julie's eyes are on me. I wonder who else might be watching. The incline stops and levels out to dirt, and at the top, I see signs of life. An abandoned black basketball shoe distended and splayed like the person who once owned it has ankles the size of posts. Opened tin cans of what might be food. Crushed BIC lighters. Cigarette butts, a rainbow of wax wrappers from Starburst candies, and chewing-gum foil line the dirt trough between the graffiti wall and the concrete slope.

Stepping carefully, I walk along the wall and edge my way around the side. A footpath cuts down the slope into some bushes. The vinegary smell of dried urine burns the back of my nose and throat. I hear a banging of metal coming from behind the bush. A woman's voice calls out something I don't understand. Pushing through the leaves I see what looks to be a base camp of sorts. Cardboard boxes cut lengthwise with sleeping bags on top of them. A white ten-gallon bucket is flipped in front of a little pit filled with garbage. A small, thin woman is bent at the waist smacking a spoon against a pot.

"Hey," I say, stopping at what I hope is an entrance. "Is Miro here?"

The woman stands up slowly. Before she turns to face me, she sighs loudly, like I've interrupted an important task. She is shockingly clean. Her face is full and unblemished. Her straight black hair is in a ponytail. She has a strong nose and high, rounded cheekbones.

"Sorry, don't know him." There isn't a mark on her yellow shirt or her jeans. Out on the street, behind me, I hear Julie leaning on her horn.

"Please, do you know anyone who might know where he is?" Maybe it's the way I plead, but she really looks at me, squinting like she's deciphering a street sign.

Recognition rides over her face. "Wait," she says. "You family?"

"Yes. His daughter. Do you know him?" The horn sounds again. I'm getting jumpy.

She ignores me, turning instead to some bushes behind her. "Oye, Chato," she calls out in Spanish. "Miro's daughter is here. Do you know where he is?" She pauses as if waiting for an answer and then turns back to me, smiling.

I peer over her shoulder. There's no one in the bushes. I worry she might be off balance.

"You know, I see it now." The woman steps closer to me, scrutinizing my face. "You look so much like him. Your nose and lips and the shape of your jawline." She touches her own face as she speaks, demonstrating what she means. "Wow." She laugh-talks in a slightly disturbing way. "I mean, I always believed him but sometimes you just don't know." Nodding at me like she's appreciating what she's seeing, she says, "So you're his daughter. Wow. Did he really play music with all those famous people?"

This is not a detail I can confirm. "Um, I don't know, really." Julie's horn blasts again. I need to get back to the car. "I really have to go, so if you don't know where he is . . ."

She holds up a finger to shush me and shouts angrily at

the bushes again. "Chato, come on, you shithead. She's gotta go. Where is he?"

I start to back away. "Could you just tell him I'm looking for him? That I'll try to come back?" I pivot quickly before she can try to keep me there. I'm halfway up the slope when I hear a male voice come out of the plants.

"What you want, mami?"

I turn to see a guy wearing baggy jeans. His rainbow-striped shirt is buttoned all the way up. He's obviously not my father. He's too young, in his late twenties. His hair is an uneven bowl cut, a white blond with black roots.

"I'm looking for Miro. I'm his daughter." It's strange making kinship claims so casually.

He holds out his hands, showing me they're empty. "Ya, well, you can see he's not here at the moment." He speaks impatiently.

"Do you know where he is? Or when he might come back?"

"Listen, mami, this ain't the Radisson and I'm not his secretary. He comes and goes. We don't keep tabs on each other." He folds his arms across his chest like he's daring me to ask him another question.

The woman in the yellow shirt comes from behind him, smiling at me. Pointing to the overturned bucket, she says, "Come, sit. He might be back later. You can wait here."

"Okay, well, I . . . just tell him his daughter was looking for him." Chato's back is already turned, but the woman smiles eagerly like she's ready to dole out hospitality. I contemplate staying, imagine my father coming out of the bush with a face that looks like mine. But I'm not sure I want him. All the anticipation, the driving around, the poking into dark alleys, the stench, the bleakness of the place, the reduction of humans to street animals, it breaks me.

Julie's white Lexus is parked near the camp's entrance. She starts the car the minute she sees me emerge from the bushes. She unlocks the door only when my fingers touch the handle.

"It fucking took you long enough," she says as she pulls away. She's too angry to say anything else. I'm grateful for her silence.

The sun is lower in the sky. Pale yellow light casts off the low-rise buildings, elongating shadows. As we drive out of LA, I scan the streets for my father and don't stop until Julie gets gas in Lake Elsinore.

Later, at home that night, lying on my bed's thin mattress, I wonder if my mother might be right. That the reality of my father is too complicated, too difficult for me to handle. In my mind, I am back at the overpass. The filth, the smell, all the ways other people step over you, or worse, treat you like a piece of shit on the bottom of their shoe, like the way I treated that homeless guy, like the way, surely, my father is treated. And to talk to Miro, daughter to father, and say what? Sit where? On a flipped milk crate? A cinder block padded with cardboard? And I wonder, between sips from cans of Coke, brought for the occasion, a derelict approximation of afternoon tea, would Miro even be up for a fatherly conversation, and would he be the kind of father who could dole out advice, or would we just talk about the weather? I already know the answer. I try to breathe slowly, take all of this in. And I can't stop myself from crying. Because I don't want my own father. This makes me a terrible person. A weak person. Because I know I will leave him out there on the streets, to have to carve out the semblance of survival, that even on the good days when he remembers to stand in line for food and on the bad days when he is snatched up again by police for vagrancy or trespassing or something more, he will know that I looked for him exactly one time and that I never came back.

9

Stay away from men who are too nice, too helpful. They are also controlling. An eager smile on the face leads to a hand in your wallet.

Charles is over. He's visiting my mother. He leaves his poems with her and she sits with him, red pen in hand, slicing up his pages, asking for meaning. Their heads bend together at the kitchen table, a stack of books, borrowed and returned, between them. The table is cluttered with plates and empty vodka glasses, an overflowing ashtray. A bag of American Spirit loose-leaf tobacco and Drum rolling papers are Charles's contribution to cool.

She's telling him about 1983, her first year in America. She had just arrived in New York, a city, she promises, that is "without charm." Yevgenia got off the plane with a mission to find "America's intellectuals."

"Can you imagine?" she squeals. "That's like trying to find a pot of gold at the end of a rainbow. Impossible."

From my spot on the sofa, they make an odd-looking pair. Yevgenia's recently dyed red hair is thin and shocked into a shoulder-length bob. Shiny silver plastic-looking leggings and a black tube top make my mother look like she works at a sex shop on the Strip. Charles sits up straight, the collar of his white button-up poking out of his sweater. With his pressed pants and brown shoes, he's dressed for a college interview.

There's no way I'm not resentful. I don't know who to blame for this: Charles for gaining the approval I've never received or Yevgenia for turning my friendship into hers.

Charles asks my mother questions about her life in an eager way that allows her to be magnified and embellished, holding her in the moment. As a child, I too learned to keep my mother talking. If she was talking, she wasn't ignoring me. She might even remember I hadn't eaten lunch. Through her stories, my mother beamed a little light on me. She included me in her laughter. Touched my hand every now and then to make sure I, her audience, was still with her. I clung to those moments, confusing her sharing as intimacy until I got old enough to see that the stories and the secrets were all told in the same way, with the same laughter, to anyone who would sit at her knee, drink with her, sleep in her bed.

She will eventually disappoint Charles as she disappoints me.

Soon, he'll realize that all her talking is not reciprocal. That, in the end, she is a shallow listener. That her interest in others is only as deep as lending advice, to chastise, to prod people to her way of thinking. And then I will be there, sloppy seconds but reliable, my ears filling with his hurt feelings, his complaints, offering weak sympathy while suppressing an *I told you so.*

This evening, a greedy bitterness swells within me. I decide I'm not going to warn Charles. I'll let him find out on his own. I stand on the sidelines, waiting to drag him off the field when Yevgenia is done with him. I watch. Listen. Hear stories that I already know. They are repackaged but have the same general plot: Yevgenia, regardless of the circumstances, emerges smarter and scrappier than anyone. A heroine.

"So, tell me how you met Lara's dad." Charles turns in my direction, his smile an offer, a slim cut of meat tossed to a patient dog. He knows I'm still mad at him for not showing up when I went to look for my dad. He thinks it's his fault I have already given up my search.

Yevgenia stands, starts doing her "exercises," a series of stiff bends, stretches, and marches that seem to come straight from an overcrowded Soviet prison yard.

Even before she starts talking, I feel myself retreating. The subject of my mother and father troubles me too much. As Cold War refugees, that my parents found each other here in the land of the sworn enemy seems like a bona fide act of desperation. The reality of my parentage, the fantasy of it. I brace myself for what she will say and for the things she won't.

THE STORY OF my mother and father starts with a loneliness so acute, it becomes genetic. The two of them were derived from the homesickness of people who faced permanent exile. They couldn't go back home, and as my mother tells it, "When we spoke, we couldn't make ourselves understood. And it was strange because we both spoke enough English to get by, so we thought it was our accents." Even now, Yevgenia seems genuinely confused by this. "We were internationalist, something Americans have no understanding of, so there was a collision, the locals didn't know what to call us." Meaning that my father became Black and therefore unfit for human designation. My mother became white and therefore well positioned for luck if she played her cards right. And of course, in marrying my father, she played them all wrong.

"Your father and I searched for places where we were

understood, so we checked out of America"—she sweeps her right arm over her head—"to what we hoped would be more manageable places: Little Cuba. Little Russia. Little Havana. Little Moscow. And it was even worse than moving to an Alabama swamp."

All that I know about my parents' time together as a couple in America is stored in my blood. Together, my parents were awkward. This was made worse by the fact that even before their separate arrivals from their separate countries, my parents—my mother's rage, my father's mental illness—made them interlopers in the cities where their first words were spoken.

Yevgenia hasn't come to that part of the story. She's still on the moment she met Andrei, her first Russian boyfriend in America, shortly after she moved from Rome.

"Andrei was what you would call cultured—but he lacked a real education," Yevgenia is saying, her voice high, animated, showing signs of drink. "Sure, he read Pushkin, of course Dostoevsky, a bit of Brodsky. Not at all terrible for a U.S. State Department dog. The trouble was that he had not read much else." She pauses long enough to take a swig. There's a clunk of glass against Formica and she starts up again. "I had to get rid of him, though. You see, he fucked like a Catholic, silent and scared like the pope or the KGB was watching. In truth, Andrei was nothing like the men I had known back home. He was a *rossiyski nemets*, a Russian German. Too much of a pussy for my purposes, but he kindly took me to all the parties."

I stop listening at this point. I know how the story goes from here. How Yevgenia contemplates the virtue of New York's snow over Moscow's; how the New York streets lack the glamour of the ones in Rome, of course with the exception of the drag queens she follows around in the Village. I wonder what Charles is thinking. Whenever my mother tells me stories, I can't tell if she's happy reliving a time or just bragging about what I will never access. The travel, the freedom. As if the whole world favorably bends toward my mother but not to me.

In her telling, my mother's voice is flooded with joy and alcohol-induced cleverness. She lays it on thick.

"I was standing on the corner of Seventh Avenue, I remember. A soft thudding of drums came up from behind me, licking the nape of my neck. I had not heard music like that before—nothing quite like this." Yevgenia is gripping the back of the dining room chair. Charles pushes back from the kitchen table, his legs extending out in front of him, feet crossing at the ankles.

I get up and lean against the wall next to the kitchen, my eyes on Charles. The drink and her demand for his attention show on his face.

"I'll be fifty before she actually gets to the part about meeting my father," I say, trying unsuccessfully to draw Charles away.

He smiles graciously, but turns back to my mother. Yevgenia gives me a weak acknowledgment, turning her body slightly in my direction, an invitation to listen.

"The Village Vanguard is famous. Have you ever heard of it?" She doesn't wait for a response. "Well, until that night, I never had." She was drawn by the unfamiliar music she heard coming from the club. It was languid. It rubbed against the walls of the Vanguard. She took the only table left, a small one off to the side. Her view of the stage was partially obstructed by a large, ugly speaker. She could count seven musicians, the sweat on their skin reflecting the stage lights so brightly they sparkled. But it was their music, the sound of which took on a distinctive shape. It spiraled up overhead and burst out like rays of sun. It was exuberant music, evoking a language of the sea spray against the Malecón and fruit so ripe, the sweetness of it is carried in the wind.

"I tell you, I'd never seen grown men caress and cradle something that wasn't a lover the way these men did with their instruments. I recognized the moment as an opportunity." She pauses artfully. "I would have one of them."

So she picked Miro. Maybe because he was the youngest. Maybe because he was a drummer. Drummers, she had heard, were an easy lay. But she claims there are other reasons. "Lara's father was a poet, not a good one." She looks over at Charles like she's trying to reassure him. "Miro's real artistry came from his music." She reaches for her pack of cigarettes. I hold my breath, hoping she won't light another, because if she does, she'll be staying home awhile. Yevgenia takes the packet in her hand, turning it as she speaks. "You know, Miro is a synesthetic and he had musical hallucinations. Everything was in sounds and colors. Musical notes lit up his mind in different shades. It seems amazing, right? But it tormented him. Maybe because of his mental problems. He would spend weeks grasping, reaching for music that haunted him in his sleep, waking him or stalking him in broad daylight."

Yevgenia's hands are working the cigarette box like it's a rosary, turning it methodically. "He had a kind of celebrity, Miro did. There was a time, just before Lara was born, when it seemed like everyone wanted to work with him. Lionel Richie, Madonna, Billy Ocean, Lisa Lisa and Cult Jam. I traveled with him everywhere, trying to keep him together, you know. The money was good. The real American dream." She sighs, looking around our trailer, remembering more lucrative days. "But Miro was not meant for this world and certainly not for America with its thirty-one flavors of ice cream, Big Gulps, and all-you-can-eat buffets. It was too much." She circles her hand in the air, the cigarettes rattling in the half-empty pack. Yevgenia looks over at me. "Your father was a genius, so he was troubled."

Suddenly she slams her hand on the table. Forks and knives jump on plates. "I have to go," she says. She stands, gathering her ring of keys and her white plastic platform shoes. She reaches for the bottle of vodka on the table. "You want any more of this?" she offers to Charles.

"No, I'm good," he says, his voice slowly breaking from his trance.

She drags the bottle off the table, walking to the door. "See you later. Don't do anything illegal." Her laugh is crude, jagged. The sound of her bare feet stomping down the steps stays in my ears.

"Where do you think she's going with that bottle?" Charles asks.

I shrug. On a night like this, my mother might make the long drive out to the beach, drink to her thoughts, the person she used to be. She'll drink until a cop knocks sharply on her window with the butt of his flashlight and tells her she can't park in the empty lot. Or she'll hit a bar, scan the leftover men plunked on the barstools, her body a metal detector, waiting for the signal to go off.

"You want to watch some TV?" I ask, ashamed that I have none of my mother's excitement.

◆

They say a man's hands or feet tell you everything about their sexual capacity. But I say watch how they eat. It will surprise you.

It's the end of November. Half of the students are buzzing with plans for winter break. The other half are trying to figure out what they'll do without free lunch for the next two weeks. Charles and I walk to the bus together, smashing through bits of conversations. *Are you going to Tahoe or Big Bear?* Or, *Oh my God, Jenna and Brittany are going to the Bahamas together.* Then the perfunctory squeal and the jumping up and down.

"Fuck integration," Charles says, scowling at a group of white girls.

I hadn't thought about it before. "Why do you say that?"

Charles nods in the direction of the winter-break kids. "Look at them. This is all designed to mess with our minds. Put us in reach of shit that we can't have, can't afford, or are structurally barred from."

"Yeah, I guess you're right."

"Please." Charles clicks his tongue. "You know I'm right."

We wait for a few students ahead of us to climb on the bus. When we approach the steps, Mr. Curtis, the driver, looks at us askance.

"What? The two of you ain't driving with Miss Daisy?" He flashes his missing tooth.

Charles blows out a puff of air, annoyed. We don't get the reference but we know he's talking about Julie. She isn't at school today. She's out looking at colleges with her mom.

Charles and I don't talk about it but I figure we both know Julie's parents are wasting their time. Julie isn't college bound. She has neither the grades nor the interest. She doesn't even want to go to community college. I don't get how she stands by and lets all that opportunity circle the drain. "Hell no," she always says. "When school is done, I'm done. I want to be out in the real world." Her dad promises her an internship at some client's PR firm in LA this summer if she manages a C-plus average. She sets her sights on that and doesn't budge.

"This sucks," Charles says as he slides into a seat.

"Yeah," I say, settling in next to him, already preoccupied with thoughts of having to get a job. "I wish I had rich parents who took me around to schools I couldn't get into." I'm mean. Petty. Trying, in that way my mother has taught me, to test the limits of his loyalty. Not to Julie but to me, our friendship. This trick, drawing a line, forcing people's hand, making them choose a side, is something Yevgenia claims is necessary. *Eliminate all the wan, spineless people,* she encourages. *Always know where you stand with the ones you call friends.*

Charles looks at me. His brows scrunch together, a slight frown on his face. For as much as Charles picks things apart and, I will discover later, rests easy with being the instigator of various half-truths, his moral compass prevents him from speaking badly about Julie or anyone he cares about. Perhaps that's why, in the months of hanging out with him, it doesn't take me long to understand that Charles's is the friendship I most want to cultivate. He is more difficult than Julie. Unlike her, Charles makes you work for everything—a laugh, an inside joke, a knowing glance. And so, when you get them, you know you earned it.

"Shit, I wish I had parents," Charles says, quickly looking

out the window. He won't say any more. His mother died giving birth to a second baby that didn't make it. A few years after that, his dad was crushed to death by bricks at his job on a construction site. Charles tries to pretend that he doesn't live with his aunt, Ms. Eunice, who seems old and cranky enough to be his grandmother. Whenever we see her on her electric old-lady cart, patrolling the few paved roads of the Oasis, he glances down and never talks about her either.

"Fucking plebeians." Charles nods toward the kids loitering outside their cars in the school parking lot. Their doors are open, their music blasting. "They're all in training for watercooler small talk. Idiots."

I nod, saying nothing. The kids in the parking lot wear looks of anticipation, like every moment holds the possibility of some big adventure. They gaze from one person to the next, calculating who is likely to have a key to the magic door. We would be right there with them, doing the same thing, if Julie were around.

"So, listen," Charles says, his voice going low, slightly official. "Did I tell you that Ms. Kim nominated me for an 'opportunity' scholarship?" His two fingers make scare quotes when he says the word *opportunity* with rueful disdain.

"Oh yeah?" I'm jealous even before I know what the scholarship is about.

"Yeah," he says. "I probably won't get it but it's nice of her."

"Oh please, I bet you get it." My voice is pitched high, like I'm straining against resentment. "What's it for? A new computer or something?"

"Well, it's . . ." He seems to be sifting for the right words. I can already feel his regret. "It's for a private school. Actually, a boarding school."

"What, you mean like in England or Switzerland or something?"

"No, nothing like that."

"In New York or someplace?" I interrupt him. I hate the way my voice sounds in my own ears, cloying and prying, like someone afraid of being left behind.

"No." He laughs and I feel small. "It's nothing like that. The scholarship is for the Idyllwild Arts Academy."

I shake my head. I've never heard of it. "You're going to live there and what, like, paint or something?"

Charles pulls back from me with a look of utter amazement on his face, his eyes moony. "Shocking." He shakes his head; the trail of peach fuzz above his lip pulls down, nearly dejected. "Painting? Have you ever seen me paint before? No. It's for writing." Charles is thoroughly put off. "Honestly, sometimes you make me wonder."

"Wonder what?" I ask. We're both annoyed. But worse, I'm jealous he's going to get the hell out. "So I made a mistake, okay? I didn't know writing was considered 'art.' I just thought it was, you know, writing."

"Forget it," Charles says, brushing me off. "I probably won't get it anyway."

"Yes you will," I say, but really, I hope he doesn't.

WHEN THE BUS drops us at the crossroads where the Circle K meets the road that will turn into Route 74, I match Charles's steps until we march past my place and are halfway to his.

"What are you doing?" he says over his shoulder when his longer legs finally outpace me.

"Walking with you."

"Naw, you don't have to." Charles tries to downplay his discomfort. "I have some things to do, you know, so I'll just see you tomorrow." He walks away from me at a quick pace, but I'm on his heels, determined.

I jog to get in front of him, forcing him to stop. We're standing in the middle of the narrow lane, the broken asphalt jutting like seismic calamities beneath our feet.

"You don't get to do this to me," I say.

"What are you talking about?" He's annoyed. This is starting to feel like drama and I sense the power behind it.

"Come over to my house and hang out with me and my mother, see the inside of my fucking life, see all the shit-filled corners, and then not invite me into your house, your life." I'm panting from speaking too fast.

Charles looks at me in that way I hate, with silent furious eyes, like he's listening but throwing up barriers, locking the windows and doors because there's a crazy person trying to get in. "'Shit-filled corners'? Really?" he asks. "That's disgusting. You need to rethink your imagery."

"Fuck off," I say. "You're supposed to be my friend. This is an exchange. I'm out here fully exposed. But not you. It's not fair."

"My God," he says, shaking his head. "I'll show you the great fucking existence I'm keeping you from." If Charles could make the soft soles of his sneakers blast and boom his way to his trailer, he would.

WHEN WE ENTER his house, the living room is dark. Heavy bloodred curtains are drawn across the windows. The wood-paneled walls seem even darker. I spot the sofa first. It's deep brown, and plump to the point of parody. Next to the enormous armrest is a walker. It takes me a minute to connect the image flashing on the large television screen with the unfamiliar language filling the trailer. In front of the TV Ms. Eunice is swallowed into the sofa, her bright yellow tracksuit clashing with the brown. She pays us no attention when we enter the room. She's riveted by the soap opera she's watching with the subtitles on.

"This woman and her Korean shows." Charles rolls his eyes, but I'm guessing it's mostly performative, because he walks quickly over to her and gives her a peck on the check.

"Hi, Mama!" he shouts over the earnest Korean coming from the TV.

Ms. Eunice hardly looks at him as she nods briefly and says, "Baby."

Charles motions me to go down the hall.

"I thought you said she was your aunt," I say.

"She is, but the woman's been caring for me since I was eight." He's giving me a sideways glance, like he's not sure what I'm trying to say.

I quickly change the subject. "That's cool she speaks Korean."

"She doesn't. But for some crazy-ass reason the woman has to listen to it at a volume like the whole world does." Charles pushes his bedroom door open and we're in a room that would make a librarian blush. First there are the bookshelves, metal utility ones meant to be screwed and unscrewed, packed up and moved in a matter of minutes. These shelves are stacked two and three rows deep with books of all kinds. Then there's the collection of gay art that Charles will explain to me later, calling it "tasteful porn from the ancient world." Most of it is posters, like Nisus and Euryalus in marble at the Louvre, or postcards of Greco-Roman artifacts of men with oversize dicks resting on the legs of boys, or miniature Mughal men with cocks up asses and photocopies of Qing dynasty men embracing and Egyptian rulers kissing.

"Impressive," I say, and my hand goes to a ceramic dick, erect like a stick shift, in the display area of his bookcase.

"Don't touch that," Charles says, smiling. "He's my part-time lover."

I draw my hand back quickly. "That's gross."

"I'm just playing." He laughs. "Sort of."

Then Ms. Eunice is calling out for Charles. "Baby. Baby. Come out here and help Mama get up from this damned couch." There's struggle in her voice.

"Shit," Charles says. "Stay here."

I keep staring at the art on his walls. The miniatures, I decide, are my favorites. I hear Charles coming down the hall. He's talking to Ms. Eunice. They seem to be arguing.

"Mama, it's okay, she's not staying. She just came by to get a book." Charles appears at his door, livid.

Ms. Eunice is grumbling something I can't hear.

"Grab a fucking book and get out of here." Charles motions me to hurry as he moves to quickly grab the large poster of Nisus and Euryalus off his wall. "Sorry," he adds. "Normally, she never comes in here, but she's worried that we're doing drugs or something." I understand my mistake. My presence, the upset of daily routine, invites scrutiny. He's trying to hide his life not from me, but from his aunt.

"What are you doing over here?" Ms. Eunice blocks the doorway with her walker. She's chewing loudly on something, like gum, but then she brings a piece of red licorice to her mouth, biting into it roughly. I look to Charles, waiting to see if he can give me a clue as to how to respond.

"Well, I'm waiting." She tears another piece of licorice off. I bite my lower lip. The worst part of me wants to laugh. She's kind of like a hardened cowboy in the slightly bent body of an old Black woman.

"The cat got your tongue, girl?" She looks at Charles, flips her hand up in disgust. "What's wrong with your friend? She's standing there with a dumbass smile on her face. She on drugs or something? Buncha shithead junkies up in here." She looks back at me. "You taking drugs? Because I do *not* condone drugs."

Charles looks at me like he might laugh too if not for his anger. "Mama, she's fine. She's, like, the last person to be taking drugs." He scrunches his eyebrows at me and gestures for me to speak.

"I'm Lara," I say, stepping forward, holding out my hand.

"That wasn't my question. I know who you are. You the daughter of that Russian lady. Both of you boy crazy." Ms. Eunice is sanctimonious in a way I will come to recognize as the hallmark of a life lived in sharp, jagged disappointment, cleft with just enough humiliations to breed honest resentment.

"Excuse me?" I can hardly believe her. "I am *not* boy crazy."

"Well, I've seen you chasing after that blond fella so you can't be a queer."

"Okay, here's the book you wanted." Charles's voice is falsely cheery as he places it in my hands. He pushes me toward the door so I'm pressed against the bars of Ms. Eunice's walker.

"Boy, where's your manners?" Ms. Eunice spits fiercely at Charles. "You bring a stranger into my home and want no questions asked? You don't even introduce us?" She backs out of the door and her nylon tracksuit swishes as she pushes her walker down the hallway. She's wearing red high-top Reeboks that were popular more than a decade ago, but they still look brand-new.

Charles ushers me back through the living room, where he pauses in front of Ms. Eunice. "Mama, I'm sorry. This is my friend Lara. She lives down the street from us." He turns his body slightly in my direction. "Lara, this is my aunt Eunice."

"You can call me Ms. Eunice or, if you have to, Ms. Bell." Ms. Eunice holds her hand out to me as if what happened in the other room took place in a parallel universe. I take her hand. It's a thing of contradiction. The wrinkled fingers are rough but her palm is like the smooth underbelly of a kitten. Her knuckles are hard, cold, and yet her hand is small and delicate. I worry that I will crush her hand in mine.

"Charmed," she says without any irony.

"Same." I believe we have started over on friendly terms. And then I notice her scrutinizing me.

"So, your father has the African blood?"

"The what?" My attention is drawn to the TV. There are two Korean women sitting in a nearly empty room. The woman in purple plastic curlers is wagging her finger at the other woman. The TV is on mute but the subtitle reads, *You only have three chances in life. You just blew the first one.*

Ms. Eunice sighs. "The African blood, your father."

"Yes." I give her my attention.

"Mm-hmm, thought so." She looks at Charles, nodding as if there's evidence for him to examine. "That's how it usually goes, the Black man with the white woman." She trains her eyes on me again. "He's not living with you?"

"No, I . . . I never met him." I don't know why I offer this information.

"That's a shame. Know any of his people?"

"No." It's my turn to glance at Charles, who just shrugs.

Ms. Eunice grunts some kind of confirmation to herself. "Yeah, I figured as much by that hair of yours."

I purse my lips together. I had given up on my braids, four days in. My mother wouldn't stop riding me, so I caved. I was back to wearing my hair in a mass of dry curls tied back into a stubby ponytail at the base of my neck.

"Oh!" There's surprise in Ms. Eunice's voice. "My program is on." She moves to her spot on the sofa faster than I think possible for a woman with a walker.

Charles guides me outside and escorts me to his chain-link fence and opens the gate for me. "That sucked," he says.

"Yeah," I say, my thoughts still on my hair.

"I guess we'll be hanging out at yours going forward?" There's no mistaking Charles's voice rich in *I told you so*s.

10

Fuck the rich, eat the rich. It doesn't matter. They own your house, job, and car, so they fuck you.

We stand on the corner across the street from the bookstore. Through the window, I see people taking their seats. Everyone seems to know one another. Charles rolls his shoulders back like he's about to enter the ring and starts toward the store.

My hand shoots out, grabbing him by the arm. "Wait." All the confidence I had on the way over evaporates. My mouth is dry.

Charles spins quickly, impatient. "No. Fucking. Way. You are not about to ruin my night. You want to go home, go. But I'm doing this."

"Yeah, but . . ." My eyes bounce from Charles to the patrons in the bookstore and back to Charles. He's right. He's prepared himself for weeks, from his new pair of fake tortoiseshell glasses, new white T-shirt, the artfully trashed Euro blue sport jacket, but most important, his hours and hours of practicing a breathy British accent he picked up from repeat viewings of two grainy episodes of *Upstairs Downstairs* from the 1970s burned onto a disk someone gave him. For all his efforts, Charles sounds more Down Under than Eaton Place, but he's determined.

It's his big night. He got accepted into his boarding school and this is how he wanted to celebrate. A literary reading followed by an open mic at Minerva Book Store in Santa Monica. It took us forever to get here by bus. But Charles says it's "the place writers go to get discovered."

Whatever. He pestered me to join him, saying, "Come on, Lara, let's do something different. Let's get the fuck out of here. Or do you only want your big life experience to be attending some redneck junior prom?"

He was right. So, eventually, I caved. But now, looking in on the mingling patrons, women in outfits of studied cool, the young in vintage dresses and the older ones in leather pants and pristine motorcycle boots, men with groomed facial hair and manicured nails, they all seem so much better than us. I hang back.

Charles stands next to me. We're both watching people in the bookstore settle in. "Look," he says, starting in on what is becoming his daily mantra. "I'm a gay, poor, skinny Black boy. We don't even live in the fucking ghetto, so I got no street cred. Kissed one hick on the school playground when I was twelve. Parents died of natural causes. You think these white people are interested in *my* stories?"

We've gone over this a million times.

"What's the best book right now?" he asks, like a coach trying to fire up the team.

"*Harry Potter,*" I say without feeling.

"Who's *the* Black writer of the moment?"

"Zadie Smith."

"And where's that Black writer from?"

"England."

"Right. I'm riding this moment, okay?" His jaw is firm. "Think historical. Think Richard Wright or James Baldwin."

He points to himself, then turns his finger on me. "And Josephine Baker." Popping the collar of his blazer to reset his determination, he adds, "Remember, you don't say a word."

I roll my eyes behind his back as we cross the street. Even I know that Wright, Baldwin, and Baker are terrible examples because they lived in France, not England, but I say nothing. What's important is how I play my role. I'm to be a visiting French artist and woman of mystery. I'll smile blankly at people and turn to Charles to translate their English into his even slower English and rapid hand gestures. It's stupid, but he needs me. According to him, the literary world is a closed country club driven by a "Euro-American mythos" and "a culture of unexamined privilege and soft-core rage viewed through the lens of first-world problems." I'm not exactly sure what he means but he protests against it incessantly.

Charles sits us down smack in the middle of the venue. A woman with stringy hair and an annoying, high-pitched voice takes the podium to introduce the writers, two women, twentysomething empyrean nymphs with vacant eyes, and one very unhappy-looking middle-aged man with thinning hair. They're all white. Charles kicks my foot as if to say, *See, told you.*

"There's a sign-up sheet going around for the open mic," the woman at the podium shrills earnestly. "If you read last week, put your name at the bottom of the list to give others a chance to share their voice."

When the list gets to Charles, he scratches out a name toward the top, writes in his name, and then puts the other writer at the bottom. He turns to no one in particular, saying, "Bloody jet lag," in his fake accent. "Just flew in from London.

Don't think I'll last, you know." Then he hands the clipboard to the person next to him.

I burn with humiliation. We already stand out as the obvious newcomers. Why does he have to be so bold, draw attention? It reminds me of Yevgenia. I can imagine her sneering at me just now, ridiculing my sense of propriety as being very "middle American" and my desire to go unnoticed as "weak." I think about this as the various writers read from their work, falsely humble, full of their words and impressed with their self-expression. When it comes time for Charles to step to the mic, I feel myself sliding down into my seat. He speaks each well-rehearsed word, clipped and efficient.

"Autopsy Report," he begins, clearing his throat. His voice performatively switches inflections between official diction and melancholy whisper. His face scrunches in a practiced pathos as he holds out in front of him a small black sketch-book, bought for this moment, though he recites his lines from memory:

> The body, identified by toe tags, is that of an embalmed,
>   refrigerated female, Black.
> *Under bright lights*
> Examination of the eyes reveals irises that appear brown
>   in color.
> *In the air of the room you are not*
> The genitalia are that of an adult woman. The anus
>   is edematous and shows pooling of blood in
>   subcutaneous tissue.
> *Living warmth of black bird wings, quicken*
> The body in a state of moderate decomposition.
> *After, when your voice leaves*

The scalp and hair easily slough with slight pulling.
raucous talk climbs over walls
naming mountains in the dark.

Slinking farther down into my seat, I can't help but bris-
tle at him. He's so fucking dramatic. It's like he's auditioning
for a Shakespearean role. Mostly, I'm furious at his desire to
be anybody but himself. I see his aspirations as corrupt, his
longing for success a blight. I set accusations in my mind that
damn him, rather than the people at the bookstore, all of us,
for making Charles work so hard for acceptance. But by the
time he is done reciting his poem, I'm the one who's wrong.
He doesn't need me, or my pity or my rage. They love British
Charles. I can see from the way the audience leans forward in
their seats they think he's good, or at least good enough. And
this is all he needs, for now.

He steps away from the podium and a woman touches
him on his back in appreciation, and then another person and
a few others as he makes his way to his seat, smiling widely.
Within me, a brewing concern that admiration is an ambush.
I want to collect the small pieces of Charles, those that belong
to the regular Black American kid that he leaves on the floor
when he walks off the stage.

After the event Charles wants to linger in the bookstore
with the others. We're standing near the exit. I'm trying to
decide how we're going to get home. Charles pretends not
to scan the room for people he considers "famous" when a
white man approaches us.

"Hey," he says to Charles. "Thank you for that. That was
really good."

Charles does something I've never seen him do before.

His hands come together in prayer and he bows ever so slightly, like an urban Buddhist monk. "I'm absolutely chuffed. Thank you." Charles is inflated, full of himself, but flustered. I can see why. The man standing in front of us is unsettling. He's as tall as Charles, broad shouldered, slender, his brown hair impeccably windswept, his teeth very even, very white. He looks important, wealthy.

"My name is Cameron, by the way," he says, extending his hand. Charles takes it like he's not sure it's real.

"Charles. Pleasure."

The man turns to me, his hand out. I look at it and look at Charles for direction.

"This is my friend Lara. She's visiting from France, so her English isn't great." Charles gives me a hard look. *You better not fuck this up.*

"*Ah bon? Enchanté, Lara. Comment ça va?*"

I hesitate. "*Estoy bien . . .* ah. *Je suis bien.*" I feel my face go hot.

Charles laughs it off for me. "She's been in California for a while." I move away from them quickly but stay close enough to eavesdrop.

"So, which part of London are you from?" Cameron asks.

"Kensington," Charles says. I stiffen. This is not what he has rehearsed with me.

"Really? Kensington is exquisite." To my ears, Cameron sounds both impressed and unconvinced. I turn to watch as I suspect I may need to dive in and save Charles.

"Yes. Yes, it is," Charles says, nodding, having exhausted all he has to say on the subject.

Then Cameron's face sparks surprise, like he's just re-membered something. "But I suppose that depends, if you're from North Kensington. There are some housing estates there, right? What street are you on?"

Charles hasn't spent much time constructing his backstory for his English accent. For him it's enough to sound different, to be something other than an ordinary Black boy. "Americans love British accents," he said to me weeks before, when he planned this whole charade. "Everything sounds smarter when you speak like the colonizer."

I cough a little, walking up to Charles, putting myself in his line of vision.

Charles starts to backpedal. "Well, you know, I'm really from all over London. We moved houses a lot." I motion to Charles, pointing to the door. He looks past my shoulder, like he can't see me, so I move to stand next to him.

"There you are, Cam." An older woman approaches and links her arm through Cameron's.

"Nina." The woman introduces herself as if we've been waiting for her. "Loved what you read. Your work is really promising." She leans over to pet Charles's arm. She's a malnourished midsixties wearing a soft sweater that begs to be touched.

"Yes, Nina would know," Cameron says. "She represents three of the four authors here tonight."

"You're a literary agent?" Charles stumbles over his British pronunciation of *literary*. His eyes grow greedy.

Nina presses her lips together and shrugs. "For the right talent." I think she seems smug.

"She's the best in the biz. All about the stars." Cameron turns to her like he just had the greatest idea. "Ni, why don't we have them over to the house?"

Nina gently sways her body, as if the suggestion is so

powerful it might knock her over. Her eyes narrow. Then she shrugs as if to say, why not?

"We're having a little soiree," Nina explains, reaching out and petting Charles's arm again. "It'd be lovely to have you. Both." She glances at me.

"Sounds brilliant. That'd be great." I can see Charles trying to put a tight lid on his excitement, to no avail. "Only, I just arrived via taxi, you know. No one drives in London, so I'm without wheels."

I roll my eyes. I can't help myself. I can hardly stomach the three of them. Charles's outright lies, and Nina and Cameron's self-importance. After they arrange for us to ride with one of the waifs who read earlier in the evening, I pull Charles toward the exit.

"What the fuck are we doing?" I ask.

"What?" He acts innocent. "It'll be fun. Relax."

"This is really stupid. I want to go home. It will take us for-fucking-ever on the bus as it is."

"Lara, are you kidding me? She's a fucking agent. *An agent.* I need this."

"Who cares?" I whisper harshly as our ride starts to move toward us. "She's creepy, rubbing up on you like that."

"She is *not* rubbing up on me. Why you gotta hate? They like my fucking work. Is that so hard to believe?" He pushes away from me, leaving me in the corner, waving down the girl who's driving us to the party. I watch him switch on a smile and his accent.

Her name is Emily. She has a face Charles will later characterize as "forgettable." It's a harsh truth. I spend the first few minutes in the car trying to remember the story she read. It doesn't matter anyway. She doesn't require polite conversation. As she winds through the hills she angrily complains about the event. How they didn't have as many copies of her book on display as the others, how she resented having to share the stage with "cloying amateurs."

"I mean, what kind of event has an open mic after *published* authors read from their work? It was just pitiful. Like they didn't think me or Noah and Megan were enough to draw in a crowd."

Charles sits up front, listening quietly to her assault, occasionally offering a word of agreement. I sit in the back, staring down on the winking city lights as we speed through the hills. Enclosed in the air-conditioned car, removed and moving further from a known reality, it occurs to me that Yevgenia might be somewhere down in the valley. I can't stop myself from wondering what she's doing in the same moment.

Nina's house is a slender glass box built into the side of a hill. The driveway is a long, narrow concrete strip with fewer cars than I think should be at a party. Charles isn't speaking to me even though I can tell he finds Emily's diatribe on the difficult life of a "debut novelist" tedious.

I walk a few paces behind them, glancing out onto the vista below. There are other houses around Nina's, hidden, but you can feel the presence of human proximity. The front door is already open. Just inside are two small benches with shoes organized on them. Emily bends, removing hers, replacing her shoes with a pair of guest slippers. Before she leaves us, she points at my tennis shoes. "You'll have to take those off. Nina's a real stickler for her floors."

I give Charles a look of irritation, hoping that he will forgive me and reinstate our friendship. But he puts on his slippers and goes off to fulfill his dreams of being discovered. Sighing, I sit on the bench, untying laces. I pull a shoe off and instantly regret it. The corridor starts to fill with an earthy combination of boiled broccoli, wet dog fur, and rotting cheese. A panicked shame engulfs me. I quickly hobble to the front door, one shoe on, the other in my hand. Crickets scratch out songs of derision as I wedge my shoes between a large planter outside the door. As I grab a pair of house slippers, I notice Emily's shoes. Pretty brown flats of the softest-looking leather I've ever seen. Listening out, I carefully pick up a shoe, turning over the barely worn sole. The scalloped edges and the slight heel are delicate in my hand. The leather footbed is embossed with an Italian designer's name. I slip it on my foot, or try to. It's a half size too small. I pull it off quickly, fearing I'll stretch it out, and I go off to find Charles.

Everything in the living room is white. White walls and furniture, white people. With Yevgenia, who is ignorant, really, when it comes to the ways that race operates in America, I'm a dark coincidence. Maybe it's because my mother is Russian and raised Soviet that she thinks a person's class is more important than their race. Her kind of thinking is too advanced for life in the U.S. I've known now for a while that Yevgenia's faulty racial neutrality straightjackets me. Once, when I was seven, I was walking through the corridors of the nursing home where she worked for several weeks washing the shit-stained sheets of old people and stealing dead people's clothes, and a senile, balding white woman, bent and withered like a broken flesh-covered tree, pointed a spindly finger in my direction and shouted hysterically over and over again, "Nigger! Nigger!" I didn't know what a "nigger" was but it scared me, not only because the woman resembled a ghostly demon, but because the way she said it told me that a "nigger" was the worst thing to be in the entire world. I was shaken but Yevgenia laughed it off, saying, "She's just a mindless puppet toeing the party line. That's her job as a poor white in a capitalist system. If Marx saw this, he would say that race is the opiate of the masses." This became the logic my mother used to shape my sense of self. She'd have me believe that my difference was no difference at all, just the problem of other people. But I knew otherwise, not just by the cold stares or cruel sideways glances that told me I was not welcome, but also by the way a teacher would accuse me of "being a liar and a cheater" because I knew words that she didn't. My mother wanted to believe she could explain away these experiences, chalk them up to "dumb people who just so happened to call themselves white." But she couldn't explain other things, the casual violence that seemed without roots—a grown man pitching a beer bottle at me as I waited on the corner for my mother, the teenagers in the building next door who screeched like monkeys when I sat outside playing by myself. And because she couldn't explain it, we didn't talk about it, leaving me confused and alone.

THE WHITE PEOPLE at the literary party aren't like the old woman at the nursing home, nor are they like Julie's parents or any of the white people I have ever been around. These are white people who hang art from Africa, discuss Japanese graffiti artists, wear Bedouin jewelry, travel to India. Their world is unapologetically global. Here, any culture or dress or religion or food is fair game. These are not white people I have any understanding of, nor have I read enough Marx to theorize them. What I do know, from watching Charles sip from a glass of wine and throw his head back, laughing easily, is that he has stumbled upon his kind of white people.

Cameron spots me standing at the top of the steps of the sunken living room; behind him is a glass wall of windows and lights of the huddled city.

"There you are," he says, holding up a champagne glass. He says something else to me in what I guess is French. I feel Charles's eyes on me. I glance in his direction. He stares through me before turning, giving me his back.

Cameron places his hand on my elbow and passes me the glass of champagne. His touch is light but I don't like it. He smells of manufactured citrus, sharp but clean. "Ursula," Cameron says to the woman he ushers me to, "meet our guest—" He pauses, looking at me expectantly. The hired jazz trio starts up outside.

"Lara," I say flatly, staring into the glass.

"Yes, Lara. She's French," he says. I see his smirk. He turns to Ursula and says with flourish, "Lara, meet the fabulous designer Ursula, though I know you're *French* and very young, you might have read the feature about her lamps in the *Times* last week."

I shake my head, watching Charles go out onto the balcony with Nina and two other hangers-on.

Cameron and Ursula chat. I get tired of listening. They put words together, forming sentences. That much I understand, but their words are meaningless to me, even though they're in English. Maybe it's the champagne I've been nervously sipping. My head starts to hurt with the strain of being out of my depth. I feel too loose and slightly out of control of myself. It's excruciating.

"Excuse me," I interrupt abruptly, and walk away. On the cool white marble countertop of the open kitchen, two platters of food are on display. Fruits of the brightest colors and fresh-cut vegetables raw and bulbous are the most beautiful I have seen. Next to this food, I am decomposing leftovers. I notice two young men, dark and small and trim, in black pants and black T-shirts, going in and out of the kitchen. At first, I think they're guests, until I see them offer food, take plates, fill drinks.

"Do you know where the bathroom is?" I ask one of them as he passes.

He points hurriedly to a wall behind him. "It looks like a wall but there's a door. See where that lady just came out?" His words are accented and perhaps this is why I say what I do.

"Gracias."

He clucks his tongue, as if offended. "I'm Portuguese," he says, shaking his head, rushing off to fill another glass.

I push through the hidden door, trying to leave my mistake in the other room. I walk down a corridor, windowed on one side, a white wall with three black-and-white abstract photos hanging on it on the other. At the end of the hallway is a bedroom lit by a bedside lamp, sparsely decorated in an expensive generic Asian sort of way. Off the bedroom is a smaller room, another white box with black accents—a black lacquered desk and black chair, white bookcases. A window seat, plush and pillowed, overlooks a rocky hill. The room is dimly lit. I skim the books on the shelf with my fingers, pulling one off without looking at the cover. I snap on the desk lamp, which fills the space with accusatory light, suggesting that the room is being used for the first time. I sit on the win-

dow seat, flipping through the pages of the book, until a pas-
sage toward the end grabs my attention.

> And when you die, a stranger will lay you out in a
> hurry, grumbling impatiently. No loving hand will
> touch you, no one will bless you or sigh for you.
> All they'll be thinking of is how to get rid of you as
> quickly as possible. They'll buy you a cheap coffin
> and carry you out as they carried that poor woman
> today, and then they'll go off to a tavern to have a
> drink to your memory. In the grave—nothing but
> slush and mud and wet snow—who'll bother about
> the likes of you?

Death has not been on my mind, so I know that the pas-
sage has pulled me in with its honest assessment of living.
Who'll bother about the likes of you? Of course, this exact sen-
timent, the tone of it, I've heard from Yevgenia. The finality
of judgment, the "don't get your hopes up or set your dreams
too high." It's as if her voice is ringing out from the page. Like
she's conspired with the author to impart more of her lessons.
I flip to the cover, suck my teeth when I see *Notes from Under-
ground*, by Fyodor Dostoevsky.

It figures.

I examine the book again. Its unbent spine, the crisp pages.
An untouched Signet Classic. My eyes drift to the bookcase.
Black typescript words against a white backdrop look down
on me. The books are debutants lining up at the ball. This
is no reader's bookshelf. Here, the books are tchotchkes, se-
lected for their font, color, and size. These are books held one
time in the hands of a designer, judged only by their covers.

An aggravation begins to lift the edges of my emotion. I pick up the Dostoevsky, rip the page out of the book, and stick it in my bra. My mother would be mortified by the defilement. But I do this in her name. Wouldn't she be disgusted by the nonreaders who turn books into a banal commodity? I replace it on the shelf, spine side facing inward. Then I turn another and then another and soon I work in a frenzy, turning all the books, as many as I can reach, spine facing inward. In my mind, I'm freeing them from their status as mere objects of display, another collection for the vacant people who keep them. I step back, admiring my effort. A patchwork block of brown, white, and yellowed paper spatters the wall. It's a collective cold shoulder, a fuck you, a detachment from being owned. Being seen but not read. Snapping off the light, I go to get Charles.

I move through the quiet, dark house, until I reach the empty living room. Outside on the terrace, the trio takes a smoking break. Silhouettes speak with heads lowered. Emily, the author, is hip to hip with the middle-aged guy who also read earlier. Both of the waiters are out there, sitting by a pool I didn't notice before, sharing a joint with Ursula. No Charles though.

I go up the stairs to the second floor and stop at the softly lit landing. A faint smell of sweet rose hangs in the air. In front of me is a door left slightly ajar. Voices come from behind it. It sounds like Cameron.

I peer around the corner. A delicate mound of silky clothes lies on the floor. A single lamp is illuminating Charles in half-light as he stands rigidly against the floor-to-ceiling glass. Cameron is kissing his neck. Nina, naked except for a pair of underwear, stands behind Cameron, rubbing her hands under his shirt. Charles, to my relief, is still fully dressed, but I can see, from the way his clothes are being pulled, that he won't be for long.

"Get down on your knees," Cameron demands. Nina turns his head to kiss her.

"I don't know," Charles says. I hear the conflict in him, the confusion. "I'm not sure." His voice is quiet, like he's talking to himself.

Cameron says, "C'mon, I want to feel those full lips of yours around my cock."

"Loosen up, sweetie," Nina says. "Take another one of these. It will liberate you." She leans to grab something from her bedside table and holds her palm out to Charles.

"No, please," Charles says. His English accent is gone. His resolve slips away, the eager belief in himself from earlier squeezed out by this encounter he does not want.

"Here, let me touch you." Cameron unzips Charles's pants. Nina comes around to his side, pulling at his blazer.

"Hold up, don't, don't do that." Charles is trying to push away from them.

I step into the bedroom. "Charles, I'm leaving," I say. Cameron and Nina turn, not at all surprised to see me.

"We were waiting for you." Nina holds out her arm, motions me with her hand. "Come. Have fun with us." Nina's breasts are perfectly round, hard globes. She's a small woman, muscly. But her skin sags at her knees, her ribs protrude. Nina approaches me, her arms stretched out like some drugged-out sex zombie. As she stands in this hotel-quality bedroom with its high ceilings, the white carpet, the wall of windows, for some reason lines from an Anna Akhmatova poem erupt from my mouth.

Pale, slender lady,
The narrow antique frame
Compresses you in a golden oval,
A Negro stands behind you with a pale blue fan.

It's called "An Old Portrait" and I memorized it when I was eight, shortly after my mother returned from those missing years. Then, I hoped to impress Yevgenia with my young literary talents so she wouldn't leave me again, but she only shook her head, irritated, and said, "There's no translation. Russian poetry is only beautiful in Russian."

But now, Nina stops as I pelt the words at her. I look over her shoulder and say to Charles, circling my finger in the air, "Let's get the fuck out of here."

Charles looks stunned. He glances from me to Cameron. Finally, he pushes past him, staggers as he tugs his jacket over his shoulder. We bound down the stairs, Cameron's loud pleading behind us.

"Come on," Charles says, hurrying me along like we've just robbed a bank. We get to the front door and he's wobbly as he stoops to put on his shoes. Without thinking, I grab Emily's designer shoes and cram them on my feet. We run out of the house, leaving the front door wide open.

The sun is rising.

Neither of us says a word until we're on the bus marked *Inland Empire.*

"So, what happened?" I'm vague, hoping Charles will address any number of things, especially the way he treated me back there. But he wants to talk about Cameron and Nina, so I let him.

"I followed him up the stairs because he said he would

give me books and, I mean, I kind of knew what he actually wanted, because I wanted it too. But then that Nina woman comes out naked and suddenly it's like, they're both on top of me. They planned the whole fucking thing. That's all they wanted. Black dick. And you know, at first I thought it could be okay. I thought I'd go along with it. It's just, I didn't know how it would make me feel." Charles shudders. His face is toward the window. He isn't crying but I can sense his distress.

"Are you okay?" I ask after a while, scared of what he will say.

"Yeah. I'm okay, I guess." His voice comes out ragged. "I'm so fucked-up, Lara. Really."

"No, you're not," I say, grabbing his hand, squeezing it.

"I am." Charles seems annoyed that I don't believe him. "You know what I was thinking the whole fucking time? I was thinking, you know, maybe doing something like that, being with Nina, would, I don't know, get her to represent me." Charles lets go of my hand. "And there is no confusion. I'm not into women."

I sit quiet for a few moments. "But they already liked your work. Why would you do something you don't want to do just to get an agent?" I can't understand wanting something as much as Charles wants his own success.

"Don't you get it? Look at this," he says, pointing out the window. We're heading east on the 10 freeway. The valley floor is flat and dour with gray, drying tufts of weeds sprouting between the boulders and asphalt. "This is shit. No art comes from a place as barren as this."

"That's not true." I say it, but even I don't believe it. "What about—" I have to think for a moment. "*Ramona*?"

"*Ramona*? As in Helen Hunt Jackson? As in my sixth-grade play that condemns the Cahuilla to noble savagery and whitewashes the Spanish missionary genocides?" Charles clucks. "Oh my God, you *are* helpless. But you just prove my point."

"What about *The Grapes of Wrath*, then?"

Charles sighs. Putting his head down in his hands, he groans melodramatically. "I'll never work in this town again." He's sobering up. "I should've just been their Mandingo, and had sex with them."

"All I know," I say, trying not to sound too judgmental, "is that if you lie yourself into your accomplishments, betray who you are, you will never know if you or your work were good enough on their own terms. You'll always be trapped."

He frowns and pulls his blazer closer to him, as if protecting himself from a cold reality. The sun streams through the bus windows, landing on Charles's face. He looks like shit. His eyes are bloodshot and puffy, his skin dull. I know that whatever he's feeling wasn't worth the cost of what he put into the evening. The weeks of practicing an English accent. The hours thinking up a backstory and formulating justifications for his lies.

It's then that I know something essential about myself. I will not live a lie. I will not contort to the will of others. Or adhere to their vision of what I should be doing or how I should be acting. It seems to me that the trouble begins when people, like my mother or Charles, can't accept that they may be insignificant. And maybe, for people like me, we don't control as much as we think we should.

Charles leans his head against my shoulder. "I'm really tired. Aren't you tired too? Having to explain how your existence is even possible?" I can feel him looking up at me. This is what we share. The impossibilities of ourselves.

"You know, for my application to the academy," Charles says, snuggling into my shoulder, "I submitted a story about a Black boy growing up in the desert. How the heat and the inhospitable landscape bred in that kid an isolation so immense that he couldn't see his own reflection. And you know what the committee said? They called the story a 'cutting-edge account of race and disability,' as if I was writing about a Black boy who was blind. They thought it was a memoir, hoped it was. That's why they admitted me. A sociological experiment in categorical disadvantages. I wasn't going to go, but you know who told me I should?"

"Who?"

"Your mother. She said"—Charles's voice shifts as he tries to mimic Yevgenia's accent and register—"'Americans like to believe powerless people have no inner lives. You go. Show them.'"

Outside the window, the mountains are approaching. We will leave one valley and enter another. "Yeah, sounds like her," I say, not really wanting to hear about my mother's special ability to encourage other people, when I just want her to stretch herself out for me.

"Wait a sec." Charles sits up, fully awake. "Why the fuck did you take that girl's ugly shoes?" He stares at my feet. "They don't even fit you."

I look at the shoes. In the bright light of morning, outside the context of a home in the hills, the shoes are like two homely ladies who lost their way to a luncheon at the golf course.

A smile spreads across his face. "That's fucked-up."

"I know, right?" We both begin to laugh like lunatics. At the parts we played for the evening, at the selves we are in that moment. We bend over each other, gasping for air, slapping each other's knees.

A deep, sleepy voice calls out from the back of the bus, "Yo, man, keep it down. This here is public space. Respect."

11

"Free-market capitalism" is the greatest propaganda machine ever created.

California's desert air in winter grips with the surprising force of an old woman on her deathbed. The mountains hide behind sheets of fog until afternoon. Nocturnal animals take their chances sourcing food in broad daylight. Trailers at the Oasis Mobile Estates are spineless metal carcasses sagging under the weight of the damp cold. Each day, my neighbors wearily park their cars and drag their feet until they hit the carpeted floor inside. They stand themselves in front of the electric furnace. *You're blocking all the heat*, they squawk at each other, angry and disappointed in yet another year passing brutally with low-paying jobs or no jobs at all. Addictions that leave them prostrate. Another warrant. Another arrest. Another day stacking up against all the others.

Our neighbors know, before my mother and I do, that winter at the Oasis is a hateful season.

January is its traditionally ridiculous time at my house. Yevgenia loves what she calls the "New Year's Holidays," celebrated in the "Russian way," which means it's sort of a combined Christmas and New Year's starting December 31 and going until the money is drained, usually around midmonth. My mother's version of Russian "Christmas" brings good things, like her laughing without the aid of intoxication and an armistice between the two of us. We exchange gifts on the thirty-first and I listen to my mother belt out what has to be the saddest Christmas song on earth, "Step da Step Krugom." Basically, the lyrics are the last will and testament of a man freezing to death in the snow. After that my mother and I toast each other. Vodka is too harsh for me but my mother always has me drink it, even just a thimbleful, every year since I can remember. "You want me to die young?" she says. She's always so melodramatic. "Because that's what happens when you toast with water or with your eyes closed."

Every Christmas holiday is the same. My mother shows me how to make a proper krendl bread while reciting stories of Ded Moroz—the Russian Santa—and Snegurochka, who my mother calls a snow maiden. I admit I find the pair creepy. Depending on my mother's mood, Ded Moroz is either the snow maiden's grandfather or her boss or her lover, and Snegurochka is made of flesh or snow. What did shape my understanding is that Snegurochka is a motherless daughter. Like my mother, and maybe a bit like me. It's Snegurochka who brings about Yevgenia's stories of Katya, her own mother.

"Here's something you don't know about parenting." My mother is violently kneading dough as she speaks. "It shackles. Turns you into a person that you never wanted to be. A mother, your mother, my mother. You never met your baba, Katya, that cold bitch, so be grateful for one less obligation." She punches the dough, flattening it.

"You're overworking it," I say.

My mother pinches the dough, nodding. Wiping the back of her hand across her brow, ignoring me, continuing her tirade, lost as she is in her own story, she says, "Yeah, well,

Katya's response to everything was, 'You're as ugly as an old man's ass, but work hard, and be loyal to the motherland.' But who was she to talk? Okay, she had nice legs. Everyone said so, even the head of the neighborhood association, Comrade Luski. Every day up until the day he couldn't get out of bed anymore, that man would throw open his window and call down, 'Katya Borislava has the best legs in block twelve.' Even my grandmother, a silent half-blood Dzhugi—who we called Mina—would raise her eyebrows and nod in wordless agreement. Trust me, this was a big deal. My Mina was a true old-fashioned Soviet trash-talker. She was mostly mute, you see, but that woman could scare scales off a fish just by looking at them.

"Of course, because of this, Mama would not be deterred by snow piles three meters high or below-freezing winter. She worked at the Moskvitch car factory. I remember looking out onto the street from the only window in our apartment trying to spot her as she walked to the bus stop on those typical Moscow mornings when wet, fat snow came in sideways. So my mother would be in her black factory-issued coat like the others but she would be the only one in a skirt and heels. True bourgeois conventions.

"Anyway, Katya was proud of her legs and she was going to make damn sure that she showed them off every chance she got. You see, it was also a known truth that the beauty of Mama's legs did not extend to her face." Yevgenia looks at me, frowning as if to show the seriousness of this unfortunate fact.

"My mother had inherited the fleshy nose and pock-marked skin from her father, Yevgeny. These features were only made worse by the ignorance of your great-grandmother

Mina, who was raised in southern Siberia and mostly educated in a gulag. Mina never knew about the benefits of dental hygiene. As I understood it, even after the state-issued toothbrushes appeared, Mina could be seen using them to scrub the dirt off potatoes but never her daughter's teeth.

"That my mother didn't smile was a disappointment to me, yes. I used to lie awake at night dreaming up ways to bring my mother a small dose of joy. Nothing worked. In fact, the more I tried to charm my mother into a smile, the more she pinned her lips together as if I had offended her. It was not until I was thirteen that I realized that Mama didn't smile not because of her disappointing life but because of her rotting teeth. This revelation was made when I was sitting next to her one evening in our room. I was looking at a Komsomol booklet and Mama was sawing away at a beet when the knife slipped and tore into her hand. She screamed so loudly that even our neighbor, Irina Drukev, who was nearly deaf, heard it and came running out of the communal kitchen, shouting in that tin-pail voice of hers that sounded much like the caw of a crow, 'What? What? Are you home, Alexey? I made *sbiten*!'

"Anyway, I remember thinking about getting bandages for my mother's hand but instead, I sat frozen, mesmerized by the three or four worm-bitten nubs that blackened my mother's mouth. It wasn't the shock of seeing her teeth, nor was it the powerful stench that came from her, as if someone had just torn the lid off rotting garbage that kept me stuck to my chair. No. It was really seeing my mother, like it was the first time, you know, unrestrained, free from her straightjacket, that made me realize I could never live her life. It would kill me or I would kill myself. And here I am, domesticated."

I scoff at this last bit. "Domesticated?" I glance at her skimpy red pleather shorts. "I don't think so."

"See, this is what I mean." Yevgenia holds her wrists out in front of her face. "Handcuffed." She jerks her wrists like she's bound.

"Anyway"—she leans back against the kitchen counter, reaching for her pack of smokes—"before then, it had not occurred to me that I could ever be anything other than my mother's daughter, a kind of by-product of her pathological failings. But you know, when she cut herself, her bleeding hand was the most interesting thing that had happened to either of us since that day we found my asshole father dead on the sidewalk"—my mother bends slightly toward the sink and spits her disrespect of him like a TV baba—"the piece of shit threw himself off the roof of our apartment on Barkhatovoy."

I know not to ask anything of Katya or Boris, my grandparents. As far as my mother is concerned, she's a scorched-earth orphan, she wants nothing of her family by choice. My mother teaches me that stories have value and only the owner can determine their worth. It's the only thing they have. I might speculate, and I do, that my mother's story is of a father who violates a daughter and a mother who refuses to speak of it. But I'm not the owner of that story.

Yevgenia pushes herself off the counter with her hips. "I need a drink."

RUSSIAN "CHRISTMAS" ISN'T just about Snegurochka or family wounds. It's a time for Yevgenia to host, invite others in. I don't protest when year after year she invites as many people as she can to our house. And I mean everyone. Our neighbors and their friends, people from the bar she works at, the guy from the grocery store, her exes and whoever they're dating, even strangers sitting in their cars, waiting for the light to change. One year my mother invited the cast and crew of a porno film who she met at the hotel where she was working in housekeeping.

My mother greets everyone at the door with equal enthusiasm. Pours them drinks. Feeds them food she makes for days in advance. Later, she clears a space on the floor in the living room or outside, turns on some Lida Goulesco or some other Gypsy music, breaks out her black floral shawl and long red skirt. As a former dancer, Yevgenia has a strong sense of the theatrical. She knows how to make an entrance, slowly and in tempo with the music. She stands off to the side of her makeshift stage with the shawl stretched out on display, nods slightly in my direction, signaling that I should turn the music up to full volume, slowly, like we practiced. My mother steps lightly, her gaze fixed on a threshold of an exit. The shawl extends like airplane wings, dipping back and forth over her head. The music and the shawl's fringe beckon. Then comes the transformation. I will feel it. We all will. My mother is with us bodily but otherwise she's gone, disappeared behind a veil that marks time and memory. Her slight smile holds primal mysteries accessible only through blood. My mother arches her back, letting the shawl go as the tempo picks up, her chin jutting out with pride, her beauty feral. The shimmying of her shoulders quakes her breasts in time with the music. Whoops and claps come from some idiot she probably slept with once, as if he's at a strip club. He breaks my trance but not my mother's. Yevgenia is untouchable.

This Christmas, I look around our trailer, assessing the crowd. Gus from two houses down sits across from me, holding his cowboy hat against his knee, his foot tapping. His wife, Lourdes, is next to him in the folding chair they brought. Lourdes catches me looking, smiles, nodding her approval at my mother's dancing. I smile back. She gives my mother rides to work whenever our car breaks down. I like her but we don't have much to say since my Spanish is so bad and she's too shy to speak the English she knows.

Papa Bear stands uncomfortably by the door, his face ashen. He's a cool guy but still, he collects the rents, posts eviction notices, and calls the cops on people. It may be some sort of campaign to humanize him to the residents but my mother has convinced Papa Bear to sing a few songs at the party. I give him a thumbs-up, a corny gesture, but I worry that he may be sick on our floor and I'll be the one to clean it up.

When the music is over, my mother bows dramatically to the applause. Her face is stoic, masking the triumph coming from the rise and fall of her chest. As our guests coo over her, Yevgenia motions for me to turn on the Blondie CD that she has teed up. She pulls herself away from her friends and heads toward her room to change as Debbie Harry ardently sings "One Way or Another."

EVENTUALLY, YEVGENIA EMERGES for the third time this evening after a full wardrobe change and is now in her "festive" tiny red wrap dress and matching stripper platforms. She enters the living room and turns down the music screaming from the borrowed boom box. She moves confidently to the center of the room, clapping her hands. "Special guest, special guest," my mother announces, pulling Papa Bear through the circle of people formed around her. My mother always acts with the confidence of the prettiest woman in the room, whether she is or not.

Papa Bear holds the neck of his guitar, glancing timidly at my mother, seeking assurance. As he sits in a straight chair, smack in the middle of the circle, I wonder if it's a good choice. But he begins playing and we all watch him intently for a few minutes. Our attentions don't make a bit of difference to Papa Bear. He strikes me as one of those behind-closed-doors kind of crooners. A shower singer. A mirror chanteur. With his mournful esoteric lyrics that could have been written by Descartes and Carlos Castaneda, it's not clear who he's singing for but it's not us. Papa Bear has a strong voice. But it's where the voice is coming from, likely an empty pit tremoring with raw need. It's just too much. We all begin to shuffle uncomfortably.

Through a sheet of shiny, freshly combed black hair, Papa Bear's eyes follow my mother intently. He's in love with her. It cannot be helped. My mother encourages his feelings, dangles herself and her affections. In the five months that we've been at the Oasis, she's turned Papa Bear into her mostly all-purpose man, her handyman, her ATM, her cigarette dispenser, her shoulder to cry on, her driver, her audience, her friend. But no sex. *Too nice. Too poor. Too much trouble.* Whenever I mention Papa Bear's crush, she sneers, "Never screw someone who will cry and carry on when you kick them out of your bed." And so, as Papa Bear bleeds his feelings out, a distracted Yevgenia moves to the dining room in search of smokes. She starts hunting around the table, lifting plastic plates, digging through piles of discarded napkins, searching for a lighter that works. I wonder if Papa Bear knows when to surrender, if maybe now he sees for himself that none of his horizons include my mother. But he keeps playing. And I gain more understanding of how weakness repels.

From the corner of my eye, I see Brody absentmindedly pick his nose, then wipe it on the floor. He's a filthy shit. I've forgotten he's at the party. He sits cross-legged on the floor with his back against the sofa. He wears a white ketchup-stained T-shirt that reads WASSUP HATERS? and the same pair of blue shorts he always wears.

Terri is sitting on the sofa. I make note to Febreze the hell out of it because she looks like something dead pulled out of the ground. Her dirty blond hair is stringy. An arm is flung across the backrest and her hand dangles off the sofa. She is what Julie calls a "messy binger," the kind who drinks or takes drugs to obliterate demons. Terri fights to keep conscious but the undertow of whatever she's on drags her back down. Her head bobs until it falls onto the back of the sofa. I study the room for the arrival of Julie or Charles.

Steve comes in through the open front door. Even though my mother is the maven of goodwill during the holidays, she is still pissed at Steve. She turns her back sharply, deliberately, when she sees him. Steve looks different, a little rough maybe, like he could use a meal, but at least he's clean. Rhea says that the state sent him to some low-rent rehab after he OD'd outside some shopping mall in Hemet. Gone are the blue jeans and white T-shirt. I can't tell if he's channeling Orange County frat boy or ward of the state, wearing rumpled khakis, a button-up, and boat shoes. He moves awkwardly around my trailer, like he can't decide either.

"Hey Brody." I snap my fingers in his direction, pointing to Steve. "Your dad's here." I say it like he can't see for himself.

He grimaces and shakes his head.

Fuck. Brody won't budge, so I draw in a breath and go over to greet Steve.

"Hey, it's good to see you," I say, my voice louder than usual. "How are you? I mean, how's it going? Are you doing okay?" I'm not capable of turning my words down so they don't sound like stiff accusations. Just like I don't know how to look at him without patting him down, searching for signs of being high. If I was more like my mother, I'd walk away. Yevgenia is an atheist when it comes to second chances. She calls it dignity. She always says, "People don't make mistakes; they make choices." But Steve doesn't look like a man who has taken deliberate action; he looks like he has stumbled, in the dark, on ice, over rocks. The evidence of this is worn on his face. His eyes sink more deeply into their hollows, as if they've retreated in agony. His skin is gray, afflicted with pocks and scabs. White flakes of dead skin sprout from his cracked lips.

"Yeah, I'm good. You know, recovering, I guess they call it." Steve rolls his eyes at this idea.

"That's really great." My tone is vapid, empty. My mother walks past us. Behind Steve her face flashes me a warning. *If you don't get him out of here, I will.*

I notice that the party seems a bit tamer with Steve's arrival. The music is lower. Rhea and Papa Bear shoot worried glances in my direction. Even Gus and Lourdes shift nervously before making a quick exit. I feel bad for Steve. Before the drugs, he would be the guy people clapped on the back, cracked a beer with. Now either they want to corner him and demand all the shit he borrowed or stole or they want to forget they ever knew him. I'm grateful when Brody finally walks over.

"Hey, Dad," Brody says.

I back away from them and start toward my room. My mother's parties always end up with some jackass passed out on my bed despite the signs I've posted: PRIVATE. KEEP OUT.

"Hey, you can't leave. I just got here." Julie's voice comes from behind me. Charles is next to her, looking around the room, like he's just landed on another planet.

She smiles widely, holding up two unopened bottles of Jack Daniel's.

"Where'd you get those?" I'm relieved they came.

"The real question is, how long do we have to hang out with these plebs?" Charles says.

Julie laughs. "Screw these people. We're going to party. And these"—she wags the bottles again—"are compliments of my dad, who else? He has, like, whole boxes of alcohol that people give him that he never drinks."

I nod, half listening. Mostly, I'm paying attention to what she's wearing. A tight black skirt and a cropped sequined shirt that shows her belly when she leans left or right. She lifts her face toward my living room. "Oh my God, check this place out." She's bobbing her head in time to Eminem's "The Real Slim Shady." I glance around to see who has changed the music from Yevgenia's eighties classics. I spot him. A guy who is surely one of my mother's exes, serenading Desi, a Rusty's regular. When he starts gyrating his hips, Julie claps her hand over her mouth, cracking up. She nudges Charles.

"Oh my God, what a fucking loser." She turns to me. "Lara,

where'd your mom find all these jokers? It's like a social experiment in here."

A loud crash interrupts Julie. "What the fuck?" Terri's piercing voice, followed by her hysterical laughter, breaks over the crowd. She's on the floor next to the toppled card table.

"What the hell, Terri?" A woman I recognize from the Oasis is brushing her hands on her white halter top. "You got fucking beer on me, dumbass drunk," she shouts over Terri's maniacal cackle.

Yevgenia, sitting on the armrest of the sofa, turns to Lourdes's sons, whom everyone calls Twinkie and Snoopy, and says to them gruffly, "Show her the pavement," like she's a 1920s club owner.

"I got her," Steve says as he ushers Terri out the door.

"DUDE, THAT WAS EXCITING." Julie raises her eyebrows like there's something more titillating to say about it. I stare at her. Her dirty blond hair, her even teeth, her clear skin. Her expensive-looking clothes. I'm not sure I want to hear any more. I never meant to be the interpreter for her study on the trailer park savages.

"Here, let me take those from you," I offer, reaching for the bottles of Jack.

Julie passes me a bottle. "Only one," she says, protectively cradling the other in the crook of her arm. "This one is for us."

She means her and Charles, who I guess are friends again, and whoever else we run into on the way to a bonfire organized by a bunch of kids from school.

"That's a lot of booze for two people," I say, not so tactfully reminding her that I don't drink. And right now, I don't care if Julie or my mother or anyone thinks that I'm uptight.

"Right," she says, taking the bottle back from me. "Well, I'm going to get my drink on, and I suggest you do too. Might loosen you up. And why are we listening to this crap?" Julie asks.

"Who let the dogs out?" Two guys who appear to have rolled off the set of *From Dusk till Dawn* cup their hands over their mouths, shouting in time with the song. Soon the whole trailer is woofing in response. I cover my ears.

Thankfully, Yevgenia walks over to the boom box and cuts the music. Her laugh is throaty when the crowd boos her. She holds up her hands to quiet them down. "Okay, people, okay." It's close to eleven o'clock. Most of her friends arrive already drunk, so they're well past rowdy.

"*Cazzo!*" she screams. "*Chiudete il culo.*" Even if her friends don't know she's told them to shut the fuck up, they get the gist and simmer down. Yevgenia, smiling, curtsies a little.

"Thank you." She is pretty wasted, but not enough that she can't give her closing speech. I know that once she's done, all hell will break loose and I'll be free to go off with my friends.

"First, I want to say thank you all for coming and *s'novym godom. S'noym schastyem.*" Yevgenia raises her glass. "Meaning, to a new year and to new happiness."

"It's not midnight yet," someone shouts.

"I know, I know. It's bad luck. Fine." She waves her hand, laughing. "Unhappy new year and wishing you old sorrow. Better? Okay, I want us to all raise a toast, a glass to—" She looks around the room like she's searching for someone.

When her eyes land on me, I smile, my chest grows hot. She grins at me. "To my daughter—"

I hold my breath, confused but thrilled to get her recognition.

"To my daughter's friend Charles, who's been awarded a scholarship to go to art school." She claps her hands, trying to get others to clap along with her. Charles looks the part of an art school student in a black T-shirt that reads BAUHAUS. He stands with his back against the wall, to my mind already better than the rest of us.

The hecklers swarm like vultures.

"*Art school?*" someone calls out disdainfully.

"Hope you can eat that degree."

"Yeah, I'll see you on the assembly line, my man."

"Next stop, flipping burgers at McDonald's."

Yevgenia titters, amused. "Okay, that's enough." She raises a healthy glass of bright yellow sparkling wine, my mother's substitute for champagne. "To Charles. We are so proud of you." She blows him a kiss.

Charles smiles at my mother, then quickly glances at me. I see his apology. He knows I want this moment my mother has given to him. Her public recognition, her almost maternal pride. I want to be happy for Charles, but I'm failing. Because I'm wooden. The dumbest grin is plastered on my face, and I'm pretending not to feel embarrassed knowing that even if Charles felt sorry for me, he wouldn't ever want to change places.

People clap enthusiastically but are eager to get back to the festivities.

"Shots! Shots!" Julie starts to chant.

Charles rolls his eyes.

"FUCKING CHARLES." Julie is sitting in my tiny room reapplying her makeup. "His fat head is going to be even fatter. Fucking private school. We won't hear the end of it." She stands, swaying from too much drink. She's gripping the sides of my dresser with both hands, rocking back and forth. Prince's "1999" streams down the hall from the living room and someone shouts something about it being 2001 before the music goes off.

"If he even talks to us anymore," I say.

"What do you mean?"

"I mean it's a boarding school. He's going to live there."

"Oh." Julie thinks for a moment. "Oh well."

"It's too quiet out there. Let me see what's going on," I say.

"Then can we leave? That bonfire is going to be charcoal by the time we get there."

I bump into Charles outside my room. "Hey," I say.

"Are you guys ready to bounce? Because I am so sick of these assholes making fun of art school. It just got worse when I told them it was only high school." He looks over his shoulder like he's worried someone will hear him. "It's like the start of the Great Proletarian Cultural Revolution out there."

"The what?"

"You know, Mao. Mao Zedong."

"Oh, right, got it." I start to walk away. "Listen, you're going to have to drive. Julie's wasted. Also, have you seen my mom?"

"I think she left."

"Are you serious?" I look at Charles, who still seems

rattled by my mother's friends. There's no time to comfort him. I'm worried about me. "Now I'm the one who has to shut this down?"

Charles shrugs. "I guess. I mean, she just left."

"I'll be back in a few minutes. Wait for me."

I step out onto our landing, blinking my eyes in the dark. Our porch light is out again and I think my mother likes it that way. She's pissed whenever I leave it on all night waiting for her. It's after midnight but the Oasis shows no signs of slowing down. A wild cacophony of music—everything from the corridos of Los Tigres del Norte to Smokey Robinson streams out of trailers. Shivering against the desert's cooling night, I go down the steps and see her car parked in its usual spot. The smell of cigarette smoke that comes from the edge of the driveway tells me where she is. In the shadows, there's an outline of a man and I realize it's Papa Bear. He has my mother pressed up against a car. Her arms are snaked around his neck. They're locked in an intense, writhing make-out session.

"What the fuck is going on?" I ask. My mother is drunk but she's not one to violate her own rules. And Papa Bear is definitely one of her rules.

My mother peeks her head around Papa Bear's shoulder and says, "What's it look like, Sherlock?"

Papa Bear steps to the side. He touches my mother's arm. "Relax, Evie."

"Don't 'relax, Evie' me." My mother jerks her arm out of his grasp. Facing me she says, "I'm kissing Carlos, okay? Because I want to, because I can." Yevgenia is pointing her finger at me. She starts repeating a word I know well from childhood, "*Dastatachna.*"

That's enough.

There is an inherent meaning to this phrase between my mother and me. She feels me closing in. Feels the deathly squeeze of the covenant between mother and daughter. She is drowning in the obligatory calls for her attention. *Das-tatachna: There's not enough room to be your mother. Leave me the fuck alone. I don't want you around.*

"Carlos, let's go." My mother starts walking away from our trailer.

Papa Bear shrugs. "Sorry, Lara."

"How am I supposed to get all those people out? Her friends are fucking crazy."

My mother's voice shoots through the dark. "Carlos, let's go before I change my mind."

Papa Bear pivots and starts limping after my mother as fast as his destroyed knee will take him. He turns to me and says, "I'll come back. I'll help, okay?"

Behind me, the song "Pour Some Sugar on Me" blares from the trailer. I imagine an orgy.

Back in the trailer, Charles is standing next to the dining table, staring down with a sour expression at a nearby tray of food.

"Nasty. What *is* this?" he asks when he sees me.

I shake my head. I'm not thinking about food right now. I'm pissed off at my mother for getting drunk enough to get with Papa Bear. "Hang on." I motion to the bathroom. She's out of her damned mind. I open and close cabinets and drawers until I find it. The red notebook is crammed in with my mother's makeup. Peach-colored powder dusts the cover. Shaking it off in the sink, I start flipping the pages.

"Why are you looking at that?" Charles is hovering over my shoulder. He's so close, I can hear him breathing.

"My mother was outside sucking face with Papa Bear," I say. "Here and here." I point, handing him the Mead notebook.

◆

Never act on the advances of bosses, landlords, or mechanics. Likewise, your librarian and the guy at the 7-Eleven. With them, sex is a weapon. You don't give it, they will ruin your day.

Beware of men who offer too much of themselves. They share their friends, interests, and thoughts with you within five minutes. It can be a trick. They are either controlling or desperately lonely or both.

Charles glances at it. "Yeah, I've seen this before. It's funny. What's the big deal? Your mom broke some of her rules. So what?" He gestures to the noise coming from the living room. "Seems like you have a bigger set of issues with some of your country cousins out there."

He's right. The floor of the trailer is vibrating with a heavy, steady stomping of feet.

"Fine," I say. "You go get Julie and I'm going to try and break this shit up."

"You know, roaches scatter when you turn on the lights." Charles laughs and ducks back into my bedroom.

I'M NERVOUS. I've never broken up one of my mother's parties before but I know there's always someone who causes trouble. In the sway of bodies, I spot Brody crashed out in the imperial chair. I decide to start with him, knowing he's the easiest.

"Damn, B., you're heavy," I say, lifting him. By the time I cross the street to his trailer, I'm half carrying, half dragging him up his steps. Brody grumbles a little when I lay him on his sofa.

"Are you gonna stay with me?" he asks, his eyes still closed.

"Nope. Not tonight. I'm guessing your mother is already here," I say, looking around the messy trailer.

"Okay. Well, can you get me a blanket then?"

I sigh. "Alright." I don't need to turn on the hall light to know where Brody's room is. When I reach it, I snap on the weak single bulb that hangs overhead. Brody's room is trashed. Piles of dirty clothes dot the floor like smelly land mines. On his bed, a shiny, cheap mattress peeks out from beneath balled-up sheets and a grubby-looking blanket. *Damn*, I think, assessing the scene before me. *Would Brody's room look like this if Steve still lived here?* I grab the blanket. Since my last time here, Brody has torn pages from magazines and taped them up on his wall—photos of skateboarders soaring in the air from half-pipes and bikini-clad women draping themselves over shiny cars. I shake my head. And that's when I hear it, the creak of the floor under heavy feet, the breath that comes from a large animal. I turn, knowing already, and hating myself for it, for my stupidity, that Big Mike is standing at Brody's door.

"Just getting a blanket for him," I explain. "I'm leaving." Maybe I try to move, but I feel planted. Big Mike's eyes are bloodshot and his arms hang at his sides. I wait for him to shift.

"You think you too good for us?" Big Mike stumbles forward through the doorframe. His unstable feet tell me he's been drinking; the stench of many beers and cigarettes fills the room. I try to see my way clear of him, gauge how I can scramble past.

"I asked you a question." He jerks my arm, hard. Searing pain tears through my shoulder. Then it goes numb. A yelp comes out from my throat.

"What is it about you? I see you walking around here all holier-than-thou. You too good to give someone like me the time of day?"

I open my mouth to yell for Brody, but Big Mike slaps his hand over my mouth and nose, crushing his thumb into my jaw until my lips press hard against my teeth. I kick as hard as I can until my foot makes contact. He moves his hand and I bite. The warm taste of blood is in my mouth. That's when he hits me. I understand the phrase *seeing stars*, only it's not stars, it's flashes of light that fill my head. A sound comes from inside myself, a dull, muffled clang. It's the sound of pain and it reverberates through me. Big Mike brings his fist down again, and something tears in me. My knees buckle. He knocks me to the floor.

My mind goes to the time when I was eight and my mother showed me a book about Pompeii. Page after page of the Garden of the Fugitives, people dying in mid-escape. Big Mike lifts my hips to flip me on my stomach, my throat seems to fill with ash, my arms are pinned underneath me. I kick, I think, my legs moving wildly. Through clouded vision, an apparition. Brody standing rigidly at the door.

Big Mike falls on top of me, fumbling. Hot, stale alcohol vapors dampen my neck. The cheap fabric of the pants I wear tears easily. Big Mike's fist comes down hard again and again, punching my ears, leaving them ringing so I can't hear that he's shouting. I'm flipped again. Another fist explodes on my chest. The release of air from a tire, the hiss of being deflated, I can't breathe. I abandon my body. My mind carries me to a back room. I hide there, panting, scared while the physical me erupts into warm liquid colors I see behind my eyes. Is that a bite on my left hip? Why does a belt buckle have a needle? Why is that needle scraping my bone? Am I pulling gray hair out of my mouth or is it smoke? Are my hands birds in front of me or cat claws or cotton? Did the tar in my mouth come from blood? Do two wrists fit into his palm or just one? Where is Brody, Yevgenia? And why won't he stop?

Then there is the burning. It invades my nose. Fire is punching my brain. Snatches of distorted sound as if the volume is turning up and then down fill the room. Somebody is crying. Am I screaming? I'm trying to get the flames off my face and then I'm not. Something else beckons. The peace of submersion. The release into silence. That is freedom. I let go. Then there is the spongy beating of flesh, only this time it's not mine. Cold fingers encircle my biceps, pulling me up. I push them away. I'm drowning and I want to drown. But it's too late. I'm dumped into myself. The sound of hoarse male voices, directive. I begin gasping, choking, my lungs want to leave my body through my throat. My stomach jumps. I vomit. Tiny ants are crawling on my face, stinging. My eyes leak water. I'm on my feet, the sensation of running. My legs are thick, not under my control. My right foot is caught. I'm dragged down the stairs. My mind's back in inventory mode. Can I feel my legs? Where's my other shoe?

My body trembles. My teeth chatter, though I'm not cold. I'm in a car I don't know. Small flashing lights dot my right eye. The left is all black. Somebody is driving. A soft scraping sound of plastic bags coming together blow around my legs; I reach down and grasp at it, a down jacket.

"You're going to be okay. You're going to be okay." I hear how her voice ricochets, like one of those small rubber balls that bounces really high and fast until you lose track of it. Julie reaches out and takes my hand carefully, holding it like shattered glass.

12

Stay away from people who think they are smarter than everyone. They have a million ways to tell you how stupid you are.

I'm not me. Not even close. And now I live according to other people's schedules. Since I cannot trust myself, I trust others. It starts with Julie bringing me home to her father, who greets us at the door. Then he takes us to the hospital, where I don't want to speak, can't squeeze the sound out of my chest. A doctor comes and goes. A rape kit is not needed; I know this before the nurse orders the collection of my sample. I hurt, I say, but not there. A cop walks in. A woman in plain clothes and a soft voice. Another doctor comes as a nurse pushes a needle into my vein, turning my blood to ice. *Lacerated spleen*, he announces. *Left side rib fracture. Gross blood in urine.* I can't look anywhere but at my hands. My throat is so dry, it's as if it shriveled. Since I can't talk, Julie does. She's the one to file the report with the police while I lie on stiff white linen sheets under bright alien lights. It's Julie who presses charges. I'm given time to get the courage I don't have.

Seventy-two hours and I don't speak. I want to groan when I move. And I do. It's a collection of quiet sounds, each tempo different. Six large lumps form under my skin, my back, my legs, my arms, my chest, my eye, even the top of my right foot. Some essential platelets collide, trying to break through. Julie becomes my mouthpiece. She tells lies when the truth takes too long to explain.

I can hear them whisper in the corridor outside my room. People say that Julie is a witness but she's a victim too. Big Mike broke her nose as he reached out for her pepper spray. *Go get him*, Julie's father hisses. *Go pick up the bastard.* I imagine Julie's dad standing just outside my hospital room door in his Dockers and suede shoes talking to the police. Let him be indignant, rail against "the scum of the earth who should be put to death for doing that to girls." He doesn't know. But I do. They can't hold a man like Big Mike, not for torture and mayhem, not for hurting a girl like me. Julie's assault charge may slow him down, a speed bump, maybe even a detour. But he'll be back. And if not Big Mike, then another man.

Julie's mother is by my side. Her gold bracelets knock against the plastic bedrail. "Would you like to call your mother?" Her front teeth are slightly crooked. "I'm sure she's worried."

I shake my head. I won't tell her that I've deliberately given both the police and someone from the hospital the wrong phone number. It's a difficult choice. I fight with the loyalties of kinship, that blinding drug of obligation. But I'm not certain if I feel more secure with my mother or less.

How will Yevgenia react? What will she make of my failure to protect myself? And what of her many lists? Is there a forgotten line item for an act like this? Whatever she says, she'll be right, after all. She told me to stay away. And maybe she will brood silently for hours, days, pissed off that I don't listen to her, have never listened to her. I tell myself I can accept that. But my biggest fear is that Yevgenia will waltz into the room, bringing with her all her noise, her worries about the price of the hospital bed and the care I'm receiving. I imagine that the nurses will have to shoo her out when she starts to light a cig-arette. I fear I'll have to turn my face away from the poverty of her actions. How she will ask for a second tray of food after she's eaten my leftovers, how she will steal things, like the rough towels from the laundry cart, as she walks the ward. I think about how the doctors, the police, Julie's family might all think I'm a certain kind of girl when my mother comes in wearing a negligee, for instance, like it's haute couture. They might think I got what I deserved. I'm not ready for all that.

IT'S MY FOURTH day on the ward. Thick gray blackout curtains cover just enough of the window to let narrow slices of light sneak in. Planes cut through the sky aggressively, drowning out the squabbling and flapping wings of the pigeons nested on the ledge outside my room. Sometimes, I can hear past the coughing and rustling of my ward mates, past the beeps and chirps coming from the nurses' station, to the sounds coming from the streets where cars whoosh by in urgency to get to where they belong.

I stay with the sounds around me, tethering my mind to them. I begin to know which nurse is on duty and when from how heavy a foot falls against linoleum. I can roughly figure how many interns are doing rounds on particular days based on the volume of tentative-footed shuffles. This is how, even with the murmuring outside my door, I know from the light patter coming down the hall that Yevgenia has arrived. She is wearing her four-inch espadrilles.

I turn my face away from the door and close the eye that I still control. My mother is not alone. She brings with her the petite nurse from Trinidad.

"She's in a lot of pain, poor thing. I advise you to keep your visit short. You don't want to tax her system, if you know what I mean." The nurse sounds proudly bureaucratic.

My mother would notice the way this nurse buys into her position, believes in protocol, sees herself as the system's representative. Experience teaches me that under normal circumstances, Yevgenia will hate this display of what she calls the "false consciousness" of this nurse. Thankfully, my mother offers no snide comment, no pointed questions about overtime, fair pay, or stock options for worker loyalty.

"Is she awake? Can she hear me?" Yevgenia asks.

The soft smell of lilacs and salt water approach my bed before my mother does. Yevgenia brings with her a familiarity, a sense of my life before. I feel her at my side. With my mother's sharp intake of breath, she confirms what I know. I'm damaged. The body I'm in is a betrayal. Either I abandoned it or it deceived me. It doesn't matter. We can no longer share the same skin. If I had the energy, I would cut myself out of it, find some other place to live.

Yevgenia distracts me. "Oh my girl. No." Her breath is heavy and jagged. Her voice, slightly above a whisper, is filled with an anguish so violent that it splinters around me in a thousand dark pieces. Some place deep within me feels like it's flooding. I turn toward her voice.

I can see her but I can't reach out to her. My arm feels too heavy for me to lift. My voice is pasted to the sides of my throat. Yevgenia is in chaos. She looks wildly at my lumpy form, searching for a place to lay her hands on my body.

My mother cries. I've never heard her cry before and it scares me. Sobs thunder out of her like many small explosions. She holds on to my left foot, weeping so that her knees give way. Through my open eye, I see the nurse behind her, lifting her up. "There, darling. You've got to get yourself together. You're gonna need to be strong for her, dear." The heat of my mother pulls away from me. I can feel her in the room but can't see her anymore.

Then she's in front of me.

My mother's face is swollen and red when she comes around the side of the bed, kneeling. We are eye to eye.

Gone are the tears. Yevgenia seems like herself again. But there's a savageness that is held taut against the calm. Saliva gathers at the corners of her mouth, when she speaks to me softly in Russian, slow enough that I understand. Droplets spatter across my nose. "I will do what my mother refused to do for me. I will kill this fucker," she says, stroking my face with the back of her hand, lightly touching the gash on my lip, the bruise on my cheek. "First, I will cut off his hands, then his cock and then his balls. I will spoon out his eyes and stuff them in his mouth." She pauses to kiss the tips of her fingers, bringing them to my swollen eye socket. "Then I will gut the asshole for the pig that he is." Her fingers are cold against my skin. Yevgenia gently brushes a curl from my forehead. "I will drain him until his blood hardens around my feet. My name will be the last on his shit-eating lips." She leans closer, softly kissing the bridge of my nose. The feeble caress of stale cigarette smoke lingers.

I can't see the nurse, who probably doesn't speak Russian. But I can feel the woman's presence. How she might have taken a step back, holding herself tightly against the wall. How she might have mistaken the moment, seeing a mother's impassioned speech fiercely spoken into a daughter's ear, and assumed that they are words of sorrow, pangs of regret, loving reassurances. But any moment of compassion grew sour when my mother's tears dried. I know my mother. Yevgenia is on to revenge and she will stay there until she has satisfaction. It's like the time she bashed in the guy's car windows or keyed the manager's car when he fired her, and every response, every insult flung, every threat on the occasions when she felt her dignity has suffered. My mother always prefers the singular focus of vengeance over the multifaceted aspects of regret or grief or pain.

Yevgenia removes her hands from my face and stares at me. Her eyes clear, her determination set. "I'll get him. You'll see." She nods her head as if I've given the kill order. Violence as an act of love.

She stands, taking the index finger of my hand with the IV piercing through it. She gives my finger a quick squeeze, a gesture meant to reassure me. "I'll be back."

"Okay," I say, my voice straining against the chance that she won't.

Yevgenia walks over to the nurse. "Promise me she'll be cared for. That you won't just give her the cheap stuff."

"Yes, of course. It's a public hospital. Everybody gets the same," the nurse guarantees.

I know Yevgenia well enough to understand a decision has been made, a new pathway forged in concrete so that it's now fated.

"Thank you." My mother's voice is turning away. The soft soles of her shoes start out the door and down the corridor. I try to will her back to my side. I'm too weak without her, too unqualified to live in the world on my own. I need her. But Yevgenia needs freedom. She always has.

I say nothing as she walks farther and farther from me. To

the elevator. To the lobby. Across the parking lot. To the car. All I can do is what I have always done. I wait. And after eight days, when the time comes for me to be released from the hospital, a nurse who I've not seen before helps me step into a wheelchair, hands me a stack of release papers, and brings me to the nurses' station. She rolls me up against the wall and we chat in the pleasant, nonsense way you speak when checking out of a hotel.

"You're going home. How great is that?" She smiles and winks at me as she goes back to her desk. The white nurse is TV pretty, nice bone structure framed perfectly by short brown hair, a tattoo with the name Otis and a small heart on the inside of her pale, hairless arm.

"Yeah, it's great," I lie. "Thanks so much for everything," I say, like it's my choice to leave, like the hospital didn't just boot me from the room to make space for another helpless case. The nurse has moved on to another patient though, her eyes on the computer in front of her. I turn my face to the bank of elevators, monitoring them. My heart jumps with anticipation each time the doors open.

Ten minutes becomes twenty, and then thirty minutes of waiting. After an hour, it becomes awkward.

"Are you sure she's coming?" the white nurse asks.

"Yeah. She must be stuck in traffic," I say, trying to believe it myself. I wait. A family comes in wearing matching red T-shirts with TEAM VELEZ. WE LOVE YOU, PAPI written on the back. They're carrying a large box, which they place on the counter in front of a few nurses. More hospital staff comes over and soon everyone fusses over the treats inside. The white nurse speaks Spanish and thanks them, smiling and showing the other nurses their gesture of gratitude. I decide to dislike her, this nurse. For her charm, her easy beauty, her abilities in the languages she speaks, but I can't.

Team Velez brings out Papi, a bony, confused-looking man with white hair tufted like an egret's plume. He sits in a wheelchair. A stuffed bear holding a satin heart shares his ride. Papi is pushed by a short but muscular young man. Two older women on either side of Papi are loaded down with flowers, gift boxes, and helium balloons. The old man grins. When our eyes lock he nods at me in appreciation, like I'm somehow part of his celebration, like the love of his family is one of the pastries in the box given to the nurses, something for everyone to partake of.

The buzzing chaos the family brings evaporates when they enter the elevator. I want to yell after them, "Wait for me, I'm coming." But I don't. I stay in the wheelchair, parked against the wall until I quietly blend into it. I wait until the tattooed nurse goes down the corridor and awkwardly wheel myself over to a young Asian woman checking a chart.

"Excuse me," I say, dreading what I'm about to do. "I've been discharged and I'd like to make a phone call."

PART IV

EXPLANATORY DICTIONARY OF NIGHT

There's even a difference between the way
people speak in the morning and how they
speak at night. What happens between two
people at night vanishes from
history without a trace.

—SVETLANA ALEXIEVICH, *Secondhand Time*

13

A book will always be your best friend and your lover. There are intimacies that live in them that cannot be replicated between people.

How I manage to stay on at the Harrisons' for a month is a combination of Julie's grit and Joanne's announcement to her Thursday-night Bible study that the group will have to suspend all meetings due to a "family emergency." With the news, all those ladies bring over enough cakes, frozen lasagnas, and bean casseroles so Joanne doesn't have to worry about cooking for weeks. Julie's mom likes that bit. The break in her routine. Being the center of attention in her circle. The false urgency of her "recuperating houseguest," as she calls me in a cheery tone, as if I have just ridden my bike into a tree.

There is no comparison between my bedroom at home and the guest bedroom at Julie's. At hers, I sleep on a queen-size bed with a light blue quilt cover. It's so soft to the touch that a week after I'm there, I flip it back, looking for the tag that will identify the fabric. I've never touched 100 percent silk before. On the bedside table is a light purple orchid. It looks nothing like the fake ones in the supermarket. Beyond the room's sliding glass doors is a deck with potted flowers. Then a view of the swimming pool and a putting green. The wooden floors are not too dark or too light, a firm decadence under my feet. But it's the art that reminds me I'm a gate-crasher. Three small watercolors hanging on the wall. Real paintings, not photocopied pictures haphazardly taped up, trying to make something ugly less ugly. The framed art advertises the family's permanence, something my mother does not subscribe to.

Thankfully, the room's cable television is enough to distract me.

Every night since I've left the hospital, Julie's mother brings me food on a tray that I eat in bed while the TV's on. Julie doesn't leave my side. It's as if she's assigned to watch me. I don't say it, but I need her company. Without her, there's no sense to my being in a place like this, wearing absurdly bright tracksuits with the word *Juicy* splashed all over them, staring out at the empty pool until my eyes hurt. I wait for her. I sleep until she comes home from school. Then we sit on my bed, not speaking, watching back-to-back episodes of *Charmed* until midnight.

For a while, my days take on this pattern until hunger interrupts it. I press my ear to the guest-room door, listening for signs of life. It isn't that I need to sneak around, but Julie's mom will fuss if she sees me. Joanne's like one of those cleaning commercial housewives. She's never still. But also, I'm starting to see the signs of my stay wearing on the family. One afternoon Julie and I sit together in what her mother calls the "den." Joanne wants to wash my sheets and "air out" my room. Julie and I are playing Go Fish on the large L-shaped sofa when her brother Jason, a funny little kid who wears thick glasses, turns away from his cartoons, saying, "Are you going to live with us? Because Grandma Mary is coming soon and you're sleeping in her bed."

The pen Julie throws at him falls on the floor next to the TV, skidding under the console. "Shut up, Jason! You're a jerk!" Then she calls, "Mom, can you get Jason out of here? He's being rude." Jason doesn't mean anything by it, but it's enough to get me thinking I've overstayed. After that, I try to make myself scarce, only mediating my presence through Julie.

WHEN I CRACK open the door, I don't hear any sounds in the house. It's too much to hope that Julie's mom is out shopping or something. She isn't. I know this because she always knocks on the door and tells me exactly where she will be. "Okay," I call out feebly, understanding she will not try to start up a long talk about "getting back on my feet" or "trusting the Lord's plan" while she has her grocery list in hand or a church meeting to get to.

No, she's home, puttering somewhere in the house, and I'm determined to stay out of her sight. I wind my way around the dark formal dining room and into the kitchen. The place is a Stepford wife's dream of architectural trickery, everything hidden behind maple cabinets and speckled marble. I pull on handles only to find a trash can. Another reveals a microwave, another a split-level spice drawer. Finally, I give up and grab an apple from a glass fruit bowl that seems staged for a photograph. I start back to the guest room. I can hear Joanne talking on the phone. She's not speaking especially low but her voice is cautious. I know she's talking about me. I pause for a moment. I hate that I'm listening in, but I can't help it.

"I know, it's really awful," I hear her say.

"Absolutely. Thank God Julie had her mace. That was Jack's idea . . . A year ago . . . Yes ma'am, she's certified and everything." There is a long pause. I move away from her voice.

"You bet. Saved that girl's life . . . I know, right? It was terrible enough . . . Doctor says that she's still a virgin, blessed be."

She muffles a giggle.

"Totally. Can you imagine? What would I do with a pregnant sixteen-year-old? And to have a baby come from that in *my* house?" Another laugh. Its cruel edges stick out like a shirt tag. "Oh Patricia, stop. You're terrible."

I hurry back to the guest room, the heat rising in my chest. I understand. What happened to me only confirms Joanne and her family's place in the world. To them, I'm just a disadvantaged Black girl, a womb waiting to be filled with more charity cases.

WHEN JOANNE LEAVES for the store, I sneak into Julie's room. I want paper. The idea is to leave a note. Instead I find a pamphlet that reads, "What to Do If Someone You Know Is Raped," crammed into the top drawer of Julie's nightstand. Dread beats in my ears. There's a small highlighted section that reads, "Provide unconditional support for the victim, who after such a trauma may be filled with false questions and beliefs. The victim may ask herself, 'How can there be a God in a world so cruel?' Or she may think, 'God failed me.' If the victim receives good Christian counseling, she will feel empowered and renewed and come away with God's presence in her life strengthened."

I put the pamphlet back in the drawer, closing it quietly. It will be long-standing, this wish I feel for the certainty that Julie has. It wasn't just the constant of food and shelter. It was the matching order of her bedroom furniture, the folded clothes in her dresser, the identical hangers suspending dresses and shirts in the closet. Faith, I decide, may be easier to achieve in a plump cushion like this, the soft landing of the middle class. Because the only thing that feels certain is that I will not be saved.

WHEN JULIE GETS home from school she finds me sitting on her bed wearing a T-shirt and shorts I've taken from a box in her closet marked "Goodwill."

"What's up?" she asks, sitting down next to me. Julie's different, less familiar. What happened has changed both of us. Her face is naked. No clumped mascara or goopy eyeliner. Her hair is flat and smooth, her light brown roots filling out her crown.

"Listen," I begin. "I really appreciate everything that you've done for me." I've rehearsed this line, thinking it sounds mature, but the minute I say it, I realize how much I mean it. "You've been a great friend."

"Okay. What are you saying?" Julie looks confused.

"That I'll never be able to thank you enough." My voice quivers.

"Yeah, but you don't have to thank me," Julie says. "If this is about my brother, he's just being an ass." She gets up, starts pacing. "You could even share my room. Look, there's enough space for both of us." She points to an empty corner. "I could move my dresser over there so you could have that whole side by the window. You can have a desk."

It would be so easy to stay. I know this. I haven't spoken to Yevgenia. I haven't seen her since the hospital. There's nothing waiting for me at home. But staying at Julie's isn't right either. Her mother's laughter, from earlier, stays in my ears.

"Really, Julie, thanks, but I can't."

"Don't tell me you want to go back there. That place is shit."

"I need to go home."

"But my dad thinks you should go to counseling. He says you're traumatized." Julie's eyes are pleading.

I wonder if being traumatized might be the shy gray light, the signal of a dying tomorrow, resting in the center of my breast. "I guess," I say, "but I have to go."

I CALL YEVGENIA. I don't want to. Not after she left me at the hospital. But Julie's parents won't let me leave on my own and I don't want her dad to see where I live, so I'm in their kitchen, dialing the only number I know I can reach her at. Julie's family pretends not to watch me from what Joanne calls the "sitting room." The phone rings four times. I glance nervously up at the Harrisons. Joanne fluffing pillows. Julie's dad, Jack, doing a crossword puzzle. Jason crashing two small plastic cars into each other. The clack and smacking of their head-on collisions strain thin nerves. Julie's frowning at me, letting me know I'm making a mistake.

"Rusty's." My mother's voice, dull but efficient.

"Mom," I say, addressing her in a way I've never done before.

Yevgenia is silent for a moment. If she's surprised to hear from me, she doesn't let on. "Let me guess. Too much Son of God saving you from sin?" The sharp rip of paper tearing echoes over the phone. "Give me the address."

◆

Avoid men who are picky eaters, particular about smells or who are otherwise squeamish. They're terrible lovers.

Dusk settles against the mountains in purple and blue strips. Through the living room window, I see Yevgenia's battered Toyota slowly pass the house. Then the car lurches to a stop. The engine whirs as she throws it into reverse. I brought nothing into Julie's house, so I stand near the front door empty-handed. I hear the click of heels on the pavement outside. Through the door's glass I see her wavy, distorted figure. Julie is sitting on the stairs, sulking. Above her head, the stairwell is covered in framed family photos, vacations in Hawaii, birthday pool parties, a family shot taken in a clean white studio.

The bell rings. I'm prepared for a tight dress, or a low-cut shirt, rhinestones, fake fur, all of the standard Yevgenia fare. I inhale as Julie's mom opens the door. My mother stands with an enormous bouquet of flowers and a red gift bag, a brown box with gold writing tucked under her arm. She steps over the threshold. She rubs a palm on her gray pants before shaking hands with Julie's dad. My mother is dressed like a bank teller. Her pants and the light blue button-up cardigan that's slightly too tight are new. She glances around nervously like she's anticipating a pie in the face.

Joanne exclaims over the flowers, "Oh Eugenia, that's so kind of you but not necessary."

It's the first time I see my mother self-conscious. Her accent seems more pronounced, her movements too jittery. Standing in the neutralizing order of the Harrisons' upper-middle-class corridor, she is the immigrant, the foreigner.

"No, it is necessary. It's a thank-you." Her voice trails off, unsure of protocol. "Very good Russian chocolate." My mother passes the brown box to Jason's waiting, outstretched hands. He carries it off to the sitting room. She pulls a large bottle from the red bag. "And best vodka, also Russian." I can see the whites of her knuckles as my mother holds it by its throat.

This is a painful offering.

Julie's dad wordlessly takes the vodka from her like he doesn't know what to do with it. I almost rip it out of his grip to give it back to Yevgenia. It's an expensive bottle, and he won't drink it.

Yevgenia juts her chin at me. "Come. Let's go."

My goodbyes are quick. I tell Julie I'll call her. I won't though, not for a long time. As soon as Yevgenia is in the car, she throws the red gift bag out the open window, then she's grabbing her lighter, fighting with it to get it to ignite, the cigarette already between her lips. She tears off the cardigan like it's infested with spiders. Underneath, a tank top that's mostly cleavage allows me to relax, knowing that an alien hasn't abducted her in my absence. When we're halfway down the block she says, "I should arrest those richy *pridurki* for kidnapping and imprisonment."

"Why do you say that?"

"Because I called every day to come get you and they said no." Her voice trembles a little.

"Oh, I didn't—" What do I say? My mother has taken me by surprise. "I wish . . . I wish you would've come earlier."

Yevgenia takes her eyes off the road briefly, turning her face to me. "I thought that you wanted to stay there. Nice house, real bed, typical American family."

In a different moment, I would have interpreted her comment as an insult. But this time, I understand. We both cling to TV versions of stability, of country, of the maternal bosom of domesticity.

Yevgenia stretches her hand out over the dashboard in my direction, unsure, it seems, what to do with it. I want to reach out, grab it, but something stops me. The old calculations set off in my mind. If I grab her hand first, does it mean I'm the weak one? Or do I win if I let her come to me? But she stops short. Instead of grabbing my hand, she pats the air in front of me. She's making calculations of her own.

14

America is the only country in the world where everyone thinks they can be a millionaire.

The days are quiet at the Oasis. The nights are quieter still. In February, arid winds blow through the valley, striking parched desert grasses. Smoke from incessant wildfires becomes trapped in the hills so schools cancel recess and the county tells workers to stay indoors. At night, the news broadcasts whole towns evacuating, cars and pickups jammed to the hilt with shit nobody needs. When the rains come in March, they're met with relief, until they don't stop. The burned-out towns slide down the mountains. Expensive houses sink into wet gaping earth. The Midwestern evangelicals joyously rub their hands together. They proclaim that California, a hotbed for liberal sinners, has displeased God. The state had it coming. Through all of this my mother and I fall back into an anemic version of our routine performed in the background of Big Mike's preliminary hearing and visits to a disheveled man named Roy Roberts, an indifferent lawyer. A man my mother disliked because he always seemed to be on the phone with other, more important people each time she dragged me to his office.

On this particular afternoon, Yevgenia is especially riled, having spoken to Julie's father earlier that morning. We are sitting in Roy Roberts's small waiting area outside his office, which is simply a glorified cubicle of padded room dividers that don't go all the way up to the ceiling.

"Can you fucking believe that beast gets to request time in front of a judge?" Her voice is loud, like she wants other people to stare at us, reap the benefit of their pity. But it's Legal Aid, so I doubt there is any excess to give. "Jack says that it could take the state months, maybe years, to bring the case to court. Big Mike could be on the streets, like, tomorrow." My mother sits back in the cheap gray chair, red-faced and frustrated, the sleeves of her light blue cardigan bunched to her elbows, prominent patches of sweat under both armpits.

"Do you know that Jack says that Big Mike could spend more time in jail for hitting Julie than what he did to you?" Yevgenia raises her thin eyebrows, prodding me for a reaction.

Jack. Julie's father. We are only here because of him. Sometime after I left the Harrisons', Jack got a hold of my mother, stoked her revenge fantasies with talk of civil cases and *taking Big Mike to the cleaners*. Julie's dad hired a private attorney and encouraged my mother to do the same. And here we are. My mother pantomiming power.

I want none of this. I already told her, but she won't listen. I stay quiet, letting her prattle on with glee about all the possible horrors that await Big Mike in prison. "What if they stake him inside?" She holds a pack of cigarettes. This is something she does when she can't smoke. Almost like the feel of them in her hand transfers the nicotine into her bloodstream. "What if, like Dostoevsky says, it's the house of living death? Now that's a powerful book. God, there should be hard labor here. Who knows, maybe after twenty years Big Mike could return a man, broken and humbled. You know Americans are—"

"Do you mean *shank*?" I interrupt her.

"What?" She cocks her head, confused.

"Shank, instead of stake."

"Whatever. Either. Who the fuck cares?"

Roy steps from around his partition just then, with a relic of a phone pressed to his ear, the coil of the cord distended. I follow Yevgenia into the cramped space as we place our feet carefully between the booby traps of bloated manila file folders dotting the dirty brown carpet.

Roy pulls the mouthpiece of the phone down toward his chin. "Go ahead and move those," he says, pointing to the stack of files on the seat of a chair.

I sense my mother's anger. She hates to be instructed. Venom oozes from her long flat stare, but it's wasted on Roy. He's too busy wedging himself back into his desk, cradling the phone while flipping through files, no doubt trying to locate mine. We are sitting atop hundreds of bursting file folders. They are like unacknowledged hands reaching from the depths of hell, grabbing at our feet, wanting to drag us down with them.

The phone clangs when Roy drops it in the receiver. He starts in on the shuffling of paper.

"So," Yevgenia begins, crossing a bare leg over the other, an attempt to grab Roy's attention, "I want you to push for"— she stops and looks at a notebook she's brought—"sexual criminal contact or sexual battery." She reads slowly, like she's never put these words together before. Her voice leans harder than ever on an ambiguous accent that is neither Russian nor American but something else. Her hair is freshly dyed a deep black, curling at her shoulders. Her bangs are cut blunt, just above her brows. She's going for a French actress, like the one who starred in the movie she never watched, based on the book by a Czech author she never read—a sort of look that screams European and therefore sophisticated and worthy of American impartiality.

Roy Roberts acts like he's seen this all before, people trying to play at being legal minds in all kinds of getups. Instead of noticing Yevgenia's legs, his eyes dart to the fly buzzing around the room. He waits for it to land to jot a note on the file in front of him. "I understand what you're asking for, um"—he frowns at the paperwork—"Ms. Borislava, but I can't do that for you. You'll have to take this up with the prosecutor."

Yevgenia squirms upright in her seat. "What do you mean? Aren't you a lawyer?"

Roy doesn't so much smile as grimace. "Yes, of course I am. But as I explained the last time you were here, what you're after is handled in criminal court. Legal Aid hasn't been assigned the case to prosecute and I personally do family law. I can help you with those matters but you really should be speaking to the prosecutor."

"Last time you said you could help me." My mother's voice wavers, slightly. Her knuckles go white as she clinches the notebook. "You said you could help me seek damages." She holds out her notebook where she wrote down his words. "See."

"Yes, in a matter of speaking." He shoves his hands through his hair. "Has anyone talked to you from the prosecutor's office?"

"No."

"Okay, so let me explain how this will work." Roy's voice goes into tutorial mode. "The state will evaluate the evidence and determine if this is a matter that should go to court. And from what you told me last time, there was no penetrative sex act, is that correct?" He directs this question to me. I cannot help but feel the chill of accusation.

"No." My mother answers for me. "But what does that have to do with anything?"

"Well, I'm not the one who should be saying this, it should really come from the state, but I want to be clear about the kind of pitfalls awaiting you should you pursue Mr. Stewart in the courts through statutory rape or criminal sexual conduct. I have seen cases like these take their toll on families and I wouldn't advise moving forward with this." Roy Roberts eyes my mother as I imagine a used-car salesman would, carefully holding his breath, hoping she won't look under the hood.

She's rubbing her temples. "I don't understand. Why is this complicated? He attacked my daughter. There are witnesses." Yevgenia gestures to me. "Go on, tell him."

I open my mouth to speak but I can only hear my own heart pounding against my eardrums. Even with short walls, the air stagnates. It's suddenly too hot and I need water. "Who is Mr. Stewart?" I ask.

Yevgenia reaches over and smacks my leg with the back of her hand. "Don't sit there like a houseplant. Tell him."

"Mr. Stewart, isn't he the defendant?" Roy consults his papers again. "Michael Stewart. All I am saying is that the defendant, as a parolee, will face more time for violations than for any of the charges you want to pursue." The phone rings and Roy answers it.

When he does, Yevgenia throws her hand up. "Can't you let that go to voicemail? We're not done here."

"Call me back in five minutes." Roy quickly hangs up the

phone, annoyed, and drops the solicitous tone and spells it out for my mother. "Listen, you're asking the court to tie up time on a case that is not going to get you what you think you want. I understand your"—he turns to evaluate me with some hesitation, trying to find the right words—"*need* to preserve your daughter's reputation. I get it. But let me tell you how this is going to go if you keep pushing this. You go to court. The defendant will claim reasonable belief or mistake of age and though that's not an affirmative defense in California, it bogs the courts down. It's your time, the state's time, and puts your daughter here in the spotlight for the court to pass judgment. And they will. They'll look at her. They'll look at you"—he nods in the direction of her bare legs—"and even if they find him guilty, it's battery of a minor or, at best, sexual battery. You're looking at four to six months, if you're lucky, two years if the state can bring felony charges. But I suggest you leave it alone. Let the justice system do its job. Let the defendant go out on parole violations."

The phone on Roy Roberts desk rings again. Loud, exasperated breath streams from my mother. Roy shows both palms. He's either being held up or making peace. The three of us seem to stop breathing while the phone rings, excitable.

When it cuts, Roy looks dead at me. I'm not sure if I detect apathy or confirmation of my limited worth, but he says in a soft voice that signals the end of our meeting, "Listen, if you have no felony charges related to your ordeal with Stewart and if the crime was reported by someone to law enforcement, then I could help you file a claim with the Victim Compensation Board." He looks at his papers, muttering under his breath, "Okay, yes, I see the police report, this is good."

"You mean we could get money?" My mother narrows her eyes and I know she's trying to find the catch.

This causes Roy to start digging around in a drawer of his desk. "Hang on, it's here someplace," he mumbles.

"*Che cazzo*," Yevgenia whispers under her breath in disgust. I watch her as she deliberately slides her foot to a pile of file folders. Quietly kicking them over, she carefully spills the contents of them with her espadrilles.

I clear my throat loudly, hoping Roy will catch my mother in the act. She draws her foot back as Roy sits up, holding out some papers for my mother. "Here. This is the packet that you need to fill out for the Victims Compensation Board. I'm not going to make any promises, but it's a straightforward process and you can get money to cover some hospital bills, et cetera. It's all in there."

My mother grabs it from him, flipping through the pages. "Does it say how much we can get?" Her Marx and Engels have quickly flown out the window. Her eyes loot the information. Her fingers rush down one page and then another. "Oh." Genuine surprise catches in my mother's throat. "What's this about hate crimes? You know, he has some racist tattoos, the defendant." She offers this information in the pensive style of a detective thoughtfully assembling the last pieces of the mystery just before she rushes out the door to nab the villain. "Could we go after him for that? A hate crime? You know, my daughter"—Yevgenia motions in my direction with the papers—"she's Black. Could we get more money for that than, say, assault?"

We. The deceptive solidarity of it. Even Roy can't turn away from my mother shoving me onto the auction block.

"Ms. Borislava, Victims Compensation is no pot of gold.

If you want to file a civil suit, by all means do so. If you want to pursue a felony hate crime, talk to the prosecutor. We're done here."

My mother has been dismissed. Rarely do I see her this furious. Red and white splotches spontaneously flare up from her neck to her cheeks. Her hands are shaking. As she speaks, she tries to clamp down every word like they are daggers flying out of her mouth. "Listen, Roy, I don't give a shit that you're some hack lawyer. I am *not* looking for a pot of gold. I am looking for justice for my daughter and in your fucking country, which doesn't know the first thing about it. You think money is going to heal what she went through? You shitty man." My mother spits at the ground, and I am grateful, because a loogie, I have learned, could get a person prison time.

I try to steer my mother out of his office by pulling her arm, but she's busy kicking over files on her way out, cussing. I misunderstood. She's not callous. She's just Russian. Trying to make a broken system work the best she can. In the lobby of the building, my mother wipes away angry, frustrated tears. "I'm sorry this is so fucked-up," I say.

She shakes her head quickly, like I shouldn't say any more. "Don't ever apologize for this. I was the idiot who listened to that richy asshole, thinking we could be the same. It's my fault."

The car ride is quiet, but when we get home my mother rages blindly, throwing her fake Chanel to the floor, flinging her key ring against the plywood walls. "I came to America because there are courts of law, not a band of old ladies with vendettas deciding your fate." Her feet stomp blank grenades throughout the trailer.

"Equal protection under the law, my ass." My mother

peels off the cardigan she has worn like an invincibility cloak for weeks and bunches it into a ball, shoving it in the kitchen garbage.

While Yevgenia rages, I stay silent.

She keeps jabbing the air with her finger, saying, "That *xyecoc* will have his justice served." Although her version of "justice served" is more Stalin than Clinton, I can't get the image out of my mind of Big Mike being offered a large ice cream sundae instead of a firing squad.

Eventually, I try going back to school. It's too difficult. Charles watches me like I'm about to break. I've become a vase perched on a too-high shelf. His look makes me feel like I'm going to shatter and ruin everything. Then there's Julie. Every time I see her, she holds on to me, not physically, but emotionally, checking in, asking questions, each one a weighted backpack I can't carry. So I avoid them. Being without friends is familiar to me. It's comforting, going unnoticed. Moving through the corridors like a ghost, I think of nothing during the school day. At night, I take the sleeping pills I find among Yevgenia's things in the bathroom until they run out. Then, instead of sleeping, I pace the trailer. The night never happens. The sky turns morning blue, casting a pale light.

Charles comes by the trailer a couple of times. From my bedroom, I can hear the exchange between him and my mother in lowered voices.

"Is she going to be okay?"

"She'll be fine. And after we get him, she'll be even better." I can't help thinking that it's not me Yevgenia's talking about. Charles comes down the hall to my room. He stands outside my bedroom door, tapping on it lightly.

"Give her time, she's strong." My mother speaks firmly,

like she's trying to prove this to herself. "She's just not ready, but she's strong."

Strong? When have I ever been strong? I wonder if my mother knows that I don't have any strength without her.

◆

Generally, geography is everything when it comes to sex. For example, Americans know nothing of seduction. The Italians are premature ejaculators. The Russians are delicious animals. The French, too pensive. The Germans are not worth it. Brazilians are overrated and the Spaniards have the priest looking over their shoulder. But try them all.

Yevgenia holds it together until a heat wave in May. We had been in our little trailer just shy of a year, which is by no means a record—I mean, we have lived in places for as long as two years, or fewer than a few weeks.

"I hate this weather. It's fucking spring!" Yevgenia crashes through the trailer getting ready for work, pulling on a jean skirt and tank top. "In the normal part of the world it would be cool. In Moscow, there could be snow on the ground. I'd be wearing fur!"

There's nothing to say when she gets like this. It's not the heat and fires, it isn't even California. My mother is restless. She flips through her books, not finding the setting or the character that will carry her out of her daily existence. She sits at the kitchen table, cigarette burning to a stub, watching nothing in particular outside our window. Then she tries to kill time in other ways. She goes out with men who can't possibly interest her. A late-forties real estate agent who talks too much about boating on Lake Tahoe. An earnest guy in his midtwenties from Ohio teaching junior high school math. A few nights here and there of sex with men she picks up at Rusty's. Nothing sticks.

A dark fragility stalks my mother and me. Neither of us is fit for conversation. We find it hard to be worthy of a kindly glance. When we come into contact, we murmur efficient apologies and look at the floor. Until she stops looking at me entirely. Yevgenia will call Russ and tell him that she isn't coming in. She starts going on long drives, or at least I think she does. She's an apparition. She's gone in the car when I come home from school or pulling up to our trailer as I leave in the morning. Daily, I peek into her room, checking for the blue suitcase. A small sigh of relief once I see everything is still, mostly, in place.

Then, with her sporadic absence, our trailer becomes a body whose organs are shutting down. The landline is the first to go. It will be followed by the gas and then the electric. And it's an early weekday morning when the stillness of a house cut silent by the electric company forces me awake. Outside the sky is light gray, misty. But inside, red and blue lights shine through my living room window, bouncing off the walls of my trailer. The grumbling of codes and beeps from radios force me to stand. I look out and see the ambulance parked in front of Brody's trailer. A cluster of neighbors is gathered at its right front fender. I slide my feet into some flip-flops and join them. Gus and Lourdes are there. So is Rhea. Two other guys stop on their way to work.

When I approach, Lourdes turns and gives me a grim pressed-lipped greeting. She puts her arm around my waist protectively.

I ask, "*¿Qué pasó?*" My voice croaks with sleep. Brody's door is open. I crane my neck to see inside.

"*Ay, señor,*" Lourdes says, clutching her throat, her voice gentle, full of compassion. "*Es muy, muy triste.*" She shakes her head slowly.

Ms. Eunice rolls up on her red scooter as a paramedic steps outside the house carrying a red-and-black duffel bag.

"Oh, not good," Rhea says over her shoulder. She's talking to me and Lourdes. "That's a defibrillator. He's moving too slow for this to be an emergency." She's the resident medical expert.

"You know what that means?" Rhea asks us, waiting for me and Lourdes to tell her that we don't. "It means DOA."

The paramedic reaches the end of the carport. "Go on back home. Nothing to see here, guys."

We stare at him silently. He's a tall, skinny white man. Unexceptional, save for the gossamer puff of brown hair on the center of his head. Otherwise, he's the kind of guy who looks more important in his uniform than out of it. I watch his latex-gloved hands, wondering what kind of authority he has over us.

On the road behind him, Ms. Eunice shrugs. She carries an air of disdain, like she doesn't know what all the fuss is about. Slowly, she turns her electric scooter around and bumps silently down the road home.

"Okay," he says, like he's warned us. He walks to the back of the ambulance to put his bag away.

From the trailer, we hear a strange cry. A wounded animal. Time stops, it seems, a second, two seconds. I notice the old women, Mickey and Minnie, arms locked, as if they're holding each other up. Terri appears at the front door, in saggy cutoffs and a lime green tank top. Her hair is disheveled. Her face swollen and red. She smokes her cigarette like an addict. We stand quietly. The collective worry changes to fear. Terri flicks her cigarette to the ground.

"He's gone. Steve's gone." Terri throws up her hands angrily, slapping them on her thighs. Then she vanishes into her trailer.

My blood drains to my feet. I hear her, but I don't believe it. What does "gone" mean, anyway?

"*Dios santo.*" Lourdes brings her hand to her mouth. She loosens her grip on me and I start to back away.

One of the guys standing next to Gus turns and says something I don't understand at the time but will play in my mind for days.

"*A cada coche se le llega su sábado.*" Which is something like, Saturday happens to every pig eventually.

THE FLOCK OF bystanders is mercurial, expanding and contracting with the arrival or departure of the paramedics, the police, and someone from the coroner's office. It takes hours for the county officials to process Steve's final moments. All the movement stirs the air, filling my nostrils with the sharp smell of adrenaline. Tragedy has the tendency to crackle and then fizzle out, becoming mundane for the crowd.

I peel off early, even before they remove Steve's body. I'm unable to stand among judging neighbors, their disingenuous platitudes, their pity and relief at the suffering before them. I'm numb. I walk on hollow legs to my house and collapse on the sofa. I stay that way, two, maybe three hours, unable to close my eyes, riveted by a dark mark on the dropped-down ceiling.

Then the images begin to fill my mind. Yevgenia at New Year's, Steve riding off on his bike, Big Mike looming in the doorway. I chase these thoughts away, and then more images come to taunt me, only faster, one after another.

Later, when the cars are gone and the street is quiet, I go to Steve's trailer for no other reason than morbid curiosity. I'm at the front door and then I see my hand on the knob, turning it. It's unlocked. There's no hesitation, no feeling, no thought behind what I do next. Crossing the threshold, I see past the night of the Christmas party, past Big Mike and what he did to me. I see the interminable hours of babysitting, of waiting. There's no definition, no contour. The wood-paneled walls blur until they bleed into a long tunnel. I follow it to the back bedroom, the one belonging to Steve and Terri.

The door is open. Crumpled, yellowed gauze pads and a spent latex glove turned inside out are forgotten by the foot of the bed. A sweet-and-sour smell lingers, sugar cookies and feces. The room hums faintly, the imprint of many kinetic hands having been there and gone. A bedside table lamp is toppled onto the floor. A white T-shirt, probably cut from Steve's body, lies discarded by one of his motorcycle boots. In the middle of it all, the bed sits like a calm witness in the chaos. The knowledge of what happened lives in the wrinkled, stained sheets. I move toward the bed, running my hands over the bedspread.

A feeling that I'm not alone comes up from the floor. I sink to my knees and look under the bed. Brody's eyes are bloated shut, his face red. I get on my stomach and reach out to him.

"B., it's me," I say, touching his arm lightly. "I'm here. It's okay."

"Go away." He speaks slightly above a whisper.

"I have nowhere to go," I say, sitting up, pushing myself back against the nightstand. "If you don't mind, I'd like to sit with you."

We stay still in our silent grieving, watching the walls darken. I fall asleep, waking to the sound of Brody emerging from under the bed. He reeks of urine. Settling against my body, Brody's like a sandbag, heavy and shapeless.

He starts talking, his voice flattened by the scene he is re-living. "He didn't want me to come in, but I got hungry and I kept knocking. He was kind of like sitting up, sort of falling over. I thought he was sleeping." Brody starts to cry. "But his arm was twisted, like this." Brody turns his arm counter-clockwise, pins it behind himself. "Even if he was sleeping, it wasn't normal." He clutches at me desperately, crying into my chest.

"I'm so sorry, B." And it's the truth. I can't manage more.

Brody didn't call 911 when he found his dad and he didn't call for his mother. He just crawled under his parents' bed and didn't come out. Not even when Terri came upon Steve and was screaming and bawling and banging on his chest. He stayed put when he knew his mother was digging around in the pockets of his dad's clothes looking for money and drugs. He didn't even come out when the paramedics came, or the police, and not even when the ambulance took his dad away. Brody tells me all of this with a distant voice, search-ing, trying to make his way back to himself. He's shivering and I pull the sheet off the bed. We wrap ourselves up in it. Onion-laced sweat, Steve's smell saturates the sheet, staying in our noses.

We sit that way, falling in and out of sleep. The deep purple light of dusk edges in, nudging us to shift so blood can flow. Together, alone, Brody and I weep. His crying splits the thin wall of human decorum. Something inside me becomes unhinged too. I'm not crying for Steve. So when Brody lies prone on the carpet, calling out for his dad, I beat my fists against the floor until they bruise, seeking a singular clarity, moaning *why*. Because I am trying to understand—in the only time that I will allow myself to think about this—how *both* my body and my mind had been shaped by Big Mike's hands and how my mother's had been shaped to a kind of death, little by little, by her father.

If Brody and I didn't fully understand our place in the world before this day, the adults in our lives forced us to. What does it mean to be abandoned by people who largely neglected you in the first place? We are orphans, with and without parents, and without siblings, alone. In this moment, we only have each other. I wish we stayed that way but we don't. It's late in the evening when Terri comes home. We're standing in the kitchen, heating up a plate of food that Lourdes left at the front door. When Terri sees me, she yanks Brody from my side.

She's high. Her irises seem to be swallowed by her pupils. Her thin hands flail uncontrollably in the air. "You have some damn nerve being all up in here after what you did to my family," she says. Her hands won't stop, so she clenches the roots of her hair. It fringes out of her knuckles. There's a large tweaker welt on her chin. "You're a goddamn bitch. A lying fucking whore. He didn't rape you. He wouldn't even touch someone like you."

Brody tries to pull his mother into him. She lets go of her hair, smacking his hands away. "Don't touch me, Brody. This bitch here"—Terri points at me—"she got Mike locked up again." Flat-footed, she paces the short length of the kitchen like she's trying to figure out what to do next. "Get the fuck out!" she screams. "Get. The. Fuck. Out!" she shrieks over and over again.

"Go on, Lara," Brody says, his voice like shattering waves against rock.

I'm already at the door. Scared and trembling, I shout over his mother's screeching, "We don't have to turn into this. Brody, we can leave this place." I point at Terri. "Fucking high after your dad ODs. A real fucking role model." Terri lunges in my direction and I scramble to the door. But I don't need to. Brody grabs his mom by her waist, while she screams and claws at the air like a Hollywood zombie. Drugs have diminished her so badly, she's as thin as her son. I turn to see the strain on Brody's face as he holds on to her. "Just go," he shouts. I hesitate. I don't want to leave him.

Then there's the smack and clatter of a plate crashing to the floor. Rubber sneakers skid against linoleum as Brody wrestles his mother to the ground. "Look at what you've done," Brody says, grunting as he struggles to pin his mother's arms. "You dumped my food." Terri surrenders; she seems to melt into the kitchen floor. She starts crying. I guess it's natural for a kid to hurt when his parents are hurting, because Brody stops being an enforcer and switches back to being a son. He hugs his mother, rocks her. He looks up at me, then turns away.

He's in the same striped T-shirt and dried-urine sweatpants that he was wearing when he found his father. Nothing, but everything, has changed. If I leave, he won't be coming with me. If I stay, he will be lost to me. Brody is choosing to be tied to Terri's derailing train, and I get it. She's alive and here. And she wants him for now, if only to say that she kept him. It's a kind of love. Who am I to mess with that?

YEVGENIA JUST SHRUGS when I tell her about Steve's death. She's too preoccupied by things even closer to home. By me. By her own childhood troubles and, maybe, by the fading possibility that she will be able to have her revenge. Word gets to her that Big Mike has been moved from Robert Presley Detention to Chuckawalla Valley State Prison, putting him further out of her reach. This comes as a final blow. For Yevgenia, score settling is a debt owed to her ancestral ties, the blood feuds and animosities. Revenge is transcendent, the closest she gets to a spiritual belief. So, it isn't a surprise when, one night, Russ drives her home before her shift's over, leaving her propped up at the base of our steps.

The trailer is permanently black with the lights cut so I stumble through the house when I hear her retching and coughing outside. She's wrecked when I shine the flashlight on her. Hair matted and wet with vomit, her eyes dripping black sludge down her cheeks. Yevgenia grumbles, drunk, incoherent sounds as if she has forgotten she's human.

"Here, let's get you up," I say, lifting her by an armpit. I try not to breathe in the sour-milk smell of her stomach lining. She leans into me as we stagger up the stairs. She slurs an excuse of sorts. "They threw me out. Said I was going too far, looking for a contract kill. Fuckers."

We make it through the door, maneuvering slowly toward the sofa. "All those assholes and not a single contact in prison," she says.

"Lie down. I'll get you some water." I offer her my place on the sofa.

"No. My room." She tries to steady herself. "They kill a woman to get some pussy. But kill another man for hurting a woman? Then they have morals. I hate men." My mother hugs my waist tight as we shuffle down the hall together. We hit the edge of her bed and she falls into it, curling into herself. I place the flashlight on her cardboard-box nightstand and rummage in her dresser drawer for a change of clothes.

"Leave me." She speaks into the mattress.

"You're covered in vomit, at least change your shirt."

"No, really. I mean it. You have to go. I am my mother and you will be me if you stay."

She's shit-faced. I decide to ignore her. One of the drawers is stuck and I jiggle it back and forth to open it. The particleboard knocks hollow.

"Listen to me." She's clumsily pushing herself up. "I can't protect you."

The drawer comes loose in my hand, the bottom of it detaching from the face. "Shit. This drawer is broken," I mutter. I keep my back to her, moving to the next drawer.

"What are you catatonic? Headless?" She throws something, a book, maybe. It flaps past me, hitting the wall.

"Hey, what the fuck's wrong with you?" Her voice is rising and with it, gathering more clarity.

My fingers land on something soft and cottony. I straighten to hold the garment to the light.

"A dog bites, but not you? Be crazy with anger." Yevgenia is standing behind me shouting. Contempt laces her words. "Act!" she yells. And I feel it. Her hand hesitating for a fraction of a second before shoving me into the dresser. An ashtray, perfume, and her souvenir bottle of Russian Standard, empty, crash to the floor. "Are you fucking in there?" She grabs me by the arm, jerking me toward her.

"Act, you fucking idiot!" She's screaming. I know she's screaming but I hear her from a place more distant. Before I can stop myself, I am pushing my full weight into her. We slam against the floor, scraping against the metal bed frame. We topple the boxes of her nightstand, scattering the flashlight and her fake Tiffany lamp.

In complete darkness, we go silent. Only the heavy panting of our breath, damp and semi-noxious with drink and vomit and grief, fills my mother's room.

Eventually, I stand and speak, directing my voice toward the floor. "*Act?* You want me to act like you? Shake my ass at every stranger? Pretend that anyone gives a shit about what I think and what I read? Pretend that I have power or, what, control? Pretend that I'm not some fucking joke?" I start crying and I hate myself for it because I'm tired of feeling backed into a corner, reacting to her, waiting on her. Watching her. Listening to her. Everything about her.

"Don't worry," I say. "I *am* angry. That's all I am. Is that what you want? Because that's what you gave to me. Your bitter life lessons on what to expect from this shit-filled world. So yeah, I got it."

Shaking and spent, I feel my way to the door. Yevgenia says nothing. I'm not even convinced that she's still conscious. I run my hand along the pitch-black hallway and I remember: *The future was a dark corridor, and at the far end the door was bolted.* One year my mother greeted me with this quote nearly every morning. I was eight when I was first aware of Yevgenia reading and rereading the book *Madame*

Bovary. "God," she'd say out loud to herself as she closed the book. "Flaubert is a master at capturing the tediousness of motherhood and the trap of domesticity." After which I'd tried to make myself small and unseen.

I fight the urge to go back to her room and tell her a different version of the same truth. That damage like ours is hereditary. And another truth: my mother never knew how to be my mother.

ON MY WAY home from school, I'm listening carefully to the sounds of tires on the road. The warm tacky rubber rolling over scorching blacktop is interrupted by an engine turning over someplace in the Oasis. The start and stop of it, the hope and the death of it, frustrates the owner, I can tell. Walking down the street, I see Ms. Eunice, who sits on her scooter with a yellow legal pad on her lap and a pen in her hand. She's got her usual getup on, a nylon tracksuit in light green and a white baseball cap pulled to the middle of her brow. Ms. Eunice is lecturing Papa Bear. I hear the words *building codes* and cross to the opposite side of the street, not wanting to talk. Ms. Eunice doesn't care and Papa Bear is fussing over his truck, hood open, so he doesn't see me. I've been avoiding him anyway, because I haven't figured out a way to thank him for that night. If he or Charles or Julie hadn't come looking for me— My mind halts. The taste of vomit in my mouth is involuntary, like seeing Big Mike's face behind my closed eyes or remembering his smell. His real smell, past the booze and cigarettes mixed with end-of-day body odor. The scent of his worthless, throwaway life, the rejection, the being unseen. It's the scent that lingers. The film on my tongue.

I get home and step into my trailer, and I know. Before checking on her suitcase, before seeing the three black plastic garbage bags tossed on my bed. I know, even before I read the note she wrote on the backs of two unopened electric bills as well as an overdue notice from the library. My mother is gone and she isn't coming back.

15

Dear Lara,

Did I ever tell you about that story I read, in Argumenty i Fakty? Or maybe in the Robata?

The point is that this story comes from a reputable newspaper, I promise you. The story was about a woman in Siberia, a mother, who ate her 16 year old daughter. And not like these fake cannibals you have here in America, like what's his name, the one that everyone was so surprised about, you know, the blond one. Anyway, this mother, she was a cannibal—a fucking real deal one. She didn't just boil a few fingers and eat them. She took that daughter of hers and she ate her all throughout the winter. Served the girl up stewed, roasted, and grilled. The whole family unwittingly ate her—the father, the brothers, even a few cousins had a piece when the mother brought a plate of pelmeni to a wedding. Yes. Disturbing, but true fact.

Anyway, remember Donnie? The "Russian American"? A tall guy, dark hair? He always wore that black leather jacket? You might have been ten when I dated him. He was the guy who vomited on your shoes that time. Anyway, years ago I say to Donnie, "Do you know that there was this mother in Russia . . ." blah, blah, blah. And then I tell him about how Russians are well-known cannibals. That was the other part of the story—that Russia has among the highest incidences of cannibalism in the modern world.

So I tell Donnie, "You know, famine aside, it makes sense that Russians are comfortable being cannibals. We are passionate people. Name one Russian who doesn't love with the enthusiasm of a fanatic and fight like a lion while fucking?"

But Donnie couldn't agree. He said something like, "Shit. You wouldn't catch me eating another human being. Not even if I was the last man on earth."

What an idiot.

He probably was sitting on the sofa, wearing that fucking jacket—indoors and in the middle of summer. Anyway, he was so American. All moral high ground, what could he know? The only thing between me and the Siberian mother is a knife and a fork. Maybe too the habit of cooking. Because with genuine emotion, like deep consuming love, comes an infinite hunger. I only knew this when I had you.

You were six months old when I realized that you were not mine and that I could not keep you. You don't believe me, but then I loved you more than I have loved anything, even, and maybe especially, myself. When you slept I would admire how your soft flesh creased at your wrist, dimpled at your knees. I rolled your earlobes between my fingers, like delicate grapes. And yes, there would be occasions when I put your skin between my teeth and with gentle pressure bit slowly, tasting a faint baby sweetness that was so subtle it was almost bland. With those eyes of yours, the toothless smile, the great need you had that only I could fill, you brought out my most Russian traits. Let's just say, I would have eaten you if it were not for a misunderstanding of time.

I craved that feeling of being full with you like I was in pregnancy. You felt the same, I think. You used to crawl onto my lap. Push into my body where I was still soft from birth. Your hands would go to my belly and tug at the skin. You couldn't speak so you would whimper and grunt in a way that I could only describe as insistent. I thought perhaps you had seen enough of the world and knew it was time to go where you belonged. I would close my eyes and see our cells comingling in my body, reversing the order that brought you to life. Where once my body fed you, you would be feeding me.

To think that had I ingested you, we could have stayed as close as we had once been, and this, I imagine, is what that Siberian mother thought as she watched her daughter's flesh firm with age. She acted. Whereas for me, I realized too late, and each day put more and more distance between us.

Once you said I was a terrible mother. Yes. But my inattentions and lack of romance for the job only heightened your part in the family drama. Consider, for a moment, that you are a terrible daughter. Because who but fanatics and children believe idolizing equates love? It's impossible. There is no taking shelter in the mother because she's a home that does not exist. But that's you, my daughter, the only one I have ever loved. It's you who held me in long years of stupid terror. Your deep need to say we belong to each other. Yes. And still, we belong nowhere.

Perhaps a certain greediness, a misplaced hope, or a failure to read the omens kept me from doing what should have been done. I could have saved you from this grief, like the Siberian mother did with her daughter. Save you and keep you intact.

Remember, no apologies. I will not ask for your forgiveness. But I make a promise. I will carry you close like the scent coming from my own body.

Always,
Yevgenia

I have consulted the cards. The Six of Diamonds. You'll be fine.

◆

After my mother leaves comes the strange lucid season. I remember everything I try in vain to forget. Yevgenia walks with me through my days, wakes me at night. Her occasional soft cadence and the gnarly, bitter recollections, her shadows and demons appearing after she drinks and sometimes before, stain the floor of every room I enter. I pass her bedroom, stand in the doorway, I smell her—a clean, powdery smell layered over the ripe, musky odor of oily skin, frustrated living, and the earthy damp folds of her unwashed body. The binding scent of my childhood.

It suffocates.

I go outside cautiously, sniffing the cool, smoky air. Human sounds penetrate the night. Television voices, music, requests shouted from room to room, crying babies. The people of the Oasis are tucked into their trailers performing their usual nighttime rituals. This brings me some comfort. The shared world has yet to slip off its axis. Out across the street, at Brody's trailer, a sliver of blue and purple hues flashes against a tiny opening in their window blind. Past his trailer, down the street, are other trailers, some with lights on, others dark boxes set against the foothills. Inky black crawls out of the sky, darkening it. This is how time moves in the desert. Slow and deliberate, unseen but seen, an apparition. A mother. She's there, in the corner of your eye. You look and then she's gone.

16

"The Mother" is for promotional use only. After the commercial, they leave the woman to dig her own grave.

It's early September and the desert's heat lifts off the asphalt in slow, silent waves that pass through my body. An old woman's summer, my mother would call weather like this.

Charles and I are standing under the protection of the carport, mustering the courage to walk out into the taxing, all-devouring sun.

"Do this for me," he says, wanting to drag me around the Oasis to say his goodbyes.

"I need to get to work." The street is dead. The air-conditioned bus ride into town seems appealing right now.

Charles winces at me. "Come on, I leave in three days, can't you call in sick?" He's trying hard not to show his relief and excitement at his departure almost as hard as I'm trying to hide my envy.

"Don't become some fucking hermit." He watches me closely. "I'm not going to be around to pry you out of your cave."

"I'll survive without you," I say slowly, with confidence I don't feel. My mouth is dry, sandpaper dry, like I'm shriveling from the inside knowing that he's leaving me behind.

"You might, barely. But my aunt won't." His brown eyes glisten. I think he's a little sad too. Charles takes both my hands in his. "I know you don't like her, but promise me you'll check on her." His worry is charging through his hands. "Please."

I groan, pulling away. "Don't make me." I slump my shoulders, enjoying being needed. I want to hold on to his request as a promissory note for the longevity of our friendship. "Fine," I say. "But I don't want to wipe any asses or anything."

"You're such a bitch." Charles hugs me. "I *might* miss you." He nudges me forward. "Seriously. I'm not going over to see this little shit machine on my own."

Crystal gave birth a few months ago and is back home with the kid. Neither of us has seen it yet. I'm in makeshift post-Yevgenia training, keeping myself busy with my job at Señor Taco, mindlessly serving microwaved meals from a tiny shop in a strip mall on Market Street to dental hygienists who work in the office next door. Lucky Charles fills his summer days packing his worldly goods into three large suitcases and spending scholarship money on "dorm essentials" at a Kmart in Riverside.

"Hey, be happy that you're not the one who's going to be around having to listen to stupid baby stories all day, every day," I say, hitting him on his skinny bicep. We both know Rhea and Crystal offered to let me live with them when school starts. It's a deal I don't want to take but I'm barely affording living on my own, even working full-time. It's a safe place to land, until I can get back to Mexico and back to the dreams I began to form there. Start saving. As it turns out, I'm terrible with money. I kick at the ground carefully, glancing with mild pride and regret at my Jordan XI low-tops that consumed my first paycheck. "Alright, let's get this over with."

The Oasis is a ghost town, except for the air-conditioning units bumping and whirring around us. The sky, pale blue and cloudless, bows past the mountains, turning into hazy white particles that seem to hover just above the ridge. Without the relief of any breeze, it's like we are walking into the mouth of a crematorium's furnace. Charles and I trudge shoulder to shoulder straight down the middle of the narrow street. He's rambling about the book he's reading for the special summer course they make all the scholarship kids take. I'm listening with half an ear, trying to imagine him already gone. To miss him when he's still close is a quintessential *daughter of Yevgenia* life skill. Prepare the body, fool the mind so when Charles isn't here, I'll think he's still with me, like a phantom limb.

". . . that's fucked-up, right?" Charles stops in front of Crystal's trailer, trying to catch shade from a leafless, skeletal sycamore.

"For real," I add, nodding. I have no idea what he's talking about, but it doesn't matter. What are words but sounds that shape the here and now? And Charles is already slipping. His pending move has made him different. He's a version of a person he used to be. He's shaved his head bald. His oxfords and wing tips replaced by tennis shoes, black denim shorts, and a T-shirt with a face of Basquiat broadcast generic art student. I liked his look better when he was trying too hard.

Rhea is at the door, grinning widely. "Come in, come in. Wash your hands and then you can hold this cutie boy."

Charles gives me a panicked look, whispering, "Hell to the no, this is a vintage T-shirt." But he's up the steps and in the kitchen soaping past his elbows before I can slip off my shoes and get over the threshold.

Crystal's house is a tidy shrine to the baby. A green pleather sofa, identical to the one living in my trailer, is pushed up

against a plywood-paneled wall. An upholstered faux vel-
vet rocking chair that Crystal keeps calling a "glider" is her
throne. When she looks up from her gentle swaying, her face
is a confounding mix of youthful inexperience and timeworn sage. "Hey, how are you guys?" Her voice is hushed and
dreamy, like she's slowly waking up.

Charles is standing over Crystal, his feet planted firmly
into the carpet. He peers at the wrapped log held in her arms.
"Oh my God, he's so cute."

Crystal pushes herself out of her chair with one hand.
She's wearing a long prairie-like dress buttoned all the way up.
She holds the bundle out to Charles. "His name is Elmer John
Reyes Galang." Then Crystal looks down at the baby, nodding
her head toward Charles. "And Elmer, this is Charles."

Charles holds out his arms tentatively, like he's negotiat-
ing how to cradle a viper. Crystal laughs, confident. "Here,
hold his head like this"—she adjusts Charles's position as she
gently lays the baby in his arms—"and put your other arm
underneath, like that." The baby's whimper is a crackling
complaint against the change of location.

I watch Charles in profile as he stares down at the baby.
His face glows as if he's holding a sample of all the stars in
the galaxy. "Hey little guy. Hey. Hi." He speaks empty, meaningless words and yet the marvel in his voice is a new quality
I've never heard. I wonder if every baby, these radical, un-
formed strangers to the world, are able to convert us heretics
into believers of a charming innocence, or if it's the power of
only some babies. The babies of four names, of single, loving
mothers in a long tradition of single, loving mothers.

Crystal waves me over. "Lara, get over here. He's not going to bite."

"No, I'm okay." I've never held a baby but that doesn't stop me from having a recurring vision of dropping one. Just me, opening up my arms and releasing the child over and over again. When I was younger and still cried, Yevgenia would tell me about her favorite doll, Anna. Though taken from my mother's memory, Anna is as sharp in my own mind as if she belonged to me. She was a bald peach baby with pink bowed lips and translucent aquamarine eyes and lashes of stiff brown horsehair that closed when she was laid flat. Yevgenia had, for as long as she could remember, thought she lost her favorite doll, until I came along, a flesh-and-blood human child. "You want to know what really happened to Anna?" Yevgenia would ask me, at random intervals with a cheery singsong voice. "During a two-day train ride from Omsk to Moscow, I grew bored of the baby, so I threw her out the window and watched her smack and tumble against a snowbank when we approached Kirov. So, stop your tears."

"FINE," I SAY to Crystal finally, as if my arm is being twisted.

I kneel next to Charles, who is sitting on the edge of the glider, his knees and long legs spread slightly with Elmer resting on them. Charles is bent over the baby, who clutches on to Charles's pinky with a tiny hand. "He won't let go." Charles raises his hand up to show me how the baby holds on. "He's so strong."

Charles scoops the baby up and stands carefully. "Sit," he tells me. I push my back into the glider and he puts the baby on my lap. Elmer's tiny body, warm and pulsing against my thighs, so fragile and new, is the most valuable among us.

I run my fingers gently over the top of the baby's head; his hair is jet-black like Crystal's. The skin from his brows to his forehead is white and flaky, like he's molting. Underneath this all, Elmer's promise peeks though—the hint of brown, smooth skin, the softest I have ever felt, and when his dark eyes flutter open, the surprising depth of his wisdom is brief confirmation that all is in place. Elmer chirps as he yawns, his mouth forming a perfect O. I feel myself dragged, an avalanche sweeping through the center of my chest, clearing a path. *Stay*, I beg him in my mind. *Stay and don't ever leave.*

I look up at Crystal then, who in the process of motherhood has been given back more than what she had to start. "He's so beautiful," I say.

THE CRICKETS ARE scratching out a gloomy symphony in the warm early evening by the time we leave Crystal's trailer. She ends up putting Elmer to bed in a bassinet in her room and suddenly the world returns with a familiar weight and presence. In silence, Charles and I make our way back to what awaits us, the skewed carpeted steps, the bursts of dirt bikes and ATVs and the mountains breathing hot and sometimes cold down the neck of the Oasis.

"Oh shit," I say when I see Papa Bear's truck rolling our way. I just know he's about to ask me for the rent.

Papa Bear slows to an idle as we approach.

"Be cool." Charles's quick motion lets me know he's got me. He walks up to the driver's-side window, prepared to do all the talking.

But Papa Bear has plans of his own. He rolls down the window, looking past Charles. "Hey, you need to get in the car. Your mom just left me a message."

"What?"

"She's not in any kind of trouble or anything. But she wants us to go get her." When he pushes the gear shift up to park, the truck jumps forward before it settles.

"Well, where is she?" I can feel Charles's hand on my elbow. He tugs. It's gentle, but still he pulls my bent elbow, steering me clear.

"She said that you would know." Papa Bear reaches for the cell phone next to him on the seat. "Here. Take a listen."

It's my mother's voice pushing through the vast empty canyon, her spongy words laced with the noise of waves crashing in the background. Though she's called Papa Bear's phone, her message belongs only to me.

"Lari? Lari, listen." The halting way she says my name and the way she sniffs into the phone, the long sucking of air, the slow clearing of her throat, tells me she's cold and drunk. "The car died. Yes, it's dead, I think." Through the phone I can hear her pull her face away, maybe turning to see if the dead car is where she left it. "I'm at our beach. Come, *zaya*. We can need each other again."

Need. Because something is essential. An obligation. A want beyond want. A life-or-death requirement. I taste my need like salt on the tongue, at first, a satisfying comfort, then the gradual slide into the bitter, gagging fact that too much is too much.

It's been three months since she left me. Three months since she packed up all that was important to her, leaving me and unpaid bills behind. I press Papa Bear's phone to my ear harder, waiting for more from my mother even as the line cuts.

Papa Bear leans eagerly out the driver's-side window. "So,

she said something about a beach? I just need to stop and get gas. We could be out there in about two hours."

I blink at him, estimating the impact of retrieving my mother.

"You know where she is, right?" His worry. The searching quality of his eyes. The desperation.

I imagine driving south on the highway from here to Imperial Beach, a city I associate with my mother. We never lived there, surprisingly, but years ago, when I was ten or eleven we lived in San Francisco, a city that tormented Yevgenia with its tepid people and mercurial weather, and she spoke for weeks on end about moving back to Italy. She'd plan and save, gathering coins in a large jar. She took up a collection among her friends, who threw her a going-away party, after which we climbed into the car and drove until I fell asleep. I woke, disoriented. It was the middle of the night. I recall the relentless sound of waves crashing. She had driven to the ocean, but all I could see around me were dark boxes, beach condos they're called, stacked one on top of the other. Yevgenia was sitting next to me. She touched my shoulder. "Be back" was all she said before reaching for her bag and the bottle of booze. As she passed under the weak light of a streetlamp, I watched her thin dark hair whip against her shoulders until the black distance swallowed her.

My mother asked me to wait, so I did, until morning. The sun came up over the condos, making everything appear ugly, damaged somehow. The heat of the closed car felt like it would suffocate me, so I got out and walked down narrow passageways between the buildings. And then the ocean, like an open hand, spread out in front of me. I went up and down the stretch of beach for what felt like hours, panicked and angry, tears spilling or threatening to. I finally spotted Yevgenia propped up against the rocks, her feet out in front of her. She waved, a lazy, nonchalant flip of her hand, as if she'd been expecting me. When I approached, the empty bottle sat between her legs, an afterbirth, clean against her sandy thighs. Her eyes were beyond my figure, seeing more than what was marked. "That's Mexico over there." Her voice liminal, caught between longing and bewilderment. "Another country, so close but so far away."

I understand my mother's regrets and what she has always known. That there is no place where she could slip between me and undetectable ghouls, protecting me from harms we both know are around every corner, in every city, in every country.

Sweat dribbles from my temple down along my ear. I hand the phone back to Papa Bear. "I don't know where she is."

Then motioning to Charles to follow me, I pick my way back to the trailer, across the tall yellow grass that's pretending to be dead among the rocks, but isn't. It is just biding its time.

Acknowledgments

A Country You Can Leave was written in many places, from Hong Kong to the edge of the Great Basin in Oregon and from Barbados to New York; however, it was my supportive family and friends and especially memories of California that kept me rooted.

First, my sincere thanks to Julia Eagleton, who got the novel into the hands of my editor, Daphne Durham, whose enthusiasm and careful, critical read set me on the path to becoming a better storyteller. My deepest appreciation to Daphne and Lydia Zoells, who patiently guided me to the finish line; to Rodrigo Corral, for the beautiful cover design; to Logan Hill, Andrea Monagle, and Zach Greenwald, for their hard work in copyediting and proofreading the book, and to my production editor, Carrie Hsieh; to Stephen Weil, who has been a kind guide through publicity; and to everyone at FSG, for giving me what feels like my first "real" and collaborative publishing experience. Many thanks to Kathy Daneman, for her wisdom and artistry in literary PR. The warm welcome from Amanda Betts and Martha Kanya-Forstner and others at Knopf Canada could not have been kinder. The brilliant poet and fierce literary scholar Julia Kolchinsky Dasbach read the book and corrected my Russian. Any mistakes that remain are stubbornly my own. Without the generosity of Adrienne Brodeur, this book would not have found a home.

My boundless thanks to friends who patiently cajoled me

out of my mostly happy hermit existence—Keisha-Khan, Imani, Janet, Mel, Dasha, Marcella, Christina, Iza, and Kamala. Nimmi and Victoria read very early (too early) drafts and lent encouragement. In Hong Kong, my small community kept me going, especially Naomi Kirk. I am grateful for the space and time to write during residencies at Playa and the Djerassi Resident Artists Program, and for community during workshops at Tin House and VONA. My colleagues and students at CCNY have been a tremendous source of support.

My mother and grandmother were an unlikely duo who laid the foundation for my formal education. My mother taught me to read and, by example, to give myself over to the pleasure of books. My grandmother taught me to write, often forcing my sister and me to shape our world, one letter at a time.

There are no words, not in any language, that will be sufficient to thank Alan. I would never have started or finished the book if it weren't for Alan, who lovingly "Larry Browned" me until I was done.

Jonas, Eric, and Lida and their two dogs, their cat, and their lizards tormented me with the many ways one can spend time not writing. Thank you for the gift of your lives, your laughter, and your love.

Memories of a place and people vaguely similar and yet far away from the Oasis were shared with my twin sister, Lira, who reminded me that I never came to these pages alone.

Printed in the USA
CPSIA information can be obtained
at www.ICGtesting.com
LVHW042020040324
773502LV00004B/559